was going to say that if either of
…s is pretty, it is you.'

…nce more she'd surprised him. He couldn't hold
…ck his smile. 'Men are not pretty.'

…ice shrugged. 'Are they not? You are one of a
…nd. A darkly handsome man who exudes danger.
The ladies of the ton would faint at your feet.'

…et you deny your own prettiness when it is quite
…bvious to me?'

…'m a realist, Captain, and you've been on board
…hip for many months, no doubt.'

Her contempt for his compliment irritated like a
…harp piece of gravel inside a stocking.

…et me tell you what I see. I see a Madonna's
…lm face and eyes shadowed by secrets. I see
…sun-kissed complexion and copper glints in
…ilky hair. Intelligence sits on your brow. Your
…ps tempt mine.' He paused. 'I sense hot blood
…nning beneath alabaster skin.'

…he gasped, her eyes widening in maidenly horror.

He caught her shoulders, gazed into brown eyes
pierced by emerald-green.

Longing …

Her …
his …
her …

Author Note

For all that he was a rogue, I couldn't help liking Long John Silver when I read *Treasure Island* as a child. For ages now I've wanted to write a pirate story, but by the Regency pirates were, as they say, history. Privateers, however, were a whole other breed. Men who were given licence or letters of marque by governments to prey on enemy ships, they generally made life difficult for the opposing side. Many of them became extremely wealthy in the process, and legally too.

So I hope you enjoy this not-quite-a-pirate story. I think you will find that Michael meets his match in Alice. And, while she doesn't think she has a romantic bone in her body, there is just something about a rogue…

I love to hear from readers, so if you would like to drop me a line you can find me at ann@ann.lethbridge. gmail.com, and if you would like to know more about me and my books visit http://www.annlethbridge.com

CAPTURED FOR THE CAPTAIN'S PLEASURE

Ann Lethbridge

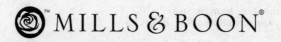

MILLS & BOON®

First published in Great Britain 2010
Harlequin Mills & Boon Limited,
Eton House, 18-24 Paradise Road, Richmond, Surrey TW9 1SR

© Michèle Ann Young 2010

ISBN: 978 0 263 87588 1

Harlequin Mills & Boon policy is to use papers that are natural, renewable and recyclable products and made from wood grown in sustainable forests. The logging and manufacturing process conform to the legal environmental regulations of the country of origin.

Printed and bound in Spain
by Litografia Rosés, S.A., Barcelona

Ann Lethbridge has been reading Regency novels for as long as she can remember. She always imagined herself as Lizzie Bennet, or one of Georgette Heyer's heroines, and would often recreate the stories in her head with different outcomes or scenes. When she sat down to write her own novel, it was no wonder that she returned to her first love: the Regency.

Ann grew up roaming England with her military father. Her family lived in many towns and villages across the country, from the Outer Hebrides to Hampshire. She spent memorable family holidays in the West Country and in Dover, where her father was born. She now lives in Canada, with her husband, two beautiful daughters, and a Maltese terrier named Teaser, who spends his days on a chair beside the computer, making sure she doesn't slack off.

Ann visits Britain every year, to undertake research and also to visit family members who are very understanding about her need to poke around old buildings and visit every antiquity within a hundred miles. If you would like to know more about Ann and her research, or to contact her, visit her website at www.annlethbridge.com. She loves to hear from readers.

Previous novels by this author:

THE RAKE'S INHERITED COURTESAN
WICKED RAKE, DEFIANT MISTRESS

and in Mills & Boon® Historical Undone eBooks:

THE RAKE'S INTIMATE ENCOUNTER

I dedicate this book to my dad, who was known all his life as Peter, though it was not his given name. He introduced me to the writings of Georgette Heyer when I was very young, for which I can't thank him enough. He always encouraged me to reach for the stars, no matter how hard the journey. I would like to thank Joanne Grant and her team at Harlequin Mills & Boon for making this a better book, my agent Scott Eagan, and my fabulous critique partners, Maureen, Molly, Sinead, Mary, Jude and Teresa, who show unfailing patience with every rewrite.

Chapter One

~~~~~~~~~~~~~~

Off Lisbon—June 1814

Repairing a gash in a man's brawny forearm on a ship's deck bore not the slightest resemblance to mending a rip in a petticoat, Alice Fulton decided. She dabbed at the dried blood around the wound with a cloth moistened in seawater.

The prospect of causing pain gave it a wholly different aspect. The ship's pitch and yaw added a further challenge. Fortunately, clear skies and a light breeze kept the motion to a minimum and the awning above their heads protected them from the midday heat.

Roped in as an unwilling assistant, her fellow passenger and best friend, Lady Selina Albright, stared grimly out to sea as if her life depended on it.

Perched in front of her on a barrel, with a three-inch gash in his sun-bronzed skin, her patient, Perkin, seemed remarkably unperturbed. But then she hadn't told the sullen fellow staring at the planks at his feet that this was the first wound she'd actually stitched herself. No sense in scaring him.

Not that much would scare this strapping sailor. Even with his head respectfully lowered and his bearded face hidden by the tangle of dark-brown hair falling around his shoulders, he had a swagger.

'When did you do this?' she asked.

'The night afore I came aboard,' he muttered, not looking up. 'I told you, miss, it ain't nothing. I'll take care of it.'

She'd caught him bandaging it one-handed when she passed the galley. On this merchant ship, the cook doubled as surgeon and he could hardly sew himself. 'It needs sutures.'

He glanced up, giving her a brief impression of a face younger than she'd first thought and handsome in a harsh, unkempt sort of way. His cheeks above the black-bearded jaw had been tanned to the colour of light mahogany. Deep creases radiated from the corners of eyes the strangest shade of turquoise rimmed with grey. Right now they held a distinctly resentful gleam. Or even anger? He lowered his head before she could be sure.

A feeling of unease disturbed her normally calm stomach. He'd been making her nervous since he had joined their ship in Lisbon, replacing their original cook who had disappeared amid the stews on the wharf. They'd certainly lost in the exchange. What Perkin knew about cooking he must have learned from a tanner. She stared at the large, strong, well-shaped hand resting on a formidably muscled thigh. At least his fingernails were clean.

No matter how bad his food or his attitude, this wound needed sewing.

'Ugh.' Selina gave a delicate shudder. 'You should let the sailmaker do it as Captain Dareth ordered,' she said in her naturally breathy voice.

Perkin nodded agreement, his strange eyes warming as they roved over Selina's lush figure.

Alice wanted to hit him.

Why, she couldn't imagine. There wasn't a man alive whose eyes wouldn't warm when they fell on Selina's dark flamboyance, whereas Alice's immature figure, nondescript brown hair and hazel eyes, rarely warranted a second look. Which suited Alice down to the ground.

'Hodges won't be off watch for hours,' she muttered, threading her needle. 'The longer the wound remains open the less likely it will heal.' And besides this might be her only chance to make use of her knowledge.

'Are you certain you know how?' Selina's voice quavered.

Certain? She stared at the bloody gash. In theory, yes. Practice was an altogether different proposition.

'This fascination of yours for surgery is positively macabre.' Selina gave another of her carefully honed shudders.

At least her friend wasn't calling her interest unladylike, as Father did. He'd always blamed it on the months she'd spent on the long round trip to India with nothing to do but follow the surgeon around. At nine, she'd been half in love with the ship's doctor. Her interest in medicine had survived the years. Love was a whole other story.

'Be ready to hand me the scissors. And don't look. I don't want you fainting.' Lord, she didn't want to faint herself.

She lined up her needle.

Prickles darted down her back. Sweat trickled cold between her breasts and clung to her palms. The needle seemed to slither in her grasp like a maggot in a ship's biscuit.

Now or never, Alice. She inhaled a deep breath. The ship rolled. She staggered.

Perkin put out a hand. Caught her wrist. 'Steady, miss.'

His palm was warm, strong, calloused. A touch that burned. His eyes flashed concern. He released her swiftly as if he too had felt the sudden burst of heat.

Ridiculous.

She braced against the roll of the ship, absorbed the motion with her knees as she'd been doing for days. She swallowed to relieve the dryness in her throat. 'Ready, Perkin?'

He grunted.

Pulse racing, she pressed the needle into the bronzed skin. It dimpled. Her hand shook.

'If yer goin' to do it, give it a good hard jab,' Perkin muttered in a growl.

Right. Alice stabbed. The needle punctured the skin. The man didn't flinch, but she knew from a hitch in his breath she'd caused pain.

'Forgive me,' she murmured.

Surprise glimmered in his blue eyes, before he looked away.

She pushed through the other side of the gash, pulled up and knotted. Mr Bellweather would have been proud. Good. And no blood. 'Scissors, please.'

They appeared in front of her, dangling at the end of lacy gloved fingers.

She snipped the thread and returned the scissors to Selina's outstretched palm.

Alice let her breath go, felt her heart steady, and stabbed again. 'Four stitches should do it,' she murmured.

Head averted, Perkin started whistling 'Spanish Ladies' under his breath as if he hadn't a care in the world. She had to admire his fortitude after hearing many a man whine like a puppy when faced with a stitch or two. His calmness instilled her with courage and in no time at all there were four nice neat knots along the puckered skin.

'Bandage, Selina, please.'

The bandage appeared under her nose.

Ceasing his whistle, Perkin inspected his arm, his expression hidden by the mass of black hair. 'Thank ye.' The tone sounded grudging.

She ignored his sullenness and smiled. 'I think it will be all right.' They wouldn't know for a day or two if the gash would heal properly. If it didn't, if she'd made things worse… Her stomach clenched. Don't think that. She'd done a good job. Carefully she wrapped the bandage around a sun-weathered, sinewy forearm strong enough to haul up a mainsail by itself, if needed. She tied the strip of cloth off. 'I will look at it later today.'

'Nah, miss. I'll look a'ter it.'

Disappointed, but unsurprised by his reticence, Alice nodded. 'As you wish. Please take more care next time you gut a fish.'

That startling gaze whipped up to her face. Not angry this time, more puzzled. 'Aye, aye, miss.' He rolled down his shirtsleeve, covering up all those lovely muscles.

Oh, Lord. Had she really just thought a common sailor's arm lovely? Was she turning into one of those eccentric spinsters who peered at males sideways and made up stories in their heads?

'That's that, then.' She rinsed her hands in the bowl and handed it to Perkin, along with the cloth she had used. He took them without a word and headed below.

A sense of disappointment invaded her chest. She made a wry grimace. What had she expected from such a surly man? Effusive thanks? She wiped her face and the back of her neck with her handkerchief. He was probably horrified at the thought of a lady lowering herself to touch him. Men of all classes were odd in that regard.

'Alice?' Selina said, a strange note in her voice. 'What are they looking at?' She pointed to the bulwark where all of the ship's officers were clustered at the starboard rail with their spyglasses directed astern. Between the master and his second officer, her brother Richard's fifteen-year-old gangly body looked distinctly out of place. Like the others, he was watching a ship drawing down on them. Its present course would bring it exceedingly close to the *Conchita*. Hairs rose on the back of her neck. Her stomach gave a roll in direct opposition to the movement of the ship. 'Oh, no.'

'What is it?' Selina asked, her face anxious, her bright green eyes wide.

It couldn't be. Not on this voyage, when they'd taken the utmost precautions. 'It's probably a ship looking for news,' she said, heading to the rail. Everyone sought news these days, with rumours of peace circulating the docks.

'Wait,' Selina called. 'Your parasol. You know how you burn.'

With a huff of impatience, Alice turned back to retrieve the lacy object from her friend. She smiled her thanks, took Selina's arm and joined Mr Anderson, her father's factotum, at the rail.

'What ship is it?' Alice asked.

Mr Anderson grimaced. 'Can't see from this angle, Miss Fulton. She's flying the Union Jack.'

Alice breathed a sigh of relief. Thomas Anderson chewed on his bottom lip. 'I think you and Lady Selina should go below.'

'Why?' Selina asked, her wide-eyed gaze turning to the middle-aged man who immediately turned pink. He'd been blushing every time she so much as glanced his way since they had left port. Not that Selina gave him the slightest encouragement. She simply took admiration as her due. Alice suppressed her irritation. She was past being interested in men of any sort.

Captain Dareth lowered his glass. 'Let's see if we can outrun her.'

The tense low mutter added pressure to Alice's already taut chest. She kept silent as the second officer rushed off shouting orders for more sail. The captain didn't need additional worries.

Richard, obviously brimming with excitement, turned to the master. 'She's fast for a brig.'

'She is that,' Captain Dareth said.

'A privateer, do you think?' Richard ask, his adolescent voice cracking with excitement.

Alice gasped. A run-in with a privateer was the worst possible scenario. With England at war with France and her allies, as well as America, too many nations had given out letters of marque. The legal document allowed greedy captains with fast ships to take as prizes any enemy merchantmen trying to slip through the blockade. They were little better than pirates, but they had the law on their side.

Until now, Fulton's Shipping had prided itself on following international law to the letter, but the situation had become intolerable, with ships being routinely stopped. She glanced up at their Spanish flag with a wince. Perhaps after all it had not been such a good idea to hide their national identity. If only they hadn't been quite so desperate to make sure this cargo reached England safely.

'Is it a privateer?' she asked.

The captain jerked his head around as if he'd only just noticed her presence. 'Miss Fulton, I really must ask you to go below. And you, too, Lady Selina. Mr Anderson, please escort the ladies.'

'Do you think it is a privateer, Captain Dareth?' Alice asked firmly, aware of the heightened clamour of her heart.

The captain's gaze shifted above her shoulder, then travelled up the mainmast to the sails being unfurled by his crew. 'I don't know, Miss Fulton. There were rumours in Lisbon.'

There were always rumours. 'But you think it might be.'

Selina gave a little squeak of terror. 'Are we in danger?'

'I must take every precaution,' the captain said.

Mr Anderson took Selina's elbow and reached for Alice's arm. 'Ladies, if you please?'

'No,' Alice said. 'Selina, go below if you wish, but it is as hot as Hades down there. Surely the *Conchita* will easily outrun her.' The ship had been specially designed for speed. Father had thrown every last penny into making her one of the fastest merchantmen operating out of England.

Clearly unwilling to argue with his employer's daughter, Mr Anderson turned his attention to Selina. He escorted her down the nearby companionway.

'It would be pretty exciting if it is a privateer,' Richard said.

The captain rolled his eyes. 'Excuse me, Miss Fulton.' He hurried off to confer with his first officer. A couple of crew members were taking down the shade awning, the rest hauled on sheets to the second officer's command in grim silence.

The pursuing brig was now close enough to see crewmen moving around on its deck.

Richard raised his glass to his eye. 'They are gaining on us.'

Boys. All they cared about was speed and danger. Hadn't he learned anything on this voyage? This cargo was Father's last hope—their family's last hope—to salvage their fortunes.

She forced a smile. 'Pray he doesn't catch us instead of cheering him on.'

Richard looked down at her, his boyish face suddenly serious. 'I'm not on his side, Alice. But you have to admire such a fine ship.'

'I'd prefer to admire it far behind in our wake.'

Richard returned the glass to his eye. 'Strange decking aft. High for a brig. Doesn't seem to slow her speed.'

Apparently not. The brig's bow was almost level with the *Conchita*'s stern. Please, please, let him break a mast, or foul his rudder. Anything, so they weren't caught. Her hands gripped the parasol handle so tightly, they hurt. She snapped the blasted thing closed. Who cared about freckles when minute by minute their pursuer narrowed the patch of ocean between the ships?

Only yards from their rail, the Union Jack on the other ship's mast went down and the American flag rose. In the stern a large blue flag unfurled bearing the image of a gryphon in gold, all sharp claws and gleaming teeth.

'I knew it,' Richard crowed.

Alice gritted her teeth, and yet she couldn't help but stare in fascination at the approaching ship's elegant lines.

A puff of smoke emerged from the privateer's bow. A thunderous bang struck their ears. Alice jumped. Selina's scream pierced the deck's planking from below. A plume of water fountained ahead of the *Conchita*. A warning shot. The maritime signal to halt.

The captain issued a rapid order to the helmsman, who dragged the wheel hard over. The *Conchita* heeled away from their pursuer. Alice grabbed for the rail as the deck slanted away.

'That surprised her,' Richard muttered, one arm hooked around a rope.

The privateer's sails flapped empty of wind.

'Oh, good show. She's in irons.' Richard hurried off to join the captain at the helm.

'Not for long,' Mr Anderson said gloomily, joining Alice at the rail. Out of the corner of her eye, Alice saw Perkin emerge through the hatch and take in the scene.

'You,' an officer shouted. 'To the yards.'

Perkin made for the stern.

With her heart in her throat and unable to do more than gaze with horrified fascination, Alice watched the privateer's swift recovery. She swung across the *Conchita*'s wake, then clawed her way up their port side. All down the length of the sleek-looking ship, black squares of open gun ports bristled with nasty-looking muzzles.

'Surely he's not going to fire at civilians?' she said.

Someone came up behind her. As she turned to see

who it was, a steely arm went around her waist and a pistol pressed against her temple. She stared at Perkin's grim profile with a cry of shock.

'Sorry, Miss Fulton,' he muttered. 'Do as you are bid and no harm will befall you.'

'Captain Dareth,' he roared. 'Surrender.' Her ears rang with his bellow.

The rise of Perkin's chest with each indrawn breath pressed hot against her back. Sparks ran down her spine and lit a glow low in her stomach in a most inappropriate way. How could she respond to this criminal with such unladylike heat?

She jabbed Perkin's ribs with her elbow. She might as well have poked a granite rock with her baby finger for all the notice he took. Come to think of it, his stomach gave less than granite, although she did hear a faint grunt.

'Dareth,' he yelled again.

The captain turned, his eyes as round as marbles, his jaw dropping to his neatly knotted cravat. He stood stock-still and stared.

Perkin cursed harshly. 'Strike your colours, man, before someone gets hurt.'

Even dazed with astonishment, Alice couldn't help but notice the change in the cook from common sailor to a man used to command.

She twisted in his grip. 'You're part of this.'

'Silence,' he snarled.

A cannon boomed. A tearing rush of air whistled overhead. Then the ship seemed to disintegrate in the sound of splintering wood and the shouts. A spar, tangled with ropes and sail, slammed on to the deck. One end knocked Richard sideways. He collapsed.

The breath rushed from Alice's throat. She struggled to find her voice, fought to break the iron grip around her waist.

'Richard,' she screamed. She stilled at the pistol's increased pressure. 'Hold still,' he growled in her ear.

'Let me go. My brother needs help.' She stamped down on his bare instep.

He uttered a foul curse, but the rock-hard grip didn't ease a smidgeon.

Beside the helm, their captain's face blanched. He gave the order to strike their colours.

'About bloody time,' Perkin muttered as their flag fluttered to the deck. 'Heave to,' he shouted. The helmsman brought the ship around and the sails hung limp. The other ship drew alongside and men leaped across the gap into the *Conchita*'s ratlines. Privateers poured on to their ship.

'Get your brother below,' Perkin said, pushing her forwards. He strode for the rail.

Heart faltering, terrified of what she would find, she ran to Richard's side. One end of the spar lay across his chest. Ropes and canvas littered the deck around his still body. A blue lump marred his temple. 'Richard,' she cried, shaking his shoulder. He didn't move.

She pressed her ear to his heart. A strong steady heartbeat. Thank God.

Now if she could move this timber… With shaking hands, she crouched and grabbed one end of the huge spar. Too heavy. It didn't move. Muscles straining, she heaved again. Hopeless. She needed help.

She looked around wildly. For all that they looked like a motley crew, the privateers were swiftly and efficiently rounding up *Conchita*'s crew at pistol and sabre point. Not one of them looked her way.

A sailor ran past. She caught his arm. 'You. Give me a hand here.' The grey-haired, barrel-chested gnome of a man stopped in his tracks. His button-black eyes blinked.

'Help me move this spar,' she said.

He glanced down at Richard. 'Aye, aye, miss.' He pulled out a knife, held it over her brother.

Alice's breath caught in her throat. 'Please. No.'

The man slashed the ropes free and glanced up. 'Did you say something, miss?'

Panting, her heart still thundering too hard for speech, Alice shook her head.

The man proceeded to lift one end of the spar and to drag it clear.

'Perkin told me to get him below deck,' she said, going to Richard's feet. 'You must help me.'

The man looked blank. 'Can't, miss. Speak to the captain.' He rushed off.

She glanced around for someone else. Within the few short minutes she'd been busy with Richard, the privateers, twenty or more of them and all as rough as Perkin, had taken command of her father's ship and were clearing the deck of torn sails, broken spars and damaged rigging. An acrid smell lingered in the air, the smell of gunpowder from the shots they had fired.

Oh Lord, what a disaster. And they could have been killed. An enormous lump rose up from her chest and stuck firm in her throat. She swallowed the rush of panic. Richard needed help. But who would give it?

A blond Viking of a man was striding aft issuing orders as he went. This must be the captain. She started towards him. He paused to speak to the traitorous Perkin, who appeared to have grown a foot since the privateers came on board. She marched across the deck and planted herself in front of both men. 'My brother needs help.'

The blond man recoiled. 'Good God. A woman? What's she doing on deck?'

A shade taller than his captain and as dark as the other man was fair, Perkin muttered into the blond giant's ear.

'You, Perkin,' she said. 'Tell your captain this is an honest merchant ship carrying civilian passengers.'

The blond giant raised a brow at his accomplice. 'Michael?'

'You know what to do,' Perkin said and strode away.

'Simpson,' the captain shouted. 'Get your sorry self over here.'

The grey-bearded man who had freed Richard ran over.

'He wants her on the *Gryphon*,' the captain said.

Her?

Simpson's eyebrows shot up to his hairline. 'Aye, aye, sir. This way, miss.'

'I'm not going anywhere,' Alice said. 'My brother is injured.' She dodged around the portly fellow and dashed back to her pale and still brother.

A hand fell on her shoulder. She jerked around to find a rough-looking sailor with a drooping moustache and a tarry pigtail staring at her from mud-coloured eyes. He grinned.

She tried not to notice the blackened stumps of his teeth. 'Take him below.'

The sailor's eyes lit up. 'I'll be happy to take ye below, missy.'

'Get away from her, Kale.'

Perkin again, with a pistol in his hand and his eyes blazing fury.

Her insides did a strange kind of somersault. The kind that shouldn't be happening for any man, let alone a pirate even if he had defended her.

'Back to your duties, Kale,' Perkin ordered.

Kale seemed to shrivel. He gave a half-hearted salute. 'Aye, sir.' He shambled off.

A rather red-looking Simpson appeared at Perkin's side. Perkin gave him a frown. 'Damnation, Simpson, get her on board the *Gryphon* before she causes any more trouble.' He narrowed his eyes and leaned closer to Simpson and muttered something in his ear.

The crewman's eyes widened, then he touched his forelock with a wink. 'Aye, aye.'

'No,' Alice said, 'not without Richard', but Perkin strode off as if she hadn't said a word.

'Orders is orders, miss,' Simpson said, his black eyes twinkling.

He grabbed her around the waist and tossed her effortlessly over his shoulder. She landed hard on the bony point. It knocked the breath from her lungs. 'Ouch, you brute! Put me down.' She thumped him on the back. Kicked at his stomach. 'I'm not going anywhere without my brother.'

The man's only response was a laboured grunt. He strode across the deck and dropped her into a canvas bucket hanging off the side of the ship. The scoundrels had rigged up ropes and a pulley between the ships, no doubt intending to steal everything of value.

Oh, God. The cargo. They were ruined.

She tried to scramble out again. 'I can't leave my brother.' Or Selina. She'd be terrified witless. Who knew what a dreadful man like Kale would do? 'My friend is below deck. You have to bring her too.'

Simpson hopped in next to her and grasped her arm. 'Be still, miss. I ain't wanting to hurt ye. Haul away,' he yelled at a sailor on the other ship handling the ropes.

She clung to the edge of the bucket, her stomach pitching like a rowboat in a storm, staring back at the *Conchita*, trying to see what was happening. Was someone bending over Richard? She raised up on tiptoes. Dash it. She couldn't see.

Simpson must have seen her dismay, because his expression turned almost fatherly. 'Don't ye be worrying about yer friends. The captain will see to 'em.'

See to them? Why didn't that make her feel any better? Indeed, her stomach churned worse than before and her throat dried as if she'd swallowed an ocean of seawater. 'You have to go back for them.'

The bucket bumped against the side of the brig and Simpson hopped out. He made a grab for her. She backed away. The twinkle in his eyes disappeared. 'Now then, miss, do as I say, or you and your friends will have more trouble than you bargained for.'

She stilled. She had no wish to bring harm to Richard and Selina.

An elderly seaman with a cherry-red nose traced with blue veins hurried up to them. Strands of greying hair clung to his scalp, his bloodshot-grey eyes looked anxious. 'Anyone hurt?' he asked Alice's gaoler.

'Yes,' Alice said. 'My brother. He's received a blow to the head.'

The man, the doctor she assumed, blinked. 'Hmm. What's she doing here?'

'Captain's orders.'

'Women. Nothing but bad luck.' He climbed into the bucket. 'Haul away, man,' he said to the other sailor.

Alice clutched at Simpson's shirt. 'He will look at my brother, won't he?'

'That will be up to the captain.' He must have seen the protest forming on her lips because he hurried to say, 'If you do exactly what I says, I'll make sure he does.' He pushed her towards the stern, towards the ornately carved walls of the strange-looking poop-deck. It reminded her of pictures of ancient Spanish galleons, only smaller.

Biting her lip, she let him hurry her along.

Simpson opened a brass-fitted mahogany door and ushered her into a chamber lit by the floor-to-ceiling square-paned window angled back over the stern. Surprisingly, the cabin's furnishings were sumptuous. A Turkish carpet covered the floor, a mahogany desk and a throne-like gilt chair occupied the centre of the room.

Beneath a skylight, an enormous bed covered in fine white sheets filled an alcove. A black gryphon, wings spread wide, curved beak open, and lion claws raking, sprang from the headboard.

The stuff of nightmares.

This must be their captain's stateroom. Why bring her here? Her heart thumped a warning. She turned to leave and found her way blocked by a sympathetic-looking Simpson.

'Make yourself comfortable, miss.'

He backed out of the door. She heard the key turn in the lock.

Make herself comfortable? Wasn't that like telling someone falling off a cliff to enjoy the journey?

Beyond the window, the azure sky and sparkling sea mocked her predicament.

Chapter Two

Eyes closed, Michael relished the cold sting of the salt-water pump as he washed away the filth of days beneath the merchantman's decks.

Luck had landed on his shoulder these past few days. He touched the talisman hanging on the chain around his neck in silent thanks. Fulton playing into his hands was one thing. Finding both Fulton heirs on board was like throwing a main.

Fulton's children at his mercy. He could kill them out of hand. Or he could make them suffer the torment of the damned he and Jaimie had suffered. The beys were always looking for infidel slaves. Or the boy could be pressed into the Navy. And the girl? She'd make a fine mistress, for a week or two.

Something dark unfurled deep within his chest as he imagined Fulton's despair at the loss of his children. Dark and triumphant and ugly.

And that wouldn't be the worst of what lay in store.

He rinsed the soap from his hair and gestured for Jacko to cease his efforts with the pump. The monkey-faced lad flashed a salute and tossed him a towel. Michael let the water cascade from his body then dried off.

'What happened to your arm?' David Wishart asked from where he leaned against the rail awaiting orders.

Michael glanced down at the puckered red line with its spidery black stitches. 'Courtesy of the *Conchita*'s cook. He argued about giving up his berth.'

'Did you make him stitch you up?'

'No.' She'd done that. Alice Fulton. Needle in hand, she'd paled beneath the freckles dusting her cheeks, but to his surprise she'd done better than many a surgeon.

He owed her for that. He hated being beholden to anyone, but a debt to a Fulton tasted bitter.

A female Fulton to boot.

And a bossy one. Even in his lowly position as cook, it hadn't taken him long to realise she ruled the roost on the *Conchita*. She'd be his key to learning about her father, not the boy. He was too much the mooncalf to be of any use. Which was why he'd had Simpson take her to his cabin for questioning.

She was certainly no beauty, Miss Fulton, with her serious eyes and plain round face. Nothing like her pretty friend. Yet beneath that mousy exterior lay unquiet currents. A maelstrom.

He'd felt it beneath his hands.

His blood ran hot, as it had when he'd had her pressed tight against his side and a pistol at her temple. As unexpected as it was unwanted.

Hell. She was Fulton's daughter. In his cabin. At his non-existent mercy. Except he did owe her a debt.

Dammit.

Jacko produced a mirror and a razor. 'Will you shave today, Cap'n?'

He'd planned to shave on this last leg of the journey to England in an attempt to make himself look more respectable, but the arrival of the prisoners on his ship required he chart a new course. 'Not this time,' he said. 'Scissors, if you please.'

He pulled a clean shirt over his head, drew on his breeches and peered into the glass Jacko held up.

'Report if you would, Mr Wishart.' He snipped at the untidy black hair on his jaw.

His second-in-command's fair brow furrowed. 'I don't like this, Michael.'

Michael didn't blame him. They'd never ventured this close to Britain's waters nor ventured into the rocky shoal of prisoners before, but Fulton, the bastard, had wandered into Michael's net. Only a fool would ignore that kind of fortune.

Idiot he was not and besides it was time he enjoyed fortune's favour. Long past time.

He dragged a comb through his hair and tied it with the black ribbon Jacko had draped over his arm. 'Report please, David.'

David took a deep breath. 'The Fulton youth and the female we found below deck are in the hold under guard, along with another male civilian, who has a broken arm. Bones is with them. Hopefully, he has something for hysterics.'

Michael glanced at his friend's pained expression and winced. 'That bad?'

David's blue eyes twinkled. 'The civilian is doing his best to keep her calm.' His first officer's face resumed its troubled expression. 'Michael, we shouldn't keep them on board. Send them to Lisbon with the *Conchita*. Prisoners are a complication we don't need.'

David Wishart had sailed alongside Michael in one of his Majesty's stinking frigates for five years. Since then he'd spent another three as Michael's first officer. This was the first time he'd questioned an order. And blast it, he was right. Michael should send the *Conchita*'s passengers to port with the prize ship. And yet an uneasy feeling swirled in his gut as he opened his mouth to agree, a sense of something about to go wrong. A knowledge that the Fates would not appreciate him letting their gift slip so easily from his grasp.

He waved a dismissive hand. 'I assume you found the falsified documents, as well as the log that proves she's operating under another nation's flag?'

David sighed. 'We did. Fulton doesn't have a leg to stand on.'

'Good. Name off a crew and send the *Conchita* back to Lisbon. Let the admiralty decide.' He shrugged into his waistcoat.

'Aye, aye,' David said. 'But I still don't like it. We aren't much better than Fulton, flying an American flag. Those letters of marque you bought won't stand up under close scrutiny and could land us in trouble if anyone takes the trouble to look.'

'They won't. You worry too much.' Michael clapped his first officer and closest friend on the shoulder.

'I wish you worried more. I'll get a crew together.' David stomped off.

At the sound of the tumbling lock, Alice ceased her pacing and retreated to the window. Her heart drummed.

Her tongue seemed to stick to the roof of her mouth, stifling the words she'd practised in her head.

The door swung back.

Perkin, huge in the doorway, searched her out with narrowed eyes. Freshly washed and groomed, he looked magnificent. A wild and untamed restless force not unlike the ocean. How could she ever have mistaken him for a simple cook?

The air in the cabin seemed to evaporate, leaving her nothing to breathe. The thunder of her heart intensified as if her chest had shrunk to half its normal size. She straightened her spine. Lifted her chin. 'What do *you* want? Where is your captain?'

His eyes widened a fraction, then white teeth flashed in his bearded face. He looked positively handsome. Her stomach gave an odd kind of lurch. Was she mad? Or just fearful?

It had to be the latter.

He closed the door behind him.

Instinctively she backed up a step, the roar of pumping blood in her ears. Fear. And it was making her knees weak and her mind an empty vessel. All she seemed able to do was stare. At his face. At the width of his shoulders. At the lithe movement of his hips as he stepped closer.

'Apparently an introduction is required.' He bowed with old-fashioned grace, almost as if flourishing a handkerchief or a cocked hat. 'Lionhawk at your service. Captain of the *Gryphon*.'

He was their captain? Her stomach sank. 'No wonder you can't cook.'

A smile lifted his lips, his eyes twinkled. 'I am sorry for my culinary disasters.'

She wanted to hit him—he looked so pleased with himself. 'So am I.'

He cocked a dark arrogant eyebrow.

Why couldn't the captain have been the Viking-looking fellow? Somehow, he'd seemed far less intimidating than this wickedly smiling man. 'So, Captain Pirate. What is it you want?'

The smile faded. 'Privateer.'

'Personally, I can't tell the difference. It is still stealing.'

'A privateer operates within the law,' he said with a scowl. 'Unlike your father. Sailing a British ship under another country's flag is illegal.'

She winced. It was so annoying that he should be in the right. Especially when it was her fault they'd flown a false flag in the first place. One of the merchants in Lisbon had suggested the ruse when they couldn't pay the inflated insurance and she'd persuaded Anderson to give it a try. In hindsight, not a wise choice. Too late to do anything about it now except bluff.

'My father is carrying on a legitimate business. He is not harming anyone.'

An eerie stillness filled the room. Although he looked relaxed, she sensed a hidden tension in his body and an underlying emotion she could not begin to fathom.

'No harm?' he uttered softly.

The chill in his voice sent a shiver down her spine. The fear she'd been holding at bay expanded in her chest. It rose up her throat. She swallowed what felt like broken glass. 'Where are my brother and Lady Selina?'

'My other prisoners are in the hold.'

Prisoners. A bone-deep tremble shook her frame. Hearing the words spoken so casually brought home the evils of their position. The nearby chair invited her collapse. She locked her knees, refusing to let him see any weakness. 'Then I demand to join them.' Infuriatingly, her words came out a low croak. She swallowed again, vainly seeking moisture and calm.

'Demand?' He prowled toward the desk. All the while he'd remained like a sentinel at the door, the force of his presence had seemed contained. Now it flooded the room, filling the corners, circling around her, no longer charming, but dark and forbidding. And if he intended his cool raking gaze to intimidate her, he was succeeding admirably.

Clearly issuing orders wasn't the most sensible thing she'd ever done, but calm good sense seemed to have gone the way of her courage. She edged closer to the window, widening the distance between them. The open window provided a measure of air and dropped straight to the sea.

'I—I am sure you are a busy man.' She gestured at his desk. 'You must have courses to plot. Orders to give. I will be in the way.'

He tilted his head on one side. 'True.'

Thank heaven. He might be a pirate—no, a privateer, no point in insulting him again—but he seemed reasonably intelligent. 'I am glad we agree. Would you care to direct me?' She headed for the door, passing within inches of his broad-shouldered frame. Close enough for a quick glance to take in the long dark lashes framing his vivid eyes and trickles of water from his bath coursing from his hairline into his beard.

Up close, he seemed impossibly large. And very male. And far too handsome. With a wince at her wayward thoughts, she turned the door handle and pulled it open. It jerked out of her hand and slammed shut with a bang.

Above her head one large hand lay flat on the panel. Damn. She whirled around, back to the door. His chest, encased in an embroidered cream waistcoat over a pristine white shirt, hemmed her in.

'No,' he said, his expression implacable.

'No?'

'No. I do not care to escort you. Not yet, anyway.'

'My brother is injured. You must take me to him.' Hating the shake in her voice, she locked her gaze with his, and instantly regretted it. The eyes fixed on hers blazed hot.

And then he smiled. It didn't make him look friendly, just wolfish, as if he'd scented something tasty. 'More orders, Miss Fulton?'

Her heart gave an uncomfortable thump. 'A request.'

'A barely civil request. You could try being a little more polite.' His deep voice ran over her skin like liquid honey. His chest rose and fell inches from her cotton bodice. Warmth permeated her skin. She inhaled the scent of ocean and soap. Clean and very male. Intoxicating.

Best not to notice his scent. Or how close he stood. Or the rapid beat of her pulse.

He placed his other hand flat on the door, framing her head within white linen shirtsleeves beneath which lay the bone and muscle she'd admired earlier in the day.

Her stomach gave a slow lazy roll. Her heart stuttered as if seeking a new rhythm. 'How is your arm?'

Lord, what made her say that? She didn't care about his arm. Would he think it an appeal for gratitude?

'Almost as good as new.' He flashed a smug grin. 'Thanks to you.'

'I wish I had chopped it off when I had the chance.' Her stomach clenched at her rudeness, but she forced herself to meet his gaze without a blink.

He stared at her for a long moment, his gaze raking her face as if he couldn't quite believe he'd heard aright. He ducked his head, pressed his mouth to hers.

Retribution. Punishment. Anger. All these things his mouth relayed through her lips. And something else. Something reckless and wild that made her insides tighten. Hunger.

She whipped her head aside. He caught her nape, held her fast, his mouth softening, teasing, wooing.

Her heart pounded. Her breathing became shallow. Her insides liquefied. She was melting from the inside out. She lifted her hands to push him away. They hovered above his chest, trembling, fingers curling with longing to touch and knowing it would be fatal.

The tip of his tongue traced the seam of her lips. Her eyelids drooped as wonderful warmth rolled over her skin.

Wickedness. Her body glowed with it. Her pulse fluttered with a longing she shouldn't even be aware of. Her lips parted to his teasing.

His tongue tangled with hers. A thrill exploded low in her abdomen. A small moan rose up in her throat.

He pulled away and gazed at her with gleaming eyes, his chest rising and falling with rapid intakes of breath. A sensual smile curved his lips.

Easy virtue. That was what his smile said. Wanton. As if he knew. He couldn't. Not from just a kiss. 'Get away from me,' she snapped, only too aware of her own humiliating shortness of breath.

He let his arms fall to his sides and straightened, looking a little surprised. 'Perhaps you'll have more care with your words in future. Then I won't feel the need to stem the tide.'

She didn't want to talk to him at all. She dodged beneath his arm, and scuttled ignominiously across the room, jerking around to face him when she reached the far side. To her relief, he made no move to follow. 'I wish to go to my brother.'

He cocked a brow.

Her heartbeat slowed and she felt more like herself. 'If you please,' she said regally.

He leaned against the doorpost, folding his arms over that broad expanse of very male chest and observed her with narrowed eyes. 'I don't please. Sit down, Miss Fulton. We need to have a conversation.'

'What can you and I possibly have to discuss?'

'Your future and that of your companions.' His voice was flat and hard and full of confident power.

Her stomach dipped, but she kept her expression calm. 'Very well.' She marched to the only other chair in the room apart from the one behind the desk. She perched on its edge, folding her hands in her lap, praying he wouldn't see how she shook inside and pinned an afternoon-tea-with-strangers smile on her lips. 'What are your plans?'

'It depends on you.'

'How?'

He pursed his mobile mouth as if deciding how to deliver bad news.

Looking into his eyes was like watching the ever-changing ocean. If eyes were the windows to the soul, his had turned the colour of storms at sea, the cold grey-green of the Atlantic in winter.

The cold crept into her blood.

He pushed off from the doorway and stalked to his

desk. He perched one lean hip on the corner. Once more he was far too close for comfort. She squashed the urge to flee.

'We might as well be civil,' he said. 'May I offer you some refreshment after your ordeal?'

Now he would play the gentleman? And would she submit meekly? Play the polite lady? 'No, thank you.'

'You won't mind if I do?' He reached down, clearly not caring if she minded or not, and opened a drawer. He pulled out a bottle and glass, poured a measure into the goblet and returned the bottle to the drawer. Every movement was elegant, unhurried, yet rife with leashed power.

It was all she could do to simply draw breath and sit unmoving beneath his cool stare.

'To the Fultons.' He grimaced and swallowed a long draught as if to remove the taste of her name from his tongue.

One booted foot swung as he observed her over the rim of his goblet. She'd never seen such long, muscular legs displayed to such heart-stopping effect. Oh, no! How could she be impressed by this an awful man? The problem was, he was too dreadfully handsome and his kisses were like a drug to her senses.

She pressed her lips together. Let him speak what was on his mind. It worked in business. It would work with him too.

'Why were you on board?' he finally asked. 'You and your brother?'

If it wasn't too strange to contemplate, she might have thought the note in his voice was gloating. 'I was visiting a friend in Lisbon. My brother loves the sea. It was a treat for him, before he goes to school.'

'A spree? With a war on?' He shook his head. 'Your father must care very little for your safety.'

'If it wasn't for men like you, our safety wouldn't be an issue.'

His dark brows drew together.

Dash it. It really wasn't a good idea to poke a lion with a stick to see what it would do, but this man had her feeling ill at ease, not herself at all. Not afraid so much as frazzled. Now she understood how an oyster felt with a bit of sand beneath its shell. Irritable. If she could only keep her gaze from admiring his manly physique, she might gather a few coherent thoughts.

'You've a sharp wit to go along with your sharp tongue, I believe,' he said. 'You used it to good effect on the merchants in Lisbon.'

Everything had depended on her forcing Anderson up to the mark in his dealings for this cargo, but she had the feeling the less this man knew, the better. And on this occasion, she didn't mind playing the female card. She widened her eyes and curved her lips in a vacuous smile. 'La, sir. Me? Engage in business?'

'And the other woman? Lady Selina Albright? Your last-minute addition to the passenger list? Why is she on board?'

She lifted a shoulder. 'If it is any business of yours, Lady Selina is a friend. She wanted to return to England early. I offered her a berth.'

Offered was far too gentle a word. Selina had showed up in tears on the night of their sailing demanding to be taken home. To make room for her, Alice had been required to leave her maid behind on the dock.

'I see,' he said.

The words had the weight of a threat.

Chapter Three

She had more courage than half the men he knew. The rays of the setting sun warmed her pale skin and glinted in the wisps of caramel hair at her temples. He hadn't expected such a prim little mouth, with its full bottom lip, to issue such blistering condemnations.

He certainly hadn't expected a gently bred, haughty English female to respond to his kiss with the passion of a tropical siren. Not that he had any interest in her kisses. He'd simply wanted to stop her words. He'd learned early that women forgot their nagging when you pleasured their senses. He'd kissed lots of them quiet. Most of them far more lush and lovely than this one.

To his annoyance, he found himself aroused. But he did not want her silence. He had uses for Miss Fulton's tongue that had nothing to do with the blood stirring in his body.

He scratched at his chin. 'Albright,' he mused. 'A wealthy family, I recollect. She would fetch a fine ransom.'

'Ransom?' The high pitch of her voice revealed her

shock. Anger bloomed rosy on her cheeks. 'Aren't you getting enough from stealing the cargo?'

Not nearly enough. 'Did you think I brought you on board for the pleasure of your company?' He flashed a smile. 'Delightful though it is, of course.'

Her eyes widened. Her body shifted. He saw worry in the way she lowered her gaze, and fear in the way her fingers plucked at her skirts.

Small strong hands. Clever hands that felt good on a man's body. Not that he'd feel them again.

Finally she raised her head. 'Why am I here?' She gestured around her. 'Why are you keeping me from my brother?'

A perfectly logical question. Something he didn't expect when dealing with females, but he'd already learned that this one had a brain when she wasn't worrying about her sibling. 'Before you return to your friends, I need some questions answered.'

'I won't tell you anything.'

'Then you will remain here.'

Her shoulders slumped in defeat. He felt more than a little guilty.

'I will tell you anything you want to know. But not until I have seen my brother,' she said, lifting her chin.

Defeated but not routed apparently 'Very well.' The words surprised him, but he'd get more from her with honey than vinegar. And he had honey to spare as she'd discover.

She cast him a wary glance. 'May I also ask for your promise that we will not be harmed while we are your…guests?'

The little minx. He almost smiled. Damn it, he did not want to admire her spirit. 'You may ask.'

'I see you take pleasure in toying with me, sir.' Her light laugh sounded like breaking glass.

The sound wrenched at something in his chest. Something he'd frozen out of existence. He forced it back where it belonged, out in the cold, ignored and unnoticed. 'Answer my questions to my satisfaction and I will consider your request.'

Moisture shimmered in her green-flecked brown eyes, but she held her gaze steady, unblinking, and nodded.

He found he couldn't look at her any more. It was like looking in the mirror and seeing your faults laid out on public view.

Hell's teeth. He wasn't the one who should feel guilty. Old Fulton was the one who had sent her into danger. He deserved the blame, for this and so much more.

'Hurry up, if you want to see your brother now, or I will insist on receiving my answers first.' He opened the door wide. 'No matter how long it takes.'

Alice stared at the privateer warily. An aura of danger hung about him. A danger she seemed unable to resist.

She should never have tried to cross swords with him. He'd met her assault with ruthless seduction as if he sensed where her weakness lay. The thought made her tremble. But if she wanted to see Richard, she had to do as he said.

He raised a brow.

With a quick inward breath to steady her nerves, she walked past him and out on deck.

'Stay close,' he murmured, leaning close. 'My men aren't used to women on board.'

She shivered, but whether from his warm breath on her cheek, or the threat he implied, she wasn't sure.

Outside the door, the squat sailor stood at attention, his black eyes gleaming.

'You met my steward,' Lionhawk said. 'He will see to my guests' every comfort. Won't you, Simpson?'

'Aye, Cap'n.'

Guests. She almost snorted. 'The only thing I would find of comfort is to be landed at the nearest port.'

Lionhawk laughed. An annoyingly seductive chuckle that hit a nerve low in her stomach. 'Come, we are wasting time.'

Time Richard might not have. She quickened her pace.

His hand in the small of her back, he guided her aft while above their heads a few stars were already piercing the velvet blue to the east. A light breeze caressed her heated skin.

A sailor coiling ropes beside the mast watched them pass with a sly grin from beneath his straggly moustache. Kale. The man Lionhawk had chased off on the deck of the *Conchita*. Other men hung in the ratlines. The helmsman darted a glance their way, and a lad half-heartedly mopping the deck saluted. She kept her back straight and her gaze firmly fixed ahead.

'What do you think of my ship?' Lionhawk asked with an expansive wave of his hand and pride in his voice.

'The truth?'

'Of course.'

'I wish I'd never set eyes on her.'

He chuckled. 'You wound me, Miss Fulton. I thought I was offering you every courtesy.'

Liar. She pressed her lips firmly together, determined not to provide him with any more amusement.

'Down here,' he said and plunged down a companionway. Highly polished wooden panels reflected her face beneath the wall-hung oil lamp. Brass fittings gleamed dull gold and without so much as a fingerprint in sight. The ship was clearly well run and it must have cost him a fortune to build.

At the bottom of the steps, he plucked a lamp from the wall. 'The crew's quarters are on the gun deck. Down here is the hold.' He bent and pulled on an iron ring in the floorboards. The trapdoor lifted with a creak.

Musty air wafted up from the dark void. She choked back a gasp. Holding the lantern aloft, Lionhawk stepped on to the ladder.

Alice shuddered. She wiped her damp palms on her skirt, grasped the rope lines on either side of the open-rung steps and followed him down.

At the bottom, his lantern cast a halo of light into the gloom. A chain swung from a nail driven into a beam like an instrument of torture in some ancient oubliette. And if she wasn't mistaken there was a strong odour of chicken manure. She grabbed at the wall to steady herself.

'Seasick, are you?'

'I've never been seasick in my life, but the stench is disgusting. How can you put people down here?'

He recoiled, his eyes flashing anger. 'I'm sorry my accommodations don't meet with your approval. We keep livestock down here on long voyages,' he said and moved ahead. 'If it is good enough for chickens, it should be good enough for a group of Fultons,' he muttered.

At least that was what she thought she heard before a sailor in a coarse linen shirt and wide canvas trousers rose from a stool beside a bulkhead door. 'All quiet, Cap'n.'

'Thanks, Del.' He hesitated. 'You did open the hatches before you put the prisoners in there, didn't you?'

'Er…Mr Wishart didn't say anything about opening any hatches.'

Lionhawk cursed under his breath. 'See to it, man.'

'Aye, aye, Cap'n.' The sailor dodged around them and was heading up the ladder in a flash.

It seemed the captain had some shred of humanity, even if he had to be reminded.

'It's the best I can do,' he said gruffly. 'I don't have accommodations on my ship for passengers.' He flashed a cheeky grin. 'I'm sure your friends wouldn't want to sling their hammocks with the crew, though I'm sure the crew wouldn't mind entertaining your friend, Lady Selina.'

It was almost as if he wanted to make her angry rather than appreciative. She sniffed. 'Fresh air will help, I am sure.'

He removed a bunch of keys from his belt and unlocked the door. He gestured for her to enter. 'After you.'

Indeed, the area resembled nothing more fearful than a smelly barn. Richard and Mr Anderson lay stretched out on two of the four cots placed along the hull. Selina, her head in her arms, drooped at a table that also held the remains of what looked like a meal of bread and cheese.

A couple of lanterns swinging from the beams provided light and the floor was carpeted with what looked like fresh straw, upon which stood their trunks. So they were not to be left in the clothes they stood up in.

'Selina.' Alice rushed forwards. Selina surged to her feet. She flung herself at Alice's breast and they clung to each other.

'Are you all right?' Alice asked, holding her friend's shaking body. 'No one hurt you? Touched you?'

'My men have strict orders not to lay hands on my prisoners without my express instructions,' Lionhawk said from behind her.

A shame he didn't include himself in his order, Alice thought, breaking free and making for Richard's still form.

'I'm quite all right, now,' Selina murmured with a swift resentful look at their captor. 'You get used to the smell after a while, but I thought I'd die of fright in that horrid swinging contraption.' She shuddered. 'I wish I had never asked you to bring me home.' She lowered her voice. 'Where did you go? I was so worried. I kept asking and asking for you.'

When Alice touched Richard's shoulder, he didn't flicker so much as an eyelid. 'Is he sleeping?'

Selina shook her head. 'He's been the same ever since we arrived in this dreadful place.'

Alice sank to her knees beside the pallet. 'Richard,' she whispered. She pressed a palm to a cheek pale beneath its tan. Cold and clammy. For one horrible moment she thought he wasn't breathing. A horrid churning rolled in her stomach. Then she felt the faint pulse beating in his throat beneath her fingertips and saw the gentle rise of his chest. Not dead. She closed her eyes in thanks.

'He's had a knock to the head,' Lionhawk said.

'Yes,' she replied. 'By a spar shot down by your men.' But why was he still unconscious? Panic tightened her chest. 'He needs a doctor.'

From above their heads came a scraping sound, the hatch covering being removed. Alice glanced up. Through the gratings, she could just see the twinkle of stars and a gust of sweet air set the lanterns flickering. She inhaled a deep breath. While the smell wasn't entirely gone, it was certainly a whole lot fresher and a great deal healthier.

No doubt Lionhawk would want her gratitude for that little concession.

'The doctor looked at your brother,' Anderson said from the neighbouring cot. He struggled up on one elbow. His broken arm rested in a sling against his chest, but he looked none too bad.

'How are you, Mr Anderson?' Alice asked.

'The sawbones seems to know his business, Miss Fulton. He set my arm. He's given your brother something to keep him calm and sleeping. I'm afraid it is Lady Selina who is not feeling quite the thing. The doctor left her some smelling salts.'

Poor Selina. She really wasn't meant for hardship.

'Mr Anderson has been a tower of strength,' Selina said, beaming at him. 'I don't know what I would have done without him.'

Mr Anderson turned the colour of a house brick. If Selina wasn't careful, she'd have him spiking a temperature.

'I am in your debt, Mr Anderson,' Alice said. 'Please send word if you have cause for concern.'

Selina gasped. 'Send word? Where are you going? Not with that disgusting pirate?' She glanced over her shoulder, tossed her head and shot Lionhawk a look of dislike.

Selina's rudeness brought heat to Alice's cheeks, which didn't make a bit of sense. 'He has questions I am to answer.'

Selina looked at her askance. 'What sort of questions?'

'I'm not exactly sure.'

'Alice, you can't be alone with him.'

No fool, Selina, when it came to men. Without her timely intervention, Alice might have married Andrew. But Alice had already given her word to provide answers in exchange for this visit and she'd have to rely on her own wits to bring her off safely. 'I won't be long. I promise.'

Selina lowered her voice. 'What about my reputation? I'm all alone with two bachelors.'

Alice frowned at her. 'Mr Anderson is an honourable married man. You know he is. And Richard is naught but a boy. Besides, they need your help. It is only for an hour or two.'

'You know more about nursing the sick than I do.' Selina's lower lip drooped in pathetically adorable fashion.

Alice pressed her lips together. 'All right. You deal with Lionhawk.'

Selina's eyes widened. *'Alice.'*

'I thought you came to visit your brother,' Lionhawk's voice grated in the thick, stale air. 'If you are done, we will leave.'

His steps echoed in the hold as he strode across the floor, his shadow looming on the curved hull like the carved gryphon over his bed. He entered the circle of light, his expression impatient and his eyes watchful.

Selina shrank back, staring at him as if he had two heads. 'Alice, isn't that…?'

'The man who signed on as our cook. Yes.' She glared at him. 'I am not ready to leave yet, sir.'

'Lady Selina,' he said with a flash of a charming smile and a bow, 'I don't believe we have been formally introduced. I'm Lionhawk, Captain of the *Gryphon*.'

A simple introduction delivered with the charm of a wolf who'd found his dinner.

Selina shifted closer to Alice, seemingly unable to take her gaze from the dark face of her gaoler.

Lionhawk bared his teeth all the more. 'Come into the light, Lady Selina. Let's take a proper look at you.'

'Alice!' Selina's voice rose to a squeak.

Alice mentally groaned. This lion or hawk or evil dragon, whatever he called himself, needed a lesson in how to treat a lady. She patted Selina on the shoulder. 'Ignore him. He's just trying to bedevil me.' She glanced back at Richard and a trickle of fear ran through her stomach. 'I would like to speak to the doctor.'

'Not tonight, you won't.' Lionhawk's voice had the implacable quality of a man expecting obedience. 'My crew are celebrating their victory. Bones won't be in any shape to look at anyone tonight and he tells me your brother will be all right until morning. Come along before I carry you out.'

Dash it all. Whoever this doctor was, he had no business leaving an injured man unconscious. The man she had seen climbing into the bo'sun's chair had looked far from competent. No wonder he hadn't seen to opening the hatch. And if he was drunk, as his captain suggested, she preferred her own ministrations. The sooner she answered Lionhawk's questions, the sooner she could return to her brother.

Selina flung herself into Alice's arms, tears running like diamonds down her cheeks. Somehow Selina managed to look like a goddess when she wept. 'Alice, what is to become of us?'

That was a line out of a play for Lionhawk's benefit. A quest for sympathy. Wasted on this man. Thankfully, beneath the weeping goddess, Selina was made of sterner stuff. Stern enough to walk out on her chaperon and jump aboard Alice's ship without so much as a by your leave.

Easing from Selina's grip, Alice lifted her friend's chin with a fingertip, capturing her watery gaze in her own. 'Do pull yourself together.' She lowered her voice to a whisper meant only for her friend's ears. 'Trust me. I'll come back soon. In the meantime, I'm relying on you to help care for Richard and Mr Anderson.'

Selina straightened her shoulders. 'I'm sorry,' she said softly. 'I didn't mean to make things more difficult. I will do my best.' She glanced quickly at Lionhawk, her eyes sharp. 'Alice, mark my words. Be very careful of that man.'

'Come along, Miss Fulton,' Lionhawk said, the sardonic line of his lips cruel in its indifference. Then he smiled, all charm again. 'Unless you would both like to join me in my cabin.'

Alice glared at him. 'One of us is all you need to answer your questions.' Somehow during the course of the evening she'd convince Lionhawk to let her raid his medical supplies. A poultice set to Richard's temple might be the best thing to bring him back to his senses.

Blast the man. By now he'd probably guessed she'd do anything to keep her brother safe. Selina was right— she would have to be very careful. Or very clever.

With one last glance at her brother, she headed out of the door.

Lionhawk closed it, pocketed the key and took her arm. Up on deck, he guided her towards his cabin. 'I'd introduce you to my crew,' he murmured, 'but they are in a rollicking mood. Not good company for a lady such as yourself.'

From the prow came the sound of a flute and deep men's voices raised in drunken harmony. 'I'll accept your judgement in that regard.'

Just how safe were the prisoners with such a crew? Thank God Lionhawk held the key.

She sucked in a breath. Did that mean she actually trusted the fellow to keep his captives safe? Trusting anyone on this ship would be like trusting a rabid dog. It would be like a green girl with stars in her eyes trusting Andrew. No longer was she green and the stars had long ago faded.

Lionhawk opened his cabin door. 'Supper awaits.'

Supper? A good idea. Men became easier to handle on a full stomach. She stepped inside.

A lantern hung from the central beam. Candlesticks glimmered on the desk. A low table had been placed in front of the window laid with a tray of bread, cheeses and cold meats along with a decanter of red wine and two filigreed goblets.

She took the chair he pulled out. He seated himself on the other side. 'It's all there is, I'm afraid.'

Alice waved an airy hand, *à la* Selina. 'It is all I need.' She picked up the bread knife.

Swiftly, he leaned across and removed the knife from her grip. 'I wouldn't want you to hurt yourself.'

He carved the half-cottage loaf into thick slices and leaned back, retaining the knife as if he thought she might have at him. Unfortunately, killing him would likely not improve her situation.

And what could he possibly have in mind that he would think she might become so desperate? More questions? Or more kisses? A skitter went through her stomach that wasn't exactly unpleasant.

A sensation best guarded against.

'Eat,' he said.

Glad to see her hands did not tremble too much, she filled her plate with bread and cheese. 'It is a while since I dined alfresco,' she said lightly. 'A picnic,' she added.

He stretched his booted feet out in front of him and frowned at her. 'I know what alfresco means. Normally, I'd provide a hot meal. There was no cooking fire today.'

'Open fires and gunpowder are not a good mix,' she agreed. 'I'm pleased to see you care about the safety of your men. It would hardly do for their ship to burn while they run down innocent merchantmen.'

A glint of amusement flashed in his eyes. 'Innocent is not a term I would use, and nor would you,' he remarked in dry tones.

Now what did he mean by that? She picked up a piece of bread. Even buttered, it tasted little better than ashes. Fear did that to a person, ruined the appetite. She added a slice of cheese. A marginal improvement. If she washed it down with wine, it might cure the trembles in her stomach.

Perhaps not. She'd need all her wits to survive the coming interview.

'More?' he asked softly, waving the knife at the bread.

She shook her head, noticing he had eaten nothing while consuming at least half the wine in the decanter. Perhaps he, too, was nervous, though she could scarcely credit it.

Simpson arrived to clear away the tray. Alice watched the knife's departure with a flicker of regret. It might have come in handy. She flashed hot, then cold. Hopefully such drastic measures wouldn't be necessary.

Lionhawk refilled his glass and cast her a charming smile. A breath caught in her throat at the threat that smile contained. 'Now then, Miss Fulton. It is time to answer my questions.'

Somehow she managed not to flee for the door. She fought to keep her face blandly enquiring.

As handsome as sin, as dark as Satan, he lounged carelessly in his ornate chair, legs outstretched, glass held loosely in his hand. Masculine power at ease to a fault, but ready to spring if she made one false move.

A heavy-lidded gaze cut her way. Seductive. Threatening. He frightened and fascinated all at once. Against all reason, she found him impossibly attractive, the way one might find a lion or tiger attractive. Beautiful, sleek and dangerous.

'What did you wish to know?' She was glad her voice didn't shake too badly.

'Everything.' To her utter confusion, he put a world of meaning in the one word and its accompanying narrowed-eyed stare. 'I thought we would start with the story of your life.'

She almost laughed. 'It makes for dull telling, sir.'

'But it is new to me. To begin with, I suppose it is too much to hope that you play chess,' he said, rather wistfully.

'Chess?' She almost slipped off her seat in surprise.

'I hear it is an acceptable pastime for men and women to play together in intimate surroundings. Perhaps you prefer cards?'

The word intimate rang in her ears. She gripped the edge of her seat. 'I do play chess. Quite well, in fact.'

He got up and prowled dangerously close. 'Quite well?' He smiled as if she'd hand-fed the wolf in him a succulent morsel. Or a piece of herself.

Her pulse tripped a warning. She gazed back boldly. 'Some would say very well.'

He leaned closer, his face inches from hers, his wine-scented breath a whisper against her cheek. 'Excellent. And while we play, you will talk.'

Clutching her goblet tight to her breast, she fought the tremble in her hands. Fear of his threat, not a wild heart-stopping impulse to taste his sensual lips again. Only by the fiercest resolve did she manage not to blink. 'It sounds delightful.'

His gaze ran from her head to her heels and a trickle of warmth beneath her skin followed its progress. She stifled a sigh of pure pleasure.

A slow smile dawned on his face. 'I must warn you, I have not played for a very long time.'

'Then prepare for defeat.'

He grinned. 'Defeat by a woman has its benefits.' The lascivious note in his voice made her insides clench. She kept her expression blank. Proper young ladies did not understand such innuendo. And it would not do to let him believe she was anything but a proper young lady.

He retrieved a marquetry box inlaid with silver from his desk. Inside, two shades of green jade pieces nestled in white satin, beautiful carvings depicting samurai and dragons and other Oriental images. Worth a king's ransom and no doubt stolen from some poor traveller.

He set out the pieces on a plain, painted wooden board that set the ornate pale and dark green jade off to perfection.

He sat down. 'Your move.'

Chapter Four

'Tell me about your father,' Lionhawk said in a lazy drawl. 'Alex Fulton.'

They were the first words he'd spoken since she'd made her opening move and the intensity in his gaze created a tightness in her abdomen. Apparently her answer was important.

'He owns a shipping line.'

The dark brows drew down. 'I know what he does. Tell me about *him*.'

How odd. She thought for a moment. 'I suppose you could say he is an older version of Richard. He is a bit heavier, not quite so tall, but they are clearly father and son.'

'Is he a good father?'

She squirmed in her seat. 'No worse than any other.'

He moved a warrior to guard his queen. 'A prevarication, Miss Fulton? I must say I am surprised a father would put his daughter on a ship flying a false flag in these dangerous times.'

When Father learned about that, he'd be horrified.

He might even disappear into a brandy bottle and never get around to raising the ransom. He'd been doing a lot of disappearing lately. A cold little breeze whisked across her shoulders from the open window. She forced herself not to rub her arms. 'It really is none of your business.'

A dark eyebrow lifted. 'I suppose he forgot to tell you of the risk?'

She gritted her teeth at the amused note in his voice. It was as if he liked the idea of Father putting her and Richard in danger.

'How many ships does Fulton Shipping own in addition to the *Conchita*?' he asked.

'What concern is it of yours?'

He straightened. 'Come, come, Miss Fulton. Surely you want the doctor to visit your brother tomorrow?'

Damn him. 'There are no other ships besides the *Conchita*.'

A derisive sound issued from his throat. 'You surely don't think me such a halfwit as to believe the great Fulton Shipping Lines owns only one ship?'

'Believe what you like. You asked me a question and I answered it.'

'Trying to do me out of my ransom, Miss Fulton?'

So that was where this was leading. 'I don't lie, Captain Lionhawk.'

'Michael.' He picked up one of the pieces she'd lost to him, a female figure in long robes. Idly, his long strong fingers stroked the elegant piece.

Strangely breathless, she watched his fingertips trace the flowing curves in a strangely intimate gesture. Heat flowed through her veins.

'A geisha,' he said.

Her gaze flew to his face. 'I beg your pardon?'

'The figure. She is called a geisha. They are trained in the art of pleasing men.'

'Oh.' She looked down at the board. The geishas took the place of pawns. 'They are lovely.'

'Yes. Are you telling me your father has sold all his ships, including the ship he'd named after you?'

He knew more than she expected. 'Would you believe anything I say?'

The movement of his fingers stilled. 'Your meaning?'

'It is quite obvious. You mean to squeeze my father for every penny. I could tell you anything, but you would have no way of knowing if I spoke the truth.'

If it wasn't impossible, she might have thought the corner of his mouth twitched with the urge to smile. 'You are foolhardy, Miss Fulton. Your brother's health is at stake, remember?'

As if she could think of anything else? She huffed a sigh. 'Very well. These past two years have been difficult for Fulton's. Insurance costs have increased sixfold. Losses to privateers have been enormous. My father has only one ship left.'

He absorbed her answer without reaction. 'It is your turn to move.'

She picked up her dragon and plonked it down in front of what should have been a bishop, but was some sort of monk.

'Tell me about your childhood,' he said. 'Where did you grow up?'

An odd choice of topic. What harm could it do? 'I was raised in Oxfordshire. We have a house there. Westerly.'

'Named after a fair wind, I presume.'

'A family joke.'

His mouth tightened. He moved his other monk to block two of her geishas.

'Did you have a happy childhood?' he asked.

'Yes. Thank you. I had loving parents and a comfortable home. Who could ask for more?'

'Who indeed?' He shook his head as if pondering the vagaries of life. 'And yet your father endangers your life on a risky venture.'

'Thank you for your concern. And what about you? If I'm not mistaken, you also are English. Where did you grow up?'

Bleakness darkened his gaze. His smile faded. 'In hell.'

She blinked. 'I'm sorry to hear it.'

'Are you? Do you care what happens to life's unfortunates? Or do you wander through your shallow life in London thinking all is right with the world? Or perhaps the mere thought of the dregs of humanity makes you nervous?'

Well, really! A thief, questioning her morals? She studied the fine workmanship of the little dragon she'd won earlier in the game, reining in a sudden surge of anger. 'Why would it make me nervous, sir, when in my exalted existence I never come into contact with any such persons? I sail through life with my nose in the air and see nary a one of them. Even on shipboard, my father's sailors only come out at night so I don't have to look at them.'

He laughed softly. '*Touché*, Miss Fulton. By the way, where did you learn to stitch up a man's flesh? I must say you did a good job.'

She glanced at the fine linen of his shirt covering his arm. 'It is healing, then?'

'It is,' he said gravely. 'Thank you.'

'I'm glad.' She felt more pleased than she ought. She pressed her lips together to hold back a smile.

He shifted in his chair, drawing up one booted foot to rest on his knee. Another display of beautiful male muscles.

Blast. She had to stop thinking about his physique or he'd mesmerise her into telling him something she did not want him to know. Like her father's coffers had a very big hole in the bottom.

'Tell me more about Westerly. Is it large? Are there stables?'

'Naturally, there are stables.' Fine empty ones these days.

He swirled his wineglass. 'Do you hunt, Miss Fulton?'

She shook her head. 'I spend most of my time in London. If I want to ride, I hire a hack. Do you hunt, sir?'

His eyelids lowered a fraction and his teeth flashed white. A pirate's grin, sly and devastatingly attractive. 'Only ships.'

Irritation warred with feminine desire. 'I imagine it is an occupation that provides little occasion for riding around the countryside.'

His smile disappeared. 'You imagine correctly.'

'You are missing a sport most *gentlemen* find exhilarating.'

Apparently deciding to ignore her barb, he inclined his head. 'Thank you for the recommendation. What do you do in London?'

No doubt he expected her to list the usual social whirl of balls and routs, but for some reason she didn't want him to think her so frippery. 'Mostly I help my father. I am also a member of the committee raising funds for St Thomas's Hospital's new surgery.'

He curled his lip. 'A sterling member of society, in fact.'

He made it sound as if she was bragging. She pressed her lips together and returned her gaze to the board.

'And you expect me to believe your father has but one ship?'

She winced. She scarcely believed it herself. 'Why should it be of concern to you?'

Candlelight danced in his bright aquamarine eyes. A mocking smile curved his lips, as if he was somehow enjoying their verbal sparring. He reminded her of a cat toying with a mouse. A very large, very dangerous, cat with enormous claws. 'I only want my due, Miss Fulton.'

'Your due?' She couldn't help how incredulous she sounded. 'How would you feel if some stranger stole the bread from the mouths of your wife and family?'

A muscle flickered in his jaw. 'I have no family.'

'A rolling stone?' She arched a brow. 'Or perhaps none you care to own to.'

'Miss Fulton, I would never abandon a child of mine. I hope, for your sake, your father is equally responsible.'

Her stomach gave a sick little lurch. What her father would do depended on whether he could raise any more credit.

He leaned forwards and blocked her samurai knight with a well-placed geisha-pawn.

'Check,' he said. 'What about your prospects—is there no wedding in your future?'

'I haven't yet met a man I prefer.'

'There was talk of an engagement a few years ago, I heard. To some minor Scottish family.' He raised a brow.

Her body stilled. Pain squeezed her chest as raw as

the day Selina had told her of Andrew's treachery. How did this pirate know? Had his capture of their ship been more than a crime of opportunity?

Her fingers shook as her hand hovered over her monk. If she tried to pick it up, she might drop it.

She returned her hand to her lap as if she'd changed her mind about which piece to move, aware that his silence required an answer.

'We did not suit,' she said carelessly. Andrew only wanted her money. His profession of love was naught but a false coin.

'Rumour has it you are an unconscionable flirt. That you were looking higher. For a title.'

Lies to cover Andrew's chagrin when she cried off.

'How would you know this ancient news?' she asked. It had happened so long ago, even the *ton* had forgotten.

He shrugged. 'I have friends. I hear gossip from time to time. Fulton's is well known among sailors.'

A truth.

Feeling calmer, she reached for the decanter and poured him a glass of wine with a smile, hoping to distract him from this line of questioning.

'Join me,' he said.

A command. She shrugged and filled her glass.

'Where did you go to school?' she asked.

He frowned at her. 'Me?'

'I assumed you received some sort of education. You don't sound like a common seaman.'

For once his insouciance seemed to slip. His lips flattened, his eyes grew hard. 'I learned all I know before the mast.' The tang of bitterness colouring his voice sent warning prickles across her shoulders. Yet she wanted to know more of this man's history. She waved a nonchalant hand. 'Why did you leave England for America?'

He grimaced. 'Not of my own volition, I assure you.'

Deported? It was possible. Britain had long been sending her criminals abroad. Or might he have fled? A horrid vision popped into her mind. 'Did you kill your man at dawn?' Over some woman.

He snorted. 'Duelling is a waste of time. There are far better ways to satisfy honour. Tell me why the *Conchita* was flying a Spanish flag?'

Another change of direction. Conversing with this man was like balancing on the edge of a knife. One slip and you'd be cut to ribbons. She found the whole thing exhausting.

'There were rumours of privateers.' A wry smile twisted her lips. 'They proved correct.'

'It was your idea, wasn't it?'

She nodded.

'Well, let me thank you for making my work easier.'

Her palm itched with the desire to slap the supercilious expression from his face. Instead, she regally bent her neck. 'Glad to be of service.'

A laugh of genuine amusement rumbled up from his chest, low and warm. It strummed a chord low in her belly. She scowled.

'You are certainly an enterprising woman,' he said.

Time to give him another surprise. The number of her pieces scattered on his side of the board proved he'd played well, if cautiously. Now she would bring their evening to a close. She moved her monk. 'Checkmate.'

He recoiled, staring at the board. 'Good God.'

Another man who thought women didn't have any

mental capacity. She smiled tightly. 'Thank you for a close-run game.'

He glanced up at her face, shock lingering in his eyes like shadows. 'I had no idea how much I'd forgotten.'

At least he hadn't accused her of cheating as one gentleman had. 'You played well enough.'

Staring at the board, he gulped down his wine, his Adam's apple rising and falling as he swallowed. He leaned forwards, gaze intent, as if replaying the game. Finally he looked up at her, with a sort of boyish eagerness that robbed her of breath. 'Where did I go wrong?'

With effort, she gathered her thoughts. 'I took advantage of your mistakes.'

He didn't look the slightest bit insulted by her honesty. She found herself liking him for that. Blast it. She really did have no sense when it came to men. 'Then I must do better. Next time.'

There wasn't going to be a next time. She hoped.

He cocked his head, listening. 'The hour grows late.'

She heard only the breeze singing in the rigging and the slap of the waves against the hull from the open window. She glanced at him questioningly.

'The men are all abed, except those on watch.'

The revelry outside had died away long ago. She'd been too intent on their game and fielding his sharp questions to notice the passage of time. She swallowed. 'I should leave.'

'I have many more questions. Drink your wine, Miss Fulton.' He gestured at her glass. 'Come, a toast.'

To humour him, she picked up her glass.

'To success,' he said.

'Yours or mine?'

'Mine.' While she sipped, he drank deeply. When

he lowered his glass the predatory expression was back on his face.

The cabin seemed stuffy all at once, airless and hot. The skin on her scalp tightened the way it did before a lightning storm and she knew she had to bring the evening to a close. Somehow she had to end this tête-à-tête on a friendly note.

She stood and carried her glass to the window on legs that felt the way they did the first moments on land after a long voyage. Like wet rags. Unfortunately, this voyage was far from over and a storm loomed on the horizon.

She gazed out into the dark, breathing in the salt air. 'I must thank you for a pleasant evening.'

Cat-like, on silent feet, he appeared behind her, his face reflected in the glass over her shoulder, his smile a glimmer of white. The warmth radiating from his body fired off a storm of heat in her own. A demented blush from head to toe, thankfully hidden in the dark reflection.

'You were right about me,' he said, his voice low, his body warm at her back. 'Once, I also had all the advantages of wealth and position.' Deep beneath the easy tone, she heard great sorrow.

She resisted the urge to sympathise. She'd heard many similar tales. It was the women she pitied. 'Did you lose your money in one of London's hells? Is that why you prey on ships? Stealing what you lost?' It happened all the time. Fortunes won and lost in a night. Men who committed suicide in the cold light of the following day.

She shuddered. At least Father preferred the comfort of brandy.

His reflected gaze skewered her like a blade. 'I can never replace what I lost.'

The depth of pain in those words scoured her ridiculously soft heart like sand carried on a desert wind. 'You lost the family estate?'

The silence stretched taut and painful. The urge to fill it, to pretend things were normal, brought words to her lips. 'What will you do when the war is over? When there are no more letters of marque? When peace allows no ships to be taken?'

The long exhale of breath, a sigh of longing he probably wasn't aware of. 'I plan to return to England where I have unfinished business.'

'You think you will be welcome?'

'A man with money is always welcome.'

A bitter truth. She said nothing.

'What about you, Miss Fulton? What do you hope for? A husband? Children?' He breathed softly in her ear. 'A lover on the side?'

Her nipples tightened, felt sensitive against her stays. Furious at herself, she spun around to face him.

Chest to chest they stared at each other. His eyes glittered dangerously. A sign of intoxication? Or anger?

He clasped his warm hand over hers on the stem of her glass. Hot against her cold skin. The diamond-sharp facets pressed into her palm. 'You tremble, Miss Fulton. I wonder why?' Holding her gaze, he took the glass from her hand and set it on the table.

His eyes turned slumberous. A sensual awareness flashed between them too strong to ignore. It had been there all night, connecting them with a filament of heat. Now, standing close to him, the minute sliver of air between their bodies practically crackled.

His lips hovered a few inches from hers. The warmth of his body washed up against her skin. He was going to kiss her. A mad kind of yearning filled her empty heart. She swayed closer. Her eyelids fluttered shut. The scent of sandalwood cologne and fresh sea air filled her nostrils.

He cursed.

She blinked.

He pressed his fingertips to his temple and squeezed his eyes shut.

'Is something wrong?' she asked.

Michael stared at her. Wrong? For a moment he didn't recognise the word as a flash of light seared jagged through the space behind his eyes.

'Are you in pain?' Her voice was soft, gentle and kind. Her hazel eyes filled with concern. 'Is it your arm?'

Why the hell did Alice Fulton have to be kind? 'I'm all right.'

Another stab, more insistent. Why was this happening now? Right when he had everything in his grasp.

She tilted her head in puzzlement. 'Perhaps a fever brought on by your wound?'

He stared at her, the words garbling in his head, the lights in the cabin unbearably bright. 'Get out.' The words came out like the snarl of a wild beast.

She backed away.

Another flash of light. Her face wavered, blurred, then righted. He had less than half an hour.

Another round of flickering stabs. This time behind his forehead. Any moment now he'd be a useless shipwreck cast up on the beach of his aching head.

Too much wine. Why the hell had he drunk so much?

The pain spiked. He rubbed his temples, seeking relief. A grinding throb set up home at the base of his skull.

No holding this one off. He grabbed for her again. 'You're leaving.'

Her eyes widened, filling with fear. He didn't care. He had to get her out of here. He would not let her see him brought to his knees.

'It's your head,' she said. 'Let me—'

'No,' he said, tugging cruelly hard on her wrist.

Anger. A hot raging beast he couldn't control crawled up his throat. 'Move.' Dragging her along, he strode for the door. He flung it open.

'Simpson,' he roared. 'Take her to the hold.' Peering through the blinding haze, he thrust her outside. Simpson would see to her. He wouldn't let him down.

God damn it all.

Thoughts whipped around in his head like storm-damaged rigging in a gale. Faces skittered across his memory. Meg falling. His beloved mother and father surrounded by flames. And Jaimie.

The light from the candles burned through his closed eyelids. Barbed arrows tore into his brain. The urge to hit something bunched his muscles. He stormed around his cabin, flinging things aside, looking for the source of his pain. The light.

The punishing light.

'Simpson,' he bellowed. 'Where the hell are you?'

A flicker of sanity gave him the answer. Gone with the girl. The daughter of his enemy.

He found the bed and ripped off the covers. Found the hooks. Nausea rose in his throat. He gripped the blanket in both fists.

'The light,' he whispered. 'For God's sake, someone douse the bloody light.'

Chapter Five

'Cap'n'll be in a foul mood today.'

He struggled to make sense of the words penetrating the thick, swirling, grey fog.

'Always is,' replied the piping tones of a boy. 'After one of they headaches.'

Who? The question bounced sluggishly in the miasma of his brain. Panic closed his throat as he stared into the surrounding heavy blackness. Who was he?

He jerked to a sitting position at the sound of a crash followed by the tinkle of shattering glass.

'Careful, lad. The Cap'n'll have your hide.'

Memories flooded in. His name was Michael. The all-too-familiar yawning pit of despair receded. He was Lionhawk. He owned this ship and he knew his name, his parents' names, his grim reality.

Michael sank back on to the mattress, safe in the dark tent of blankets put up by Simpson before he collapsed. Relief washed through him. A headache had laid him low. The momentary blank when he first awoke scared him worse than any nightmare. The rush of blessed memory, every last hellish one of them, dawned like manna from heaven.

The first episode for months. It had struck him hard. And he'd thought he was free of them. He hauled air into his lungs, gathering momentum for the task of getting up. No mean feat after a night of agony.

'Did you see the look on his face when he ordered her back to the hold?' Simpson's voice.

'Naw.' Jacko, his cabin boy. 'I only heard him roar at her.'

Her? Michael frowned and winced at the sensation of tight skin stretching over his scalp.

'I'm surprised he wanted that 'un,' Jacko said. 'T'other 'un's much purtier. Like a china doll I saw once at the market in Freeport, black curly hair and pretty pink cheeks.

Simpson grunted. 'You're too young to know, me lad. That 'un's done naught but complain. She can't hold a candle to the Fulton wench.'

Bloody hell. Alice Fulton and her brother. The pieces of the puzzle fell together in splashes of colour and light. He'd captured Fulton's ship and all who sailed in her and celebrated with too much red wine.

It put paid to his planned seduction, but he had learned a great deal more about his enemy.

In the cold light of day another truth lay before him as obvious as a steaming dollop of horse dung in the middle of a fancy soirée. Fulton Shipping had hit rough water.

Laughter balled in his chest. Served the bastard right. But just how badly off was he? Some men complained if they lost so much as a farthing.

The sounds of a scuffle broke out as Jacko and

Simpson fought for the privilege of serving him. The wily boy won and pushed his ugly wharf-rat face between the edges of Michael's makeshift cavern, grinning from one misshapen ear to the other.

'Here ye are, Cap'n. Coffee. Will ye be wanting your breakfast?'

'On my desk. And be quick about it.' The cheeky grin didn't falter, but the boy dashed off, leaving Simpson to pull down the blankets.

Michael covered his eyes with one hand and suppressed a groan.

'Might do that lad some good to feel the flat of your hand on his backside once in a while,' Simpson grumbled.

'Not on my ship. I'll turn off anyone who does.' He pressed his fingers to his temples.

'Ain't seen you this poorly since we got into the fight with the press gang from the *Dreadnought*,' Simpson commented. 'The water for your bath is on the way. Shall I call the sawbones or do you want a hair of the dog?'

The doctor could do nothing and the thought of alcohol made Michael's stomach roll. 'Coffee is all I need.'

'Cap'n?'

'Yes.'

'Er…'

'What, man? Spit it out.'

'That there Fulton lass. She told Wishart you gave orders for her and the rest of them to promenade on the deck today. Health reasons.'

Michael's mouth fell open. 'Promenade?'

Simpson rummaged through a chest for Michael's clothes. 'Sort of take a walk, like.'

'I know what the hell promenade means.'

'They're to come up at six bells. Bones agreed it would do the sick lad some good.'

So, the lad was up and about. 'I'll see Wishart in here after coffee and a bath.'

'Aye, aye, Cap'n.' Simpson held out a towel.

Absently, Michael took it. Promenade on his deck without authority from him, would she? The wench had some nerve.

But then he'd known that already. Apparently, Miss Fulton now had so little respect for him, she thought to take charge of his ship.

For some unfathomable reason, he looked forward to correcting her mistake in person. The sensation took him all abeam.

Alice stepped over the coaming at the top of the companionway and squeezed her eyelids tight against the mid-morning dazzle.

'Alice, where's my parasol?' Selina asked from the top step. In a pink muslin matched by the ribbons on her straw hat, Selina might have been preparing for a stroll through Hyde Park at the fashionable hour, instead of emerging from a dungeon. Alice smiled. One could always count on Selina to add style to the occasion.

Alice assisted her out on to the deck. 'You gave it to Mr Anderson.'

'So I did. Mr Anderson, my sunshade, if you please.'

'Here you are, Lady Selina,' Anderson said, opening the parasol. Two days' growth of beard and his arm in a sling gave the usually smart business agent a rather disreputable appearance.

A bandage around his forehead, Richard followed

him out. Mr Anderson directed them to the shade beneath the awning slung over the *Gryphon*'s deck. Mr Wishart had proved most helpful in meeting Alice's requests, once she had the doctor's agreement. Once out of the heat of a blazing sun riding high in a cloudless sky, Alice lifted her face to the cooling breeze.

Richard clung to the rail. For all his brave words, he looked as if he didn't trust his legs for support.

'Don't do too much on your first day up,' she warned, taking his arm.

'I'm all right.' He shook her off and peered over the mahogany rail into the blue-green ocean sliding by. 'You are worse than old Nanny Mills.'

And that was a bad thing? Alice curbed her tongue. Finding Richard still unconscious when she'd been hustled back to the hold last night had given her a fright. She'd bathed his temples with cool water and spent the night dozing in a chair beside his cot. Her relief at his awaking this morning with a demand for food knew no bounds.

Apart from the usual creaks and the wind humming in the rigging, the ship seemed strangely silent. No sailors aloft or on deck. She sent a sidelong glance at their captain at the helm and his nearby first officer. Now why would they send the men below?

Richard must have seen the direction of her gaze. 'Damn, but he's something, isn't he?'

'Richard, your language,' Alice admonished.

But her brother was right. At one with the elements, with his strong hands gripping the wheel, he braced against the wind and stared at the horizon as if nothing in the world existed but him and his ship. The wind played with his loose-fitting white shirt. It pulled the fabric taut and teased her with a glimpse of the sculpted muscles of his torso. Then it dove inside the shirt, billowing the cotton like a sail, emphasising his narrow hips and strong thighs in tight-fitting breeches.

Her breath hitched in appreciation of his male beauty.

It was a good thing she understood her own wanton nature, her own weakness, or she might be tempted to do more than look. But she'd followed that path before and knew the pitfalls. She was well armed to resist the handsome rogue. She hoped.

She took a deep breath. What she needed to do was find a way out of captivity that did not end in her father's complete ruin.

Lionhawk's questions seemed to hold the key, if she could just work out what it was he wanted and why he knew so much about her and her family.

'Richard, whatever the captain asks you about Father's business, tell him nothing,' she said in a low voice. 'Tell him you have been away at school and this is the first time you've been on one of these trips.'

Richard grimaced. 'You mean tell him the truth.' Once more his gaze strayed to the man at the wheel. 'What I'd give to have a ship of my own, to be answerable to no one. I want to sail, not buy and sell things or spend hours in a stuffy office pouring over accounts.'

The admiration in her brother's expression sent a sick feeling sliding around in her stomach, like the queasiness during the first days at sea. Richard was far too easily impressed. He'd always wanted to go to sea and Lionhawk was just the kind of man he'd take it in his head to emulate.

'What are you looking at?' Selina asked, joining them with Mr Anderson in tow. 'That pirate?'

'Privateer,' Richard corrected.

Selina poked her arm. 'What questions did he ask you last night?'

Richard swung around. 'What is Lady Selina talking about?'

'I had a long talk with our captain while we played a game of chess,' Alice said. 'He was prying into Father's affairs, trying to ascertain how much ransom we were worth.'

Selina shivered. 'Horrid man.'

'Yes,' Alice said, wishing her stomach didn't give a flutter every time she looked at him.

Richard bristled. 'You shouldn't have gone to his cabin.'

'Do you think I had a choice?' she said drily. 'I don't believe I told him more than I should.' If only she knew the purpose behind his questions, she might mount a better defence.

'Take heart, Lady Selina,' Anderson said. 'At least he's not thrown us overboard.'

Selina's green eyes grew round. 'Do you think he would?'

'There's no saying what a blackguard like that would do,' Anderson said. 'Preying on merchant ships about their lawful business and capturing honest citizens. He deserves to hang.'

Selina blanched.

'Oh, for goodness' sake, Mr Anderson,' Alice said. 'Can't you see you are frightening Lady Selina? It really is too bad. All the man wants is money.'

Anderson coloured. He bowed stiffly. 'I beg your pardon, ladies.'

Richard thrust out his chest and tried to look manly.

'Don't worry, Lady Selina, I'll keep you safe.' He turned an anxious pair of eyes on Alice. 'He didn't offer you any insult, did he?'

'Of course not,' she said, not quite meeting his gaze. To her shame, she couldn't call a kiss she'd responded to with enthusiasm an insult any more than she could call Andrew to account for what they'd done together.

Selina pouted. 'I want to go home. We are going to miss the Bedlingfords' rout.'

'There will be many more routs, I assure you,' Alice said.

Selina twirled her parasol. 'Do you always have to be so practical? Walk with me, someone. I need the exercise.'

Always restless, Selina would not be happy unless she was dancing until dawn and riding out all afternoon, part of the reason she had fled from sedate Lisbon society. That and a man.

'Take my arm, Lady Selina,' Anderson said, holding out his good one. 'A ship's deck is no easy matter for a delicate female. Ropes and such, you know.'

Trust Selina to bring out chivalry in a man when Alice could only manage a rough dismissal. Not that she cared. She'd been delighted to leave his cabin, even if it was rather mortifying to be thrown out like a lump of bad meat.

Selina and Anderson strolled off towards the bow.

Off the rail, the ocean flashed diamonds. Gulls dived into the water, sending up tiny waterfalls full of rainbows. The beauty of the day jarred with the turmoil in Alice's mind.

'I hate school,' Richard grumbled. 'Do you think Father will let me join the navy when we get back? I'm never seasick. Captain Dareth said I'm a natural sailor.'

If they weren't very careful, Richard might run away to sea. The thought of him joining as a common sailor chilled her blood. 'I'll talk to him when we get home.'

But when would that be? Who knew how long it would take Father to raise funds for the ransom? The trick would be to convince Lionhawk not to ask for too much, which wasn't much at all.

Completely oblivious to her worries, Richard gave her shoulders a quick hug. 'I knew I could count on you, Allie.' A rush of tenderness for the man-boy at her side filled her heart. She patted his cheek. Her fingers met hot flesh. Too hot. 'I think you may have a fever.'

Richard groaned and jerked his face away. 'The doctor said I'm all right.'

Every time she thought how close her brother had come to death, she went cold all over. She'd finally talked to Mr Bones this morning and, despite his disreputable appearance, he'd seemed to know his business. She'd ask him for willow-bark tea the next time he came to check on Richard. It would help with the fever.

Captain Dareth had taken a dreadful risk in trying to escape. Thank God Lionhawk had made him heave to before the *Gryphon* put a hole in their hull and people died, even if it did mean they'd ended up as his prize. Besides, a good lawyer might be able to prove something irregular about a prize taken by such underhanded means—if they ever made landfall to give evidence.

Against her wishes, her gaze found its way back to their captain. He looked more like a pirate than ever today in his open-necked loose-fitting shirt, black breeches and shiny black boots. Or he would, if it weren't for Selina and her fluttery pink ribbons and matching parasol parading across his deck.

As if sensing Alice's observation, he turned his head and their gazes locked. The flare of heat she saw in his piercing eyes made her tremble inside.

This had to stop. This wanton longing. It would only lead to trouble.

She forced herself to look away. When she looked back it was to see him disappearing into his cabin and Wishart alone at the wheel.

Chapter Six

Alice turned at the sound of running feet. A boy dashed by waving something aloft in a flurry of scrawny, sun-bronzed limbs.

A sailor lumbered after him a few yards behind. Kale. Alice recognised him at once.

'Give it back, you imp of Satan,' Kale bawled. He lowered his head and charged the lad. 'I'll take my belt to you, when I catches you.' He lunged. Meaty fists grabbed the boy's shirt. 'Got you.'

The boy struggled, twisting and ducking, kicking out with bare feet. Kale picked him up, dangling him like a puppy in its dam's jaws, though his intent seemed far from maternal. The shirt ripped. The boy crashed to the deck on his behind, rolled and sprang cat-like to his feet. With a crow of triumph, he pelted off. Naked from the waist up, thin arms pumping, his striated ribs expanded and contracted beneath tightly stretched skin.

Alice wanted to cheer him on, but could only watch in horrified fascination.

The lad dodged behind the mast and turned to face

his pursuer. His eyes widened, his lips drawing back from his teeth.

Kale cursed. Arms stretched wide, he lurched from side to side, blocking the boy's escape.

This was no game. No rough and tumble among shipmates. The boy was clearly terrified.

'Belay that!' Wishart roared, his face red. Good. He would stop it.

But Kale wasn't listening. He had something in his hand. It flashed metallic. A knife.

Mouth dry, her breath tangled with her voice and her shout of warning came out no more than a croak of fear.

He threw. A glinting sliver of death, turning end over end, flew right at the boy.

'Look out!' Richard cried.

At the last possible second, the boy sensed his danger and ducked. The blade whizzed over his head and landed against the bulwark with a clatter.

Thank God.

With a hoot of defiance, the lad flung himself into the ratlines on the starboard side and clambered upwards on frantic skinny limbs. Kale strode after him.

'Kale!' Wishart's roar boomed across the deck.

The seaman seemed not to hear. He hauled his burly body up on to the rail and into the yards.

Wishart roared again. 'I said enough!'

Kale turned his head, glared and then dropped to the deck, fists clenched.

Alice let go her breath.

'Stand there,' Wishart yelled. 'You heard the captain. No one on deck while the prisoners take the air. He'll be having words with you.'

The boy would come down now. Her gaze sought

him out, travelling up the ratlines and sheets, up through the timbers and billowing sails. There. Straddling the topmost spar at a dizzying height far above the deck.

Seeing his pursuer being dressed down by the officer, he leaped to his feet, shook his fist and danced a triumphant hornpipe.

The little wretch. If he wasn't careful—

His foot slipped. He grabbed for the spar. It slipped from his grasping fingers. He toppled forwards. Twisted like an acrobat. Caught one arm over the looping footropes.

Alice's heart lurched into her throat.

'Look out!' Richard grabbed her around the waist.

A large figure rushed past. Lionhawk. Alice caught the stark fear in his expression just before he flung himself upwards into the rigging, climbing like a man possessed.

Far above him, the boy's feet kicked, his free hand stretching for a rope just out of reach.

Alice pressed her hands to her mouth, unable to look away, not wanting to watch.

'Hold on,' Lionhawk yelled. His fluid strength carried him swiftly. But the boy was weakening. The rope slipped from under his armpit to the crook of his elbow. He swung wildly.

A thin wail rang out.

A gasp rushed from her throat. Her stomach knotted tight. Her heart struggled to beat. He was too little, too weak, to hold his own weight. Instinctively, she ran forwards arms outstretched.

'Please, Miss Fulton,' Wishart called out. 'Stand back.'

Richard grabbed her arm and pulled.

She couldn't move. She could only stare upwards at the figures too far apart. At the little lad's kicking feet. She could only imagine his fear. If only there was something she could do.

'Don't look down,' Lionhawk yelled up at the boy. He launched himself from one rope to the next.

'Fetch a sail,' Alice said. 'Spread it out to catch him. If he falls—'

'He's too high,' Richard said. 'Don't watch. Take Lady Selina and go below.' He pointed to where Selina stood in the stern, her face pressed to Anderson's shoulder.

Another cry from above. Against her will, her stomach so tight it hurt, Alice looked up.

The boy now hung by one hand. Her stomach roiled. She couldn't breathe or move, she could only watch Lionhawk's last desperate rush.

He hit the spar at a run.

Oh God, he would fall too. She covered her face with her hands.

'He's got him,' Richard said. 'Hooray.' He gave her shoulders a squeeze.

At the helm, Wishart cursed loud and long.

Alice felt like cursing too. And whooping. She sagged against the rail, her trembling legs refusing to hold her weight, and looked up.

Carefully, Lionhawk hauled the boy up on to the spar and pulled him against his chest, held him there, hugging him close, holding him, rocking him, stroking his hair. The lad burrowed against his solid form.

She couldn't hear anything, but she sensed Lionhawk talking to the boy the way a groom talked to a frightened horse, soothing him, calming him.

And all the while they were balanced high above

the deck on a length of wood that looked no thicker than her finger.

One false move and they'd both smash to the deck. Yet she knew he wouldn't fall, not with the lad. Not after such a daring rescue.

Time that had slowed to a crawl seemed to race. Had it been minutes or hours since the lad shot past her? Finally, Lionhawk set the boy on his feet and nudged him towards the mast.

The lad took one shaky step and glanced back at his captain. Surely Lionhawk wouldn't make him climb down by himself!

Alice's heart once more fluttered like a wild bird caught in a net.

The lad gave a little hop, then a skip, then swung down like a monkey.

Alice shook her head. Boys. Who would understand them? And now the pair was racing, Lionhawk catching the lad up, passing him and landing with a thump on the deck a good few seconds ahead with a wide grin.

They deserved to break their necks. But it was a relief to see the boy drop to the deck beside her.

Lionhawk strode over to him. 'You little rat.' He rubbed the boy's shorn head. 'I thought I was finally going to be rid of you.' The voice was hard, but the eyes were stark with an emotion Alice felt sure was fear. How was that possible?

'Let me see your hand,' she said to the boy.

He held out a grimy paw, knuckles up.

She turned it over. The skin of his palm was raw and bleeding. No wonder he'd had trouble holding on. 'How did this happen?'

''E cut me.' He jerked his head in Kale's direction.

Lionhawk's face hardened as he turned to Kale. 'What the hell were you about?'

Kale lifted his lip. 'He's a thief. The little bastard. He deserves a good whipping!'

Lionhawk stiffened. He looked at the boy. 'What did you take?'

The lad fumbled in his trouser pocket. He pulled out a silver coin.

Lionhawk's face darkened. 'Jacko. You know the rules.'

'It's mine,' the boy said. ''E stole it from me. I was just rec-recov…getting it back.'

'Prove it,' Kale snarled.

'Jacko?' Lionhawk said.

'It's the truth,' the boy yelled. 'You gave it me. When we was in Lisbon. I never spent it.' He pointed at Kale. 'I saw 'im take it, when 'e thought I weren't looking.'

Lionhawk took the coin and turned it over. 'It looks very much like the one I gave him, Kale. I want the truth now.'

'That's right,' Kale said. 'Believe your little bum boy. We all know why you favours him.'

A deadly insult.

The air on the deck stilled. Even though the sun remained high in the sky, the day seemed suddenly cool.

Wishart glowered. 'You, Kale, have been nothing but trouble since you came on board. A conversation with the cat will straighten you out.'

'Not on my ship,' Lionhawk said grimly. 'It doesn't matter who owns the coin. He pulled a knife on a shipmate.' He glared at the sullen sailor. 'Do your duty from here on in and we'll part company at our next port and no more said. One wrong step and you'll find yourself in irons.'

Kale cursed. 'See. He favours that lad over proper seamen. T'aint right.'

Wishart's handsome features twisted in a snarl. 'You heard the captain. Get below. Count yourself lucky. If it was up to me, you'd be getting off at the next port with no skin on your back.'

Kale disappeared at the double.

Lionhawk turned back to the boy. 'Next time you have a problem with one of the crew, you talk to me.'

The lad hung his head.

'Jacko.' The captain's voice was kind but firm.

'Aye, aye, Cap'n,' the boy said.

'I have some salve in my trunk that will heal his hand,' Alice said.

Lionhawk swung around as if he had forgotten all about her. 'Miss Fulton.'

'It is very good salve,' she said. 'I will give it to Mr Bones, if you wish.'

The captain gave the boy a fierce glare. 'Hear that, boy. Report to Bones and have him look at that hand. When he says you are fit, see Alphonse. You've earned yourself a day of kitchen duty.'

'But, Cap'n—'

'No buts, lad, or I'll make it two days.'

Jacko rolled his lips in as if to physically stop more words from pouring forth. He sketched a salute and walked away with dragging feet.

'At the double,' Lionhawk growled.

The boy fled.

Alice couldn't help her chuckle.

He shook his head. 'I'm sorry you had to witness that.'

'I'm glad you managed to reach the boy in time. I have never been so scared in all my life.'

Lionhawk stared at her for a moment, then let out a long breath. His shoulders relaxed. 'To be honest, I didn't think I'd make it.'

'I'm amazed you managed to get him to climb down by himself.'

'Pride is a remarkable thing.'

'And Kale?'

'Wishart is right. The man is a menace.' His lips flattened. 'The sooner he is off my ship the better.' A smile dawned on his face and turned him from stern to charming. 'Thank you for your offer of medical help for the boy.'

The burn in her face let her know she was back in dangerous waters. One flash of warmth and she melted. She kept her expression tea-time polite. 'It was the least I could do. If Mr Bones has need of the salve, have him let me know.'

'Thank you.' He bowed with old-fashioned courtesy. 'In appreciation for your kindness, I should be glad of your company at dinner tonight.'

She felt as if she'd walked into a trap. 'I did nothing.' Wrong answer. She should have said no. She opened her mouth to refuse.

'I saw you with your arms outstretched to catch him, Miss Fulton.'

'I scarcely recall what I did at that moment.'

'Kind, but foolhardy in the extreme. If he had fallen from that height you would have been killed.'

'Do you invite me to dinner to thank me, or lecture me, sir? In any case, you reached him in time, so the issue is moot.'

Michael watched her back stiffen and her face take on its disapproving expression. Prickly again. Defensive. The same as when she parried questions about Fulton Shipping. Behind that prim demeanour she was definitely hiding something, and not just the fact that she found him attractive. Tonight he would get to the truth. And…he did want to thank her.

'Since I prefer not to dine alone with such scintillating company on board,' he said, 'perhaps Lady Selina would prefer to join me in your stead?'

Her eyes narrowed, pinpoints of amber and green dancing in brown depths. Amusement or anger. 'Is that a threat, Captain Lionhawk?'

Sun-kissed wisps of hair fluttered around her serious face, her slightly askew bonnet gave her an attractively dishevelled appearance. 'Merely a question, Miss Fulton.'

'If you find our company so delightful, why not dine with all of your guests—together?'

A bantam cock in a barnyard could not have looked more ready for battle. He found himself wanting to laugh. Damn it, why did he have to like the blasted woman? She was Fulton's get and he'd do well to remember it.

'My cabin is far too small for large gatherings. No. One person only. Lady Selina it will be this evening. And tomorrow your brother.' He glanced over at the boy eagerly conversing with Wishart at the wheel. 'He's an engaging scamp. He'll make an excellent sailor, given the chance.'

'I don't see why whatever you need to discuss cannot be said here on deck, Captain Lionhawk.'

'Please, call me Michael. The ship is too small, our party too intimate, to stand on ceremony.'

Heat flushed her cheeks and she turned her face towards the empty wilderness of sea and sky.

'Do you really want to discuss the terms of your ransom now when your brother or your friend might join us at any moment and overhear?'

She sighed. 'No.'

He stifled a smile of triumph.

A dark water-slick, supple creature cleared the waves ahead of the prow.

'Oh,' she said pointing. 'A dolphin.'

He drew closer, his hand beside hers on the rail, his gaze on her profile as she admired the lithe leaps and dives.

She shivered. Michael's body warmed in response to that tell-tale tremble of awareness. Of him. It was as if he sensed every nuance of her skin, as if every breath she took had more meaning than a simple inhalation.

What the hell was he thinking? This was the daughter of his enemy.

He wasn't thinking. Not with his brain.

He had a use for Alice Fulton. And for that he needed to allay her fears.

'I hope you will find your quarters a shade more pleasant when you return below,' he said casually. 'The men are swabbing it while you take the air. I didn't expect company on this voyage or we would have made it habitable.'

She turned to face him, her face surprised. 'Thank you.'

The ship lurched on a rogue wave. He reached out a hand to steady her.

She flinched.

It irritated him, but he merely cocked a brow, kept

his voice calm. 'Surely you don't fear me, Miss Fulton?'

'Certainly not. I just don't wish for your company.'

'Your young brother, on the other hand, seems to be enjoying himself enormously.'

Her glance shot to where Richard chatted animatedly at the wheel. She paled beneath her freckles.

'What is it you really want?' she said.

Clever Miss Fulton. He would do well not to underestimate her. He placed his hand against his heart. 'I'm naught but a common sailor who rarely has the chance to enjoy such pleasant company.' He bowed and grinned at her obvious disbelief. 'And besides, you beat me at chess last night. You owe me a return match. And honest answers to my questions.'

The fight went out of her. He saw it in the resignation in her gaze, the slump of her shoulders. Damn it, now he had the urge to offer her comfort.

She held out a moment longer, chewing the inside of her cheek, giving her face a quaint, lopsided expression. 'Very well,' she said, gruffly.

'I beg your pardon.'

'I will dine with you this evening.'

The tension in his neck melted away. Until this moment, he hadn't realised how much store he'd put in her acquiescence, grudging though it was. He looked forward to battling wits with her again. And this time he would win.

She must have sensed his triumph for her hazel gaze became wary and he had the sense she might change her mind.

'I promise you an excellent dinner. I wouldn't like you to think the fare you had last night was the best the

Gryphon can provide. Simpson will come for you at four bells.'

He bowed and made his escape.

Chapter Seven

'Don't go. Tell him you are ill.' Selina stopped plaiting Alice's hair, waiting for an answer.

This was the real Selina talking, not the fragile rose of ballrooms and afternoon teas, but the lass of tough heather from her native highlands. And she wasn't about to let Alice wave her off.

'I don't have a choice. He's threatening Richard.' And you.

'Beast,' Selina hissed.

Alice bristled in the oddest way. Must be the venom in her friend's tone. Sometimes Alice thought Selina didn't like the opposite sex one little bit.

Selina pinned the plait above Alice's left ear, then set to work on another hank.

'The problem is,' Alice said, 'I don't think my father can pay the kind of ransom Lionhawk will want.'

The tugging on her head stopped. 'Oh dear.'

'Quite. Oh, you don't need to worry. I'm sure your father will pay whatever is asked.'

'If you think I would leave you here with that man, alone—'

'I have a plan.'

Selina finished pinning and came to face Alice, hands on her hips, her eyes sharp. 'And this plan involves you going to dinner with the pirate?'

Heat rushed to Alice's cheeks. 'I'm going to entice him with my half of Fulton's Shipping. He's expressed interested in Father's business and spoke of returning to England after the war.'

Selina tapped her foot. 'Why would Lionhawk— and that, by the way is such a stupid name—want a half-share in a failing….?' She drew in a breath as if to suck back the words. 'Alice, I'm sorry.'

'It's all right. It will be common knowledge soon enough. But Lionhawk doesn't know. Not the full extent. And besides, Father's good name has to be worth something. Lionhawk is rich, Selina. He's made money stealing from people like Father. Why shouldn't he put something back?'

A grin crossed her friend's face. Admiration shone from her eyes. 'You, my dear, are a devious female. I love it.'

She didn't exactly feel good about tricking Lionhawk. 'Thank you. I just hope he takes the bait. I'm banking on him taking advantage of a silly woman who doesn't know the value of what she's offering in exchange for her freedom.'

Selina's brow furrowed. She tapped her forefinger against her lips. Alice recognised the signs. Her friend was having an idea. She felt a prickle of unease. Like getting the measles, Selina's ideas were often dangerous.

'You beat him at chess, didn't you?' Selina asked. 'Can you beat him every time?'

He'd said he was rusty, but even so he had played reasonably well, while she'd played with only half of her mind because she was worried about Richard. And Lionhawk had disturbed her. It would not happen again. 'Yes, I can beat him.'

Selina frowned. 'Could you let *him* win without him knowing?'

'To stroke his pride? Make him more amenable to my offer?'

'In a way. Why not suggest a wager? You know, best of three. If you win, he forgoes the ransom and sets us free. He's more likely to bite if you let him win one game first.'

'So I let him win, then propose the wager? Fulton's against the ransom? That's thoroughly dishonest.'

Selina sighed. 'Do you think what he is doing is honest?'

'Well…' While she didn't approve of Lionhawk's chosen career, it was perfectly legal. Although he had flown a false flag and lied to them about being a cook.

Selina looked Alice up and down. 'How long do we have, before you have to go up there?'

'Why?'

'He's a sailor, isn't he? Don't they spend weeks at sea? Alone? Lonely?'

'Selina!' Alice couldn't keep the horror out of her voice, or the edge of hysteria. 'You are not suggesting I seduce him?'

'Certainly not. He likes you. I saw the way he looked at you. If you distract him, you can have him eating out of your hand.'

An image of Michael licking her palm flashed into her mind. Flutters danced across her chest, firing little pulses low in her abdomen. The base urges she had fought so hard to suppress escaped their confines in a rush of heat. She battled them down with a deep breath. 'No. I'm not cut out for having men eat out of my hand.'

'Alice, it's about tempting him with a wager and diverting his mind.'

Much as she didn't want to admit it, Selina was on to something. The wager might well be the way out of all of their troubles. With the business debts unloaded on Lionhawk, they could retire to Oxford and live quietly on half of whatever profits the privateer managed to squeeze out of Fulton Shipping.

Selina folded her arms over her chest and tapped her foot. 'I think you should borrow the gown I wore to the General's ball in Lisbon.'

'It will be too big,' Alice said, remembering the daring gown with horror.

'I may not be good for much more than decoration,' Selina said, with a bitter edge to her voice, 'but I do know how to alter a dress to fit.' She headed for her trunks.

'Who said that?' Alice asked. 'The bit about only being good for decoration.'

'I've forgotten.' Selina rummaged through her gowns and shawls, clearly not intending to say more. 'Aha.' She stood up with a wisp of white silk over her arm. 'Right. Let's get you dressed.'

An hour later, Selina stepped back. 'Let me look.'

Alice glanced down at the wide expanse of skin and very little curve above a lacy neckline. She grimaced. 'The neck is too low.'

'You are looking at it from the wrong angle. From here it looks gorgeous.' She tilted her head. 'And the colour is perfect.'

'It's white.' With pink silk roses around the hem and edging the off-the-shoulder sleeves and neckline. 'I never wear pink and white. No. I'm changing into my blue gown. It's perfectly adequate.'

A knock rattled the door of their prison. Lionhawk. A breath stuck in her throat, solid and hard. She choked it down.

'You look lovely, Alice,' Selina whispered, drawing close. 'Trust me. He'll be at your feet.'

'I don't want him at my feet. I want him stuck with Father's debts.' There, she'd said it. The whole scheme was machiavellian. Wrong.

Her friend's eyes softened. She patted Alice's shoulder. 'You can do it.' The breathy voice was back, the little girl pout she wore like a suit of armour. 'This plan turns on you distracting his attention. All you need to do is tease him a bit.'

All very well for the mistress of feminine wiles to say. The only thing flirting ever got Alice was trouble. 'I don't know.'

'Well, I do. Right now, in that gown, the poor dear will be lucky if his brain manages to get above the level of his waistband.'

'Selina!'

'You never met my mother, did you, Alice? She taught me all I know about men.'

Another knock. Louder this time.

'Come in,' Selina called out.

Dash it, there was no time to change. Alice swung around to face the visitor.

Selina gave her shoulders a squeeze. 'That's my girl.'

It wasn't Lionhawk after all, but Mr Anderson and a seaman with the key in his hand just behind him. The business agent paused in the doorway, his round face glowing, his scruffy beard gone. While she and Selina had bathed down here, the men had completed their ablutions up on deck.

'Ladies.' He bowed. And then he stared. 'Miss Fulton.' His Adam's apple bobbed. 'I—er—I—'

Well, what a surprise.

'Do come in, Mr Anderson,' Selina said. 'Where is Richard?'

He managed to drag his gaze from Alice's chest and focus on Selina, whose expression was annoyingly smug. 'He decided to stay aloft. Mr Wishart is teaching him the use of a sextant. He is doing remarkably well.'

Inwardly Alice groaned. Clearly if she was going to save Richard from a life at sea, this plan needed to work.

Dressed and ready, Michael paced the deck outside his open cabin door, occasionally glancing inside to check on progress.

His plans were set. He'd ask Fulton for an impossible sum and the man would never see either of his children again. Never know what became of them before he met his end.

It wasn't enough. Michael needed to know what drove a bastard like Fulton. Money. Power. Ambition. Then Michael would strike where it would do the utmost damage.

For that insight he needed Alice.

'La-dee-da,' Jacko chirped from inside. Michael caught a glimpse of him waltzing past the door with a broom in his arms and glowered. The men would not let him get away with this without a ribbing. They'd never guess his seduction was a means to a far different end.

Simpson stuck his head out of the door. 'Almost done. Shall I fetch her up?'

Fetch her up? She wasn't a sack of potatoes. 'No. I will escort her.' Besides, what if she'd changed her mind since this morning? Only his threats over her brother and her friend kept her under control.

'You've got less than five minutes,' he said to Simpson.

'Aye, aye, sir,' Simpson said.

Michael stomped across his deck, glad of nightfall. Glad no one would see the anxiety in his expression or his impatience.

The stooped and scholarly Bones, his strands of grey hair plastered to his bald head and his bulbous blue-veined nose redder than usual, stopped him just before he ducked down the companionway. The slight roll to his gait said he was already half-seas-over.

'How's the head today, Michael?'

'Your tea did the trick.'

'Willow bark. I used it on the Fulton lad too.'

'Will he suffer any permanent ill effect?'

Bones shook his head. 'I don't believe so. His mind is clear, the pain almost gone.'

'Good.' He wouldn't wish his headaches on a dog, let alone another human being. He bolted down the ladder, feverish, impatient.

Outside the hold's door, he straightened his cravat, took a deep breath and knocked.

A deep voice called enter. Anderson. The boy was still up on deck, following Wishart around.

He turned the key.

At first he thought it was the other woman gowned in white who opened the door, her hair arranged in some intricate series of coils above her ears and her face framed with carefully curled tendrils. But his body recognised Alice with a clench of pleasure.

Alice. Dressed as if she were going to a ball. This was something new.

He ignored the quickening in his blood and bowed the way he'd been taught as a boy. 'Good afternoon, Miss Fulton.'

When he straightened he saw puzzlement in her expression. She offered a straight-backed curtsy. A little dip of the knees.

A muffled giggle emerged from the shadows. Lady Selina, seated at the table with a hand over her mouth and her eyes dancing with mirth. Had he done something wrong? He gritted his teeth and held out his arm. 'Are you ready?'

She placed the tips of her fingers on his sleeve. They rested there so lightly he felt nothing. He wanted to growl at her to take a firm hold, but he stilled his tongue. There was something about the other woman, Lady Selina, that made him feel as if he didn't quite fit in his skin. And tonight, for the first time, he had a similar feeling around Miss Fulton. She looked too much the elegant lady. Too far above his common sailor's touch, even if he did outrank her.

Intending to put him in his place, no doubt.

He set his jaw and urged her ahead of him up the ladder. He racked his brain for small talk. The weather? Too banal. Even he knew that. Her brother's health? A bit like rubbing salt in a wound. Besides, he would be addressing remarks to her rather lovely bottom, which seemed all the more delicious because of the way the flimsy gown clung to its slight curves.

Something a gentleman wasn't supposed to notice. Who was he fooling? Certainly not Alice Fulton and her friend. He shouldn't have bothered dragging out the courtly manners he'd learned as a boy. He'd probably remembered incorrectly and that's why they were laughing.

He stiffened his spine and held out his arm when he emerged on deck where she stood waiting.

Her wretched brother dashed up. 'Alice. You'll never guess. I took a reading with the sextant and got it right second try.'

'Well done,' she said, her smile tight.

The lad seemed not to notice her lack of enthusiasm. 'I'm going to help Mr Wishart trim the sails for the night.'

Her eyes widened and she drew back. 'You are not going up there.'

The boy thrust out his chin. 'Yes. I am.'

She grasped her brother's sleeve. 'What if you become dizzy? Only a day ago you suffered a head injury.'

The lad glowered, his body tense. It didn't take much imagination to envisage him taking foolish risks just to annoy his sister. Couldn't she see too much petticoat government was making him worse? 'Leave him be. This way, Miss Fulton.'

The boy's expression changed from sullen to puzzled. 'Where are you going?'

'Never mind,' she said. 'Go and climb your stupid sails. And if you fall and break your neck, don't expect me to put you back together.'

The boy hesitated for a moment, then dashed off, probably terrified she'd change her mind.

'Can't you stop him?' she asked

He could. But he wouldn't. Not when he was angry that the lad hadn't had more concern for his sister's welfare.

Damn it. He should be glad the lad wasn't making a fuss. 'He'll be safe with Wishart.'

A sharp sigh gusted in his direction. Her brows lowered.

Wonderful. The perfect companion. A resentful female. This evening had the makings of a new low in enjoyment.

He placed his hand in the small of her back and urged her on. The small bones moved beneath his hand. Delicate, but not fragile. There was steel inside her willowy body. Resilience. It would bend without breaking. Flex against his strength.

His body hardened.

The cabin door was ajar and, to Michael's surprise, she stepped inside without hesitation. Perhaps tonight would go just as he planned, after all.

'Oh, my,' she murmured, staring at the dining table with its white damask cloth, ornate silver epergne with three branches of candles and glittering silverware.

The back of his neck went hot. He'd almost preened like some callow youth at her admiration. He didn't care what she thought of his few family treasures. He'd intended them as reminders of why this evening was necessary.

He strode across the room to where Simpson had placed a silver tray full of glasses and a couple of crystal decanters on his desk. 'Would you care for a drink? There is brandy or sherry. I'd offer champagne, but it never tastes pleasant when warm.'

'Sherry,' she said. 'Thank you.'

She strolled to the window and looked down at the side table where he had once more set out the chess board. The light from the candles around the cabin glowed on her skin. Each step she took stirred the white fabric at her hips and revealed a pair of white satin clad feet and trim ankles. Against the dark of the window, she looked untouchable, as if a marble statue had stepped down from its pedestal.

Untouchable was not good.

'Are you ready to risk another game?' she asked.

He poured her sherry into a goblet and held it out. 'Most certainly.'

She smiled up at him, her hazel eyes unfathomable. 'Are you seeking revenge?'

He froze, staring at her. Nothing in her face indicated she'd guessed his intent. It was simply harmless banter.

He let go of a long breath, forced a smile. 'Naturally.'

She took the glass. Their fingers touched. A slight brush of skin on skin, nothing to speak of, and yet his fingers tingled as if they'd been scorched.

Her little gasp said she felt it too.

'Must be a storm coming up,' he said. 'Electricity in the air.'

'Oh, I hope not.' She reached down and touched a geisha with a fingertip, revealing the valley between her small pert breasts.

His mouth dried.

She nudged the geisha one square. 'Your move.'

Simpson coughed and they both spun around like nervous cats at a dog's bark.

'Dinner is ready for serving, Cap'n.'

'Good.' It would be a relief to have something to do, something to keep his mind off her tantalising flesh. 'May I seat you, Miss Fulton?'

'Indeed you may, Captain Lionhawk.'

Blister it. She was going kill him with all this politeness. Something between them had changed.

He shrugged it off. They weren't going to be friends. Tonight he would learn all he needed to know and take the final step in her ruin.

He pulled out her chair and she sank down gracefully. He sat down. Their gazes locked above the fine linens and sparkling silver.

Alice carefully drew in a deep breath. It wouldn't do to fall out of this gown and from the grim set to her companion's face, she wasn't sure it was having the desired effect.

So much for Selina's faith in her ability to distract.

'The table looks lovely,' she said. 'The china is Meissen, is it not?'

He glanced at the plate in front of him. 'Yes.'

'Are you not afraid they will get broken if you run into rough weather?'

'Yes.' The light from the candles emphasised his high cheekbones and red highlights glinted from the dark beard. He looked almost demonic with candle flames dancing in his unreadable, light-coloured eyes. My word, her imagination was active tonight. It must be nerves.

'Simpson packs them away in straw when they are not in use,' he said in a rather off-hand manner, as if he didn't care whether they broke or not. And why would he? He could always steal more.

'My father imported china from Meissen before Napoleon gobbled up Europe.' She traced the delicate rose pattern around the circumference of the plate. 'Perhaps he even imported some of these pieces.'

She looked up to find an expression of shock on his face.

'It is not possible,' he said.

She frowned. 'It is entirely possible. Fulton Shipping regularly brought such pieces from Saxony. My father had an exclusive licence.'

His expression smoothed out. And yet it seemed to require some effort to take command of his emotions because he took a deep breath. 'You know a great deal about your father's business.'

'Yes. I do. Mother died when Richard was very young. I helped where I could.'

'Surely he has employees for that sort of thing.'

Employees who needed direction. And when the master couldn't lift his brandy-soaked head, someone had to give orders. 'A family business is best kept within the family.'

'The Fulton secret of success.' His voice had a razor-sharp edge as if he'd like to slice the Fulton name into slivers and feed it to a shark.

She repressed a sharp retort and smiled agreement instead.

The door opened and Simpson marched in, followed by Jacko and another member of the crew. The two men carried silver platters beneath covers and the boy carried a sauce boat.

Simpson set his platter down in the centre of the table and directed the other two. The boy grinned the moment he put down his jug.

'How is your hand?' she asked.

He held out his bandaged palm. 'Bones tied it up. It don't hurt none.'

'Brave lad,' she said.

He bowed and skipped out of the room. The other sailor tugged his forelock and departed just as swiftly.

Simpson's black eyes twinkled merrily. 'Dinner is served, Cap'n, Miss Fulton.' He whipped off the silver covers and beamed. Alice felt as if she ought to give him a round of applause. One platter held small fish lined up like soldiers, the other an assortment of root vegetables.

'Thank you,' she said. 'It smells delicious.'

'We have a Frenchie chef,' Simpson said with obvious pride.

'Alphonse was a chef to a French nobleman,' Lionhawk added. 'He does his best with the supplies we have available. Though sometimes his Gallic sensibilities get the better of him and he refuses to cook anything at all.'

She laughed at the dry tone of his voice. 'He certainly seems to have excelled himself this evening.' She inhaled the wonderful aroma.

Across the table, the tension in her companion's shoulders eased. He managed the faint impression of a smile, a twitch at the corner of his lips. 'Yes, indeed.'

'May I serve you, miss?' Simpson asked.

'It's all right, Simpson. I think Miss Fulton and I can manage to serve ourselves this evening. You can pour us both a glass of wine before you go.'

Simpson bowed. He removed their sherry glasses and returned with a decanter and poured red wine into the crystal glasses set beside each of their plates.

'Will there be anything else, Cap'n?'

'No, thank you. Nothing further tonight. I will ring if I need you.'

There was a bell pull? Then she noticed the little

hand-bell in the centre of the table. The silver handle was delicately filigreed. 'Oh, how pretty.'

'That belonged to Cap'n's mother,' Simpson said with his customary wink.

'That will be all,' Lionhawk said, his voice tight.

Not that it bothered the irrepressible Simpson, because he bowed again and marched in solemn fashion out of the room.

'He has ambitions to become a butler,' Lionhawk said.

'I think he would make a very good one.' If he learned not to grin and wink.

'I'll tell him you said so, though I'm afraid it will go to his head. Allow me to serve you some fish.'

'I hope my companions are enjoying a similar meal?' she said with a smile.

He lowered his brows. 'Your companions, as you put it, will eat the same as the rest of the crew.'

'Oh. What is that?'

'Weevily biscuit and gruel.'

Chapter Eight

Selina would be horrified. 'In that case, I will join them.'

He observed her over his glass. 'Do you think I'd keep my men if I fed them Royal Navy rations? I joke, madam.'

'I must say it is difficult to tell. I suppose tossing me out of your cabin after I won at chess was also your idea of a joke.' Not a tactful thing to say, by the darkening of his expression. He'd be tossing her out again at any moment and that would not suit her purpose at all.

'You think I threw you out because you won?'

She shrugged. 'I can only assume so, since you didn't offer an explanation.'

'A captain of a ship doesn't need an explanation.'

She pressed her lips together.

'What were you going to say, Miss Fulton?'

She shook her head.

'Say it. I promise I won't throw you overboard.'

This time she saw the slight twitch of his lips. Another jest. 'We sound like a couple of squabbling children.'

He leaned back in his chair, the glass to his lips, laughter fracturing the blue of his eyes, giving them the colour of tropical waters warmed by the sun.

'At least I have the grace to admit it,' she said.

At that he did laugh out loud. And the itchy sensation of discomfort fell away. Suddenly they were two people enjoying a meal, if not exactly like old friends, then like reasonable adults.

He served her some of the fish and drizzled it with sauce. She picked up her knife and fork and ate a piece of the delicate white flesh. 'This is delicious.'

'I'll be sure to tell Alphonse.'

Thankfully he did not gobble his food like a pig, or, worse yet, pick his teeth with his fork, all the things her etiquette teacher had insisted was everyday behaviour for the lower classes. Not because there was anything wrong with the lower classes, but because they were not lucky enough to have etiquette teachers.

It was not their fault.

It was too bad some of her gentlemen acquaintances hadn't been forced to take etiquette classes. They seemed to descend a level or two when confronted with food and a surfeit of wine.

This man was nothing but elegant at the table.

His fork halted halfway to his mouth and he shot her an enquiring glance. Oh heavens, she must have been staring. She tilted her head as if waiting for him to say something.

He shrugged and took another bite with his strong, even white teeth.

She filled her fork with fish and savoured another mouthful of the delicious meal.

'I'm glad you have a good appetite after your

ordeal,' he said in easy tones. 'You know the *Conchita*'s captain should never have run after the warning shot. Wishart wouldn't have fired into the rigging if he'd heaved to as ordered.'

Was he making excuses? Perhaps even an apology? She put down her knife and fork and picked up her wine. 'What I don't understand is why you were on board. Do you usually smuggle yourself on to ships you plan to take as a prize?'

'I wanted to take a look at your cargo. I planned to leave before the *Conchita* slipped her moorings. Your captain told the harbourmaster he planned to depart at first light.' The lie slid easily from his tongue.

'And we left at midnight.'

'Why?'

'We hoped to clear Lisbon in the dark and slip through the blockade.'

'Clever.'

'Not clever enough. How did Wishart find us?'

Lionhawk set down his cutlery and rang the bell. 'I hate to say this, but pure blind luck.'

'Your luck. Not ours.' She realised she sounded quite miserable and lightened her expression. 'Fate, I suppose.'

'Indeed.' He raised his glass. 'To Fate.'

The words sounded fervent. Her shoulders tightened defensively. She thrust the feeling aside. She didn't believe in luck. She believed in hard work and sensible decisions. Out of courtesy she raised her glass to his toast.

'Your father made a fortune in shipping,' he said, his gaze watchful. 'He must be a clever man.'

She shrugged. 'My grandfather established the company. My father has continued it.'

'It is unusual for a family of merchants to be accepted into society.'

'He married a Carstairs.'

'I see. Very advantageous.'

'It broke his heart when my mother died.' And that was when the rot had set in.

Lionhawk looked faintly disbelieving. 'I suppose such a rich man must have a lot of power.'

'He is well known among the *ton*.' She tried not to wince at her side-step.

A beaming Simpson entered with coffee and, of all things, sweetmeats on a plate. Marchpane and spun-sugar confections were moulded into the shapes of lions and tigers and even a giraffe.

'How lovely. He truly is an artist.'

'Yes,' Lionhawk said, sounding supremely satis-fied. 'And an excellent to'gallant man. That will be all, Simpson. Shall we take our coffee to the board and start our game?'

'Won't you be mortified when you lose?'

'You are very confident.'

'Ah, but you see I have your measure.'

Both eyebrows shot up at that and she had the feeling she'd said something a little *risqué*. Then it dawned on her what he might be thinking she was measuring. Her body blushed all over.

'At chess,' she said.

'Naturally,' he said, his eyes dancing.

Oh, Lord, now she'd really given too much away. She tried to look unconscious of his silent amusement. 'Let the duel begin.'

Only the battle would not be won or lost by way of the chess board, but by her ability to confuse the enemy.

And that gave her a rather unpleasant sensation in her stomach, as if she'd eaten too many of the sweetmeats when she'd yet to sample a single one.

Their game proceeded swiftly. Despite Lionhawk's lazy appearance, his moves were brisk, and, Alice admitted, looking at the board, devastating. It had taken all her powers of concentration to follow his strategy. A growing suspicion he'd let her win yesterday made her feel a tiny bit nauseous.

Yet there were weaknesses in his play. And the longer the game continued, the more confident she became that she had the skills to beat him. Just.

This game would finish in a moment. He would win as she'd planned. It was time to play her real hand.

'I think I have you on the run,' she said, with a smile. She leaned forwards, hopefully giving him an excellent view down the front of her gown.

Wonders of wonders, he was staring at her bosom as if he'd discovered something toothsome. Heat surged up from the pit of her belly. Her breasts tingled as if he'd touched her there. Warmth trickled through her veins.

'Do you?' he said, his gaze drifting up to her face. What she saw in his eyes both thrilled and terrified.

The heat of desire.

She felt as if she hovered on the brink of a whirlpool. If she did not take care, it would suck her down into the depths of depravity.

What she and Selina had planned was truly dangerous.

She had the feeling this man had the means to strip away her defences, break down her barriers. Fortunately, he had no idea of his power.

'Captain Lionhawk—'

'Please…' he offered her a warm smile, a smile so seductive it pinned her to her seat '…call me Michael.'

She swallowed. 'Michael. Did any of your captives fail to pay their ransom?'

He stroked his beard. 'Why do you ask?'

'I wondered, that is all.' The air in the room seemed too thin. She drew in a couple of quick breaths, aware of the rapid beat of her heart. Oh, dear Lord, she couldn't let him see she cared about the answer.

He leaned back, eyes narrowed. 'Never. But if it happened there are several ways I can make up for the loss, I suppose. The easiest is to give the relatives time to raise the funds.' His low murmur was barely discernible above the blood rushing in her ears. 'There's a man in Algiers who would, for a percentage, keep the prisoners until the funds came through.'

Algiers? Her mouth dried. She darted a glance at his face. It told her nothing. 'And if the money never arrived?'

'There are always the slave markets.'

A flash of amusement shone from his eyes. If she hadn't been watching his reaction, she might have missed it.

'Another of your jests?'

'Perhaps. Are you worried that your father won't pay for you and your brother?'

Tell him. He'd risked his life today to save a small boy. Instinct said he was not as cruel as he liked to appear.

Right, Alice. Her instincts had served her exceptionally well in the past when it came to men. Only a fool would trust a man who stole for a living. She'd been fooled by one fortune hunter, she wouldn't repeat her mistake. 'My father will pay.'

'Of course, the price goes up with every day's delay.'

See. Nothing but a pirate. He'd taken their ship, he deserved to be saddled with a foundering business.

She fanned her face and pouted. 'I'm so utterly bored with this game.'

He cocked his head. 'Because I'm winning?'

She snapped the fan shut. 'It doesn't matter who wins when there is nothing at stake.'

He curled his lip. 'Victory?'

She picked up her coffee cup and sipped the dark aromatic brew. 'Winning matters to you because you lost last time. But if you win, we are even and if I win, then I prove I am a better chess player. Boring in the extreme.'

He frowned. 'Are you saying you won't finish the game?' The frustration in his voice gave her a little thrill, the kind she felt when a patient she'd taken an interest in took a turn for the better.

'I'm saying it is dull. Ennui has me in its thrall. I thought someone like you would understand?'

'Someone like me?' He grimaced. 'And just what does that mean?'

'An adventurer. A man who craves a challenge.'

'Do you think I risk my men's lives for mere excitement?'

The gravel in his throat sent a little shimmer down her spine. Lord, but the man managed to hit that nerve, or whatever it was, every time he growled at her.

She put her cup down and widened her eyes. Selina would have been proud. 'You don't?'

'You, Miss Fulton, have no idea what drives a man like me.'

Wasn't it all about money and winning? She yawned behind a languid hand. 'I think I prefer to

retire. Perhaps we could finish our game another time.'
She pushed to her feet.

'Sit down.'

The command in his voice sent a shiver down her
spine. A delicious chill. Excitement mingled with the
thrill of the hunt. She took a deep breath, raised what
she hoped was a haughty brow.

'Please,' he said. 'Please sit down. Let us make it
more interesting. A wager. The best of three games.'

The breath she'd been holding slipped from her
parted lips. He had no idea how close she'd come to
submitting to his will. What sort of woman let a command make her weak and full of longing for things of
which she should have no knowledge? A wanton
through and through. Whatever happened, she must not
let him see her weakness or she would be lost.

'And the stakes?' she enquired with faint interest.

He shrugged. 'What would make it interesting to you?'

'If I win, you agree to let us go.'

He looked at her as if she were mad. 'Do you seriously contemplate I would wager what would obviously be an enormous loss to me and my crew?'

She yawned. 'Afraid you will lose?'

'Am I?' he said grimly. He stared at the board as if
he could see into the future.

Surely he must see he would win this game? She let
doubt show on her face. 'Of course I would have tried
a little harder from the off had I known that was at stake.'

'No matter how hard you tried, you wouldn't have
won. I learned this game from a master and he taught
me all he knew. I must admit I had forgotten much, but
it comes back to me, Miss Fulton. It comes back. You
cannot beat me.'

Arrogant man. If only he knew she didn't want to win. At least not this game. A fear unfurled in the pit of her belly, a gnawing anxiety. She'd overplayed her hand. She had asked for too much and he wasn't going to bite. 'What is the use of a wager, if one does not risk all?'

His gaze flicked up to search her face. 'And what do I get if I win?'

'You win your ransom.'

A slow lazy smile lit his face and warmed his eyes. 'I'm not a fool, my dear. The ransom is already mine.' He rubbed his jaw, his gaze skimming her body, lingering on the expanse of skin above her neckline. 'Let me think. What do I want?'

She went hot, then cold. The gown was supposed to be a distraction, not an invitation, but she couldn't help her surge of warm womanly pride at the obvious flare of interest in his eyes.

'I have an idea,' she said before her brain went up in the conflagration.

'No doubt,' he said.

Inwardly, she winced. Had she been so obvious? No turning back now. 'Why not a half-share in Fulton Shipping?'

All the languor left his body. He leaned forwards. Ah. Now she had his attention.

'You don't own a half of Fulton's Shipping,' he said.

'My dowry,' she said calmly, despite the race of her heart.

Michael didn't quite believe what he was hearing. All through their conversation this evening, he had sensed her underlying unease. A quiet desperation that had him feeling like a cur. Sympathy. A dangerous emotion females used to their advantage. This new ploy shook the wind from his sails. He narrowed his gaze on her innocent-looking face. 'Your dowry?'

'I'm not asking you to marry me,' she said with a snap to her voice. 'It is mine to do with as I wish.'

'Why would an unmarried woman risk her dowry?'

'It is not much of a risk, is it?' she said, eyeing the board.

Damn her. She really did think little of his skills. And if he refused her wager, she would think he was afraid. This second game had gone much better than the first. Some of his earlier play had been instinctive, but during this last game he'd had flashes of memory of playing as a young lad. Before he went to sea.

Memories of his father's instructions. The knowledge that he'd been taught by a master. It was like peeking through a door only slightly ajar, but he knew he'd been good enough to earn his father's praise.

Miss Fulton had no idea just how tempting her offer was, or how helpful. He'd be a fool to let the opportunity slip, especially when there was no chance she would win. 'Very well. If you win, you will go free. If I win, I get the ransom and half of Fulton's.'

'Oh,' she said. 'I thought....'

'What, that I would give up my ransom? When it is already mine? If I win, I get both.'

Clearly she didn't like his reply, for her eyes hardened and her lips thinned. She must think him witless, if she thought he'd give up what was already his by rights.

'You said, *you* will go free,' she said, holding his gaze with fierce intensity. 'All the prisoners are to be released.'

There it was again, her courage, her selflessness, bright and sharp like a sword blade angled against the sun. She would not accept anything but the release of his prisoners, he could see it in the set of her chin and the intensity in her eyes. She'd be a fool to settle for anything less, though he could probably bargain her down.

But no matter how good she was, she would not win again. This last game had revealed all the weakness in her play.

Regret flashed through him. For a moment, a very brief moment, he wanted to back down, to free her and her companions and sail away basking in her gratitude.

Perhaps if he'd been free to choose, he would have followed his gut, but he'd made a vow. If the Fates meant him to use Alex Fulton's daughter, he would not turn his back and risk their ire.

He held out his hand. 'Agreed, Miss Fulton.'

For a long moment, she stared at his hand. Finally she stretched out her small fine-boned one and he grasped it firmly, felt its warmth and light dampness against his palm. And deep in his bones, he felt the tremble. Knew her fear.

Bugger. Why did it have to be her? Why couldn't it have been her empty-headed friend, who acted no different to the countless other women he'd bedded and left happy over the years? Why did this serious-faced woman with her mysterious gaze and her hidden well of passion tempt him beyond endurance? Why did she have to be Fulton's daughter?

Because that was how the Fates worked. Giving with one hand and taking with the other. Every old salt on the ocean could give examples of their cruelty.

No matter his regrets, he had to go forwards. He could not break his oath. He released his grip. 'Have at it, Miss Fulton. The best of three.'

She pursed her lips and pushed her queen in front of his knight. A clever move.

His knight swooped in for the kill. 'Check and mate.'

Her hands clenched in her lap, the knuckles white. She nibbled her bottom lip. Slowly she raised her gaze to his face. 'Congratulations.' She sounded pleased for him. Sportingly putting a brave face on her loss. And that he admired.

He started setting up the board for their final game.

In a jerky movement, she rose to her feet and stepped closer to the window, leaning forwards to look out through the open casement.

He rose and went to stand behind her as he had the previous evening. He inhaled her scent. Sunshine in green open fields and wild flowers nodding in a breeze. Images of England he didn't know he remembered formed like freshly painted landscapes in his mind. His whole being yearned for home as it hadn't for years, even as he knew in his heart what he longed for was gone. Courtesy of Alex Fulton.

'You won, Captain Lionhawk,' she murmured softly.

'One game each,' he said, offering a salve to her pride

Through the glass, he could see the white wake and the glint of moonlit waves.

She remained still and silent, staring into the darkness. Unaccountably, illogically, he wanted her to respond to his presence.

He exhaled. A slow trickle of breath stirring the fine hairs at her nape.

She shivered. A delicate tremble of female flesh. She might not want to acknowledge it, but she knew he was there.

'What are you thinking?' he asked. He'd used the

gambit many times before. For once, oddly, he cared about the answer.

'Pondering our next game,' she murmured.

'Is that all you are pondering?'

A whisper of her indrawn breath tightened his body. Oh, yes. She was aware.

He leaned forwards, until they were cheek to cheek in the window's reflection, his face dark beside her pale complexion.

'A pretty picture,' he said softly.

Her lips parted. He wondered what she would say. She shook her head, as if willing herself to silence and he found himself disappointed.

'Surely you have not become reticent now?' he said.

A tiny laugh vibrated the air between her back and his chest; it carried her scent on ripples of air. 'I was going to say that if either of us is pretty, it is you.'

Once more she'd surprised him. He couldn't hold back his smile. 'Men are not pretty.'

She shrugged. 'Are they not? Doesn't it depend on one's point of view? You are one of a kind. A darkly handsome man who exudes danger. The ladies of the *ton* would faint at your feet. Except…'

There it was again, the secretive little shake of her shoulders that lit fires in his blood. 'Except?'

'The beard would have to go. Unless your chin is weak, which would quite undo you. Or perhaps it hides some terrible scar?'

Scars. The word bit into his mood like a whip. With rigid control, he held back an instinctive shudder of disgust and went on the attack.

'Yet you deny your own prettiness, when it is quite obvious to me?'

'I'm a realist, Captain Lionhawk, and you've been on board ship for many months, no doubt.'

Her contempt for his compliment irritated like a sharp piece of gravel inside a stocking. 'False modesty does not become you, Miss Fulton. Look at your reflection. Tell me you do not see beauty.'

Her lips pursed. 'I see a too-round face. Eyes too far apart. A forehead too high. Dreary brown hair. And if it were a real glass, I would see freckles.'

He chuckled then. 'You seek compliments indeed.'

She tried to step around him. He blocked her with his body and she let out an impatient breath. 'I state the truth.'

'Let me tell you what I see.'

She tensed. Did she fear he would be cruel, or that he would lie?

'I see a Madonna's calm face and eyes shadowed by secrets. I see a sun-kissed complexion and copper glints in silky hair. Intelligence sits on your brow. Your lips tempt mine.' He paused. 'I sense hot blood running beneath alabaster skin.'

She gasped, her eyes widening in maidenly horror.

He caught her shoulders, gazed into brown eyes pierced by emerald green. She lowered her lashes, hiding her thoughts. Keeping her secrets.

Longing hit him in the chest.

The emptiness inside him reached out in hunger.

Not the sharp hunger of the body, but something deeper, as if this prosaic creature could fill a void he hadn't recognised until now. His breath stilled in his throat. His heart thundered.

Her face tipped up and he cupped her cheeks in his hands. Before he could stop himself, he tasted her pliant velvet mouth, savoured the tang of coffee. The answering sweep of her tongue drove all thought from his mind. He enfolded her in his arms and she melded against him. A perfect fit of slender curves against his hard form.

A wildness grew inside him, a reckless urge to lose himself inside her and forget his duty.

The course to disaster.

He forced himself to let her go. 'Are you ready to finish our game?' His voice grated over what felt like iron filings in his throat.

Her gaze lowered, hiding her thoughts. Disappointment? Relief? It didn't matter. He didn't care. Wouldn't care.

When she sank on to her seat, her face was calm, showing no sign of their wild kiss, but for the rosy tinge to her lips and the flush high on her cheekbones.

She looked good enough to eat. But first he had a game to win.

Chapter Nine

The third game was not going well. Alice felt her back teeth grind and tried to relax her jaw. Tried to keep her mind clear and her gaze fixed on the play. Tried not to panic.

He'd said he was rusty. But he hadn't said that he'd once been more than a casual player. With each minute, his strategy gained a subtlety that challenged her to the depths of her knowledge.

The squares in the board wavered and blurred. With her queen in check, if she didn't find a way out of the conundrum he'd set, she'd be forced to concede.

She could not lose. Her dowry was one thing, but the ransom would put Father in the poor house. Debtors' prison loomed large, or worse, if Lionhawk made good on his threats. Richard didn't deserve either fate.

Fear had her stomach so tight she felt sick.

In her head, she rearranged her last remaining pieces this way and that, each time ending in failure.

Gambling. Was she mad? It never worked. She'd seen men lose their fortunes time and again and scorned their idiocy. Now here she was in exactly the same straits.

There had to be something this man wanted. Something he would take instead of gold. Men like Lionhawk understood trade as long as they got the best of the bargain.

She had nothing left.

Andrew had tricked her from the only thing men admire in a woman. Purity.

No gentleman wanted another man's leavings. A wanton. Used goods. She knew all the words. Andrew had flung them in her face when she had rejected his suit.

But a man like Lionhawk, a man who'd been at sea for months, might not care for such niceties.

She'd have to tell him just what he was getting. He'd probably laugh at such a poor offer.

She went hot, then cold. She couldn't do it. She clenched her hands in her lap and stared at the board. Did she have another choice?

If he agreed, there was no returning to her old life. No pretending to be a virtuous spinster. No good works at the hospital. She'd be publicly ruined. No brushing this dirt under the carpet. *A persona non grata.*

On the other hand, what she'd experienced with Andrew hadn't been unpleasant. Indeed, she'd thoroughly enjoyed herself, until she realised he'd used her passion against her, plotted with his brother to make sure she couldn't change her mind about the wedding.

Well, she had. And that left her on the shelf.

Lionhawk desired her. She could see it in the depths of his ocean-coloured eyes, feel it in the heat of his body dashing against her skin each time he drew close, sense it in her aching core. As long as she didn't think too much about later, provided she left her pride at the door, she could follow her nature. She swallowed and raised her gaze to meet his.

He leaned forwards. 'Finish the game, Alice.'

When had he started calling her Alice? After the kiss, she supposed. She arched a brow. 'Are you so anxious to lose?'

He grinned. 'Still fighting? Good for you. But it is time to pay the piper. One more move and the game is mine.'

'Don't be so cocksure, sir,' she said, lingering over the words as if to taste them on her tongue. 'Why not up the stakes?'

He cast her a perplexed look. 'What are you about?'

'Making the game more interesting?'

'It is quite interesting enough for me.'

He wasn't going to bite.

'I don't want to spend weeks in Algiers waiting for my father to raise your ransom. And nor does Lady Selina. You talked of resuming a life in England, but believe me, Lord Albright will see you hang if you treat his daughter with such disrespect.'

'Are you saying I should trust your father for the money? Let him owe me?'

Her heart picked up speed, drumming against her ribs like the hooves of a runaway horse on hard-packed earth. She couldn't swallow, her mouth felt so dry. She took a deep breath and forced the words past her teeth. 'You can certainly trust Lord Albright to pay his part of the ransom.' She lowered her voice. 'I, on the other hand, would sooner find a different way to pay off the price on my head. One we could both enjoy.'

She put down her glass, reached across the table and

ran the back of her hand along the beard-soft line of his jaw. 'There is more between us than mere conversation, Michael. Why waste it?'

A glint of emotion she could not read flashed in his eyes. Triumph? It hardly seemed likely.

'It's a high price for something I can have for free,' he said.

'Not from me.'

The words hung between them, stark and ugly.

He let go a long breath. 'I see.'

He said it as though she'd made some great revelation. Which she had in a way. Heat stole up her cheeks, despite her effort to appear unconcerned. She smiled. 'I'm glad you understand. But let me be clear. If you win this game, you own half of Fulton's Shipping, and you will have your money, but I will use my influence with Lord Albright to ensure you never set foot in England.'

He recoiled, his expression dumbfounded. At least she had the element of surprise.

'I realise you will lose money if you accept my proposition, but I will do everything in my power to help smooth your path into society when you arrive in London. I swear it. As will Lady Selina, if I ask her.'

Her hands convulsed in her lap. She stilled them. No backing down. No weakness. She curved her lips in a woman-of-the-world knowing smile. 'Is it a bargain?'

He looked unconvinced, even bemused.

She forced her point home. 'Be assured, with the right introductions, perhaps you will find a rich wife.' She let her gaze run over his person in the same manner he had looked at her. 'You shouldn't have too much difficulty attracting a wealthy female.'

His eyes danced then. 'A rich wife and a mistress to

boot.' He cocked his head on one side. 'Can you guarantee my acceptance in society?'

'With Lord Albright in our pocket, I can. As long as no one learns of our arrangement.'

He lifted his coffee and took a deep swallow. 'I have to say you are the most devious-minded woman I have ever met. If you were a businessman, I would fear for every penny in my pocket.'

Was he laughing at her? She wished she could read his reaction. Trying to feel like Cleopatra instead of plain Alice Fulton, she batted her eyelashes and cast him a seductive sideways glance. 'Admit it. You are tempted.'

'I'm tempted by your offer of an introduction to society.'

So much for seduction. But then she was at a disadvantage. You didn't need to practise flirtation while you were the richest woman this side of the grave. She forced herself to look on the bright side. She had found something he wanted, even if it wasn't her. She ignored a pang of disappointment. It was no different to Andrew wanting her fortune. For him, a position in society, as well as Fulton's Shipping was not a bad bargain in exchange for keeping her father out of prison.

'A wise choice,' she said. 'In the long run, it will do you far more good than a bag full of gold.' She arched a brow. 'Do we have a bargain?'

He brushed a finger over his lips, his gaze thoughtful. 'My ransom money in exchange for an introduction to society and a few nights with you. Is it worth it?'

She held still, tried not to let the mortification show

on her face, or the eagerness of her body's response at the thought of him in her bed while he looked her up and down. Heat flared in his eyes. He tried to hide it with a cynical smile. 'Why would I be interested in an untried mistress?'

'Untried, sir? Did I play my role too well?'

The words hung in the air like a lady's undergarments on the line on washing day. Available for all to see should they desire.

Michael couldn't quite believe what he was hearing.

Not innocent. Blood sang in his veins. The erection he'd been fighting all evening hardened to rock. Damn her. She was lying.

And yet passion was as natural to her as breathing. He'd sensed it from the first. But experienced she was not. She kissed with the enthusiasm of a maid, her body flaring to life under his hands, her pulse beating in her lovely throat, her body melting, but a skilled courtesan would have had him buried to the hilt long ago.

Blood rushed from his brain and thundered in his loins at an image of her slight, naked body beneath him. He fought to retain some semblance of rational thought.

Not an innocent? He almost smiled, she looked so prim as she awaited his answer.

'The game is not yet finished,' he said.

'If you will agree to my offer, I will concede.'

'Because you know you can't win.'

She raised a brow. 'There is always a chance…'

He glanced down at the board. There wasn't.

She was as good as offering herself to him without reservation.

Or he could let her win and attack Fulton on another front. But if Alice and her brother spoke true, Fulton loved his children and their downfall would cause the bastard to suffer as Michael and Jaimie had suffered.

The perfect revenge.

But he would not take her unless she was truly willing. 'You say you are experienced. Prove it.'

A delectable wash of colour stained her face, her gaze searched his. 'How?'

Conscienceless beast. 'Seduce me.'

She swallowed and slowly rose. She walked around the table, her steps hesitant, but her gaze fixed firmly on his mouth. Fascinated, he watched her lips part, her small bosom rise and fall. The tip of her tongue moistened her lips. The anticipation of what she might do next caused his heart to beat harder, his blood to heat, and his erection to strain against his breeches.

Then he looked into her eyes and saw the shame. Shame at the thought of bedding a crude rough bastard like him. He felt anger at Fulton rise like bile in his throat, burning and sour.

Tell her no, a small voice whispered.

His body protested. He held both urges in check. He would do nothing to help her down this path. It would be her choice.

She placed her hands flat on his chest. Did she feel the thunder of his pulse through the layers of cloth with that feather-light touch?

When he made no move, she raised herself up on her toes, brought one hand to his nape and drew him down to her mouth. For a moment or two he felt the puff of her quick little breaths on his lips.

He wanted to enfold her in his arms, crush her hard

against his body, demand, plunder, and ravish, like the cur her father had made him.

His lip curled in self-disgust and he willed his body into perfect stillness, let the hot dark urges slip away on a slow exhalation.

Prove it, Alice. Make me believe. Good God. Was that hope or a prayer?

The pull of small hands on his nape brought his mouth level with hers. Her lithe back stretched and arched. A touch of lips. Whisper soft. A flicker of tongue against the seam of his mouth, over in less time than it took to blink.

So gentle. So blasted maidenly.

She kissed the corner of his mouth, his bottom lip, the other corner, a parade of little touches, and licks and nibbles. Achingly sweet. Unbelievably seductive.

His lips burned to take command. Begged for firmer, more masterful contact, while hers teased and darted like butterflies, never settling anywhere for more than a second.

A soft purr emerged from her throat. The sweetest sound he'd ever heard. It hit his groin like a lightning bolt. Hot. Searing.

He fought the lust.

She sucked on his bottom lip.

Reason raced away like a rip-tide in full flood. He clung to it by a thread.

Her tongue swept his mouth, her fingers speared into his hair, caressing his scalp as her tongue danced away from his. Before he could think about what he was doing, his hands were on her shoulders, drawing her close, dragging her on to his lap, while his tongue followed hers into the sweet warmth of her mouth.

She suckled, holding his tongue captive, while she pressed her body hard against his length, her breasts flattened against his chest, her buttocks cushioning his erection.

Every breath he took was filled with her scent. Every inch of his skin felt nothing but her body, her warmth, the beat of her pulse. She filled his world. The here and the now. And he never wanted it to stop.

Slowly she eased away. 'Take me, Michael,' she whispered.

His body shook with the effort of remaining still. Never had he desired a woman with such bone-deep intensity. Answering heat blazed in her gaze. A dangerous combustible fire that transcended mere physical longings and spoke to something deeper, far more elemental.

He was an instrument of justice and she was the perfect tool. A weapon forged in the fires of lust for his use, no matter how it burned in his hand.

'Alice,' he murmured, the name tasting sweet on his tongue, 'be very sure.'

Her shoulders straightened and courage shone in her face, but no matter how she denied her innocence, he saw shame in the forest green and browns of her eyes, and the taut skin over her cheekbones. Deep inside, like a buried blade, he knew she had decided to sacrifice herself to save her father from paying the ransom. The question was, why?

'I am sure,' she whispered.

'Then there is one last detail required.'

A rapid little swallow disturbed the muscles of her throat. He ached for that tiny gesture of nerves. 'A contract,' she said, nodding her understanding.

'Yes,' he agreed.

He strode for the door.

Trembling, Alice watched him let in the dark from outside.

He stepped out into the night and whistled. Simpson arrived at the double.

Alice couldn't hear what he said to his steward, only the deep rumble of his voice, but she couldn't help but wonder why he didn't just take a piece of paper from his desk.

Beyond the door more voices joined the conversation. Arguing. Perhaps his crew didn't want to give up their share of the ransom. Pirates ran their ships by vote. She didn't know if privateers operated that way, too. Would they mutiny? Or change his mind?

The voices were still muttering when the door opened and Michael returned. 'What is happening?'

He didn't answer.

Simpson scuttled in after him with another sailor. They shoved the table against the bulkhead, clearing the centre of the room. The dishes, cups and glasses were whisked away.

A grim-faced Wishart entered with a tussled, sleepy Mr Bones. Eyes bleary from sleep behind his spectacles, his thin hair sticking up, the doctor carried a large black book under his arm. A Bible, she saw when he placed it on the table and riffled through the pages.

Was this how they recorded their agreements? Would he have her swear on it?

Solemnly Michael and Wishart moved to one side of Bones, standing shoulder to shoulder.

'Simpson, bring Miss Fulton over here,' Michael said curtly.

With a twinkle in his eyes, Simpson took her arm and walked her to stand beside Michael and then stepped back.

This was the oddest contract agreement she'd ever seen. Not that it would stand up in court whatever form it took. Not signed by a woman.

Bones picked up the Bible.

'Make it quick,' Michael said.

'Will you, Lionhawk, er, Michael Preston, take…?' He paused and looked at Alice.

What? Mouth open, she stared at him.

'Your name,' Michael muttered. 'Give him your name.'

'Alice…' Simpson prompted helpfully.

'Alice Primrose,' she said.

'Primrose?' Michael gave her an amused glance.

'Take Alice Primrose Fulton as your lawful wedded wife as long as you both shall live?'

'I will.' Michael's voice rang out clear and firm.

A wedding ceremony? She tugged on his arm 'What on earth are you doing?'

'It's a dowry, Alice. It comes with a bride.'

'No,' she said. 'I never meant that and you know it.'

Bones tapped the book. 'You can't force her, Cap'n.'

Michael's face darkened. 'Give us a minute.' He took her by the upper arm and dragged her to the window. With his back to the room, her arm firmly in his grasp, he leaned close to her ear. 'Do you want me to tell your brother you intended to prostitute yourself?'

His fierce expression said he would do it. It seemed her pirate had ethics. A moral code that didn't include ruining respectable females. Or was it something more? She would keep her honour, her respectability. What did he have to gain? 'Why?'

'You said you'd introduce me to society,' Lionhawk said in low, harsh tones, clearly angered by her hesitation. 'What better way than as your husband?'

Her husband. The thought made her foolish heart tumble. She felt dizzy, and breathless, and reckless with longing. But longing was a liar.

He gave her arm a little shake. 'Where is your courage, Alice?'

Courage. Was that all it took?

Why was she hesitating? He was clearly a wealthy man who could put Fulton's back on its feet, the whole purpose for her wager in the first place. Balancing the position of mistress against that of wife barely made sense. And yet she hesitated.

Dare she trust him? Probably not. As long as she kept that in mind in their dealings, then his offer was far better than she had any right to expect after her attempt at seduction.

She squared her shoulders. 'All right.'

If she hadn't known better, she might have mistaken the breath he exhaled as a sigh of relief. It was probably just frustration.

Tucking her hand under his arm, he drew her back to stand in front of Bones, who raised a brow. Michael gave him a nod. The seedy man looked at Alice and repeated the all-important question.

She glanced up at Michael. He gave her an encouraging smile.

Something inside her seemed to click into place, like a lock sliding home. It seemed…right.

'I will,' she said and her voice sounded strong.

'I now pronounce you man and wife,' Bones announced. He beamed.

She blinked. She was married. To the man at her side. A man she barely knew, but who made her heart beat faster, and her pulse race. In the past those wicked feelings had been her downfall. She'd do well to keep them in check, to remember this was a marriage of convenience. A bargain struck purely for financial gain.

'Congratulations,' Wishart said. 'I think.' He grasped Michael's hand and slapped him on the shoulder. 'I hope you don't live to regret this night's work, my friend.'

'So do I,' Michael muttered. 'That's it. You can leave.'

A chill ran down Alice's spine. Was he already having second thoughts?

The grinning Simpson, the tired-looking Bones and the grim-faced Wishart filed out. They were alone.

Her head felt suddenly light, dizzy with surprise. She was married.

'I think you are supposed to kiss the bride,' she said.

'Blast,' he said, looking uncertain. 'I was supposed to do that in front of them, wasn't I?' he scowled. 'This is the first wedding I've attended.'

Her insides softened at his obvious attempt to hide his chagrin. 'Better late than never.'

Before she ended the last syllable, his mouth was affixed to hers.

He kissed her well and he kissed her thoroughly and it was only when he stopped that her senses returned.

'Now,' he said, his chest rising and falling almost as fast as her own, 'where were we?'

'The wedding night?' she murmured.

He laughed, kissed her again, his fingers fumbling with the fastenings down the back of her gown, while his tongue swept her mouth and his lips worked their magic.

Married. To this gorgeous, if somewhat frightening, man who wreaked havoc with her senses. Delicious rippling pleasure shimmered beneath her skin and fluttered deep inside. Trembling with urgent desire, she turned to give him easier access to her back.

Blast it. She should be cool, unaffected, not panting with desire. This was merely the sealing of their bargain. Did she have no control at all?

Tomorrow. She'd resist him tomorrow. Tonight she'd pretend they were lovers.

His fingers freed her hair and the buttons of her dress.

He slipped her gown from her shoulders and pushed it down around her waist and went to work on her stays. In no time at all, he cast them aside, ran his hands over her back, swept her hair aside and was kissing her nape with a reverence that sent shivers down her spine.

Now he would see what sort of bargain he'd made.

Would he be disappointed in her boyish figure and lack of curves when he realised her stays were designed to fool the eye into thinking she had more on offer? Men preferred lush curves to bony ribs, unless they came with a nice plump pocket. She winced. He was going to be disappointed in both.

Resisting the temptation to cross her arms over her breasts, she turned and faced him. He groaned low in his throat and she followed his gaze to her tightly budded nipples beneath the fine lawn of her chemise.

Shameless. Heat blazed across her cheeks.

'Lovely,' he whispered.

Effortlessly, he swept her up and in three swift strides carried her to the bed. She felt like a doll in his strong arms. Vulnerable, yet safe. An odd, unsettling combination.

Gently, he laid her down. In one swift motion, he pulled her gown free of her hips and legs, then stretched out alongside. Cradling her neck on one strong forearm, he gazed into her face, searching her expression. For what? Permission?

It seemed that underneath all the arrogance, her pirate was an honourable man. She smiled and he bent his head and took her lips in a searing kiss.

Warmth rippled under her sensitised skin. She wanted to feel him against her. She arched into him. Pressed her hips against his, ran her hand through his hair, down his shoulder, over his back.

Her tongue tangled with his, dipped into the wine-sweet cavity of his mouth. He sucked on it.

Sweet agony. Payment in kind. She moaned.

He drew back, his eyes slumberous. 'What a surprise you are,' he murmured. 'A perfect treasure trove.'

He trailed a path of dizzying kisses down her jaw, nuzzled her neck, his lips traced her collarbone until she thought she would go mad with the exquisite, unbearable, building tension.

Through her chemise, his thumb grazed the underside of her breast. His touch sent a shock of little thrills to her core. Delicious. Intriguing. Like nothing she'd ever felt before.

Panting, she combed her fingers through his hair, caressing, encouraging.

He kissed the rise of her bosom. His tongue flicked across her nipple and it tightened in pleasure at his attention through fabric rough against her sensitive flesh.

He drew her nipple into his mouth and suckled.

Desire hit hard and fast, like a lightning bolt. Her body clenched, then flooded with heat. She moaned. A chuckle rumbled in his chest and he slid a hand over her stomach, down her thigh, small gentle circles, moving closer to her centre, moment by moment. Teasing when she ached.

And then his hand, warm and heavy, cupped between her thighs. A burst of pleasure made her gasp.

His hot, wet mouth left her nipple. It tightened with the sudden chill as he licked his way across the valley to plunder her other breast with delightful, taunting effect.

She tilted her hips and ground against his hand, seeking increased pleasure.

'Patience, princess,' he murmured, laughter in his voice. He sat up on the side of the bed, ripped off his loosely tied cravat and worked at the buttons at his throat.

At some point, she must have pulled his ribbon loose because his hair hung dark around his face, brushing his shoulders. It wasn't as black as his beard. It was dark mahogany with sun-kissed streaks of honey.

Married. The thought sparkled like a diamond, too bright to look at too closely. Long ago she'd given up thoughts of marriage and children, devoting herself to Father and her work at the hospital. And now, to be married to such a handsome virile man under such odd circumstances, seemed fantastical. He'd tried to destroy everything she loved with his plundering ways. She should be treating this as a duty, not a pleasure. She should be angry because he'd given her no choice.

She didn't know if she wanted to weep or laugh, she felt so confused.

He unbuttoned the neck of his shirt, revealing dark sworls of hair in the opening. Her stomach rolled lazily. Her insides tightened.

Lord help her, she couldn't resist him.

Her doubts would have to wait until morning, because right now the wanton part of her had taken control.

She tugged the fabric from his waistband, eager to see more of his magnificent form.

He slipped from her grasp, leaping up from the bed. She followed his progress around the room, snuffing the candles one by one, filling the room with the scent of warm tallow and shadows.

The oil lantern hanging from the centre beam was the last to flicker out, leaving the room dark and warm.

Slowly her eyes adjusted. Above her head the round face of the moon peered through the skylight. The sheets glowed white, while the gryphon grew in stature and menace. It all had a rather Gothic feel.

The maid and the pirate. It would make a wonderful title for a Minerva novel.

Only they were husband and wife. A blush stole up her body as the darkest shadow in the room loomed over the bed. She prayed that it wouldn't end in disaster.

Chapter Ten

The sight of the small vulnerable figure staring up at him with huge eyes swelled something in Michael's chest. Pride of possession. Beneath it, he felt a deeper emotion. One he refused to acknowledge.

For one horrible moment, he'd thought she'd refuse to wed him in front of his men. He wasn't sure what he would have done. But in the end her resistance had collapsed and she was no longer a Fulton.

It was all that mattered.

Tonight he would seal their bargain. Cleave her to him. The marriage had been a spur-of-the-moment idea, another way to separate the daughter from the father. And, if the truth be told, it meant he could accept her tempting offer with a clear conscience.

Perhaps he hadn't lost all trace of honour.

He gazed down at her. Practical little Alice with the middle name of Primrose. If he thought hard he could actually remember primroses from his youth. A quiet little flower with sunshine in its face. It suited her. His wife.

He sat on the edge of the bed and took in the delicate

curves and hollows beneath the transparent shift, the swell of small breasts, the peaking nipples, the darker triangle at the apex of her thighs. His to enjoy.

He heaved his boots off, tossed them across the cabin, and turned to her. 'One of us is definitely overdressed.'

She laughed softly. The sound reached out like a gentle caress. He might even be able to make her happy, Fate willing.

He pressed a kiss to her knuckles and heard her seductive sigh.

Not an innocent.

An odd burst of anger caught a breath in his throat. He shoved it aside. The past didn't matter. She was his from this day forwards. In one smooth motion, he yanked his shirt over his head and stretched out on the bed. She arched into him, warm, delicate, with sweet softness in all the right places. The scent of her arousal filled his senses.

He brushed her mouth with his lips. They parted to his tongue. He nibbled and licked and played with their soft fullness. Delicious. Honey-sweet. He thrust his tongue into her mouth and tasted her, wet and warm and softly welcoming. Her moan of pleasure pulled at the taut rope of desire he'd been holding in check for hours. Nay, since the moment she dragged him out of the *Conchita*'s galley.

He broke the kiss to gaze at her face. Shadows hid her eyes and highlighted her cheekbones. She looked fragile beside his large frame; breakable.

He wasn't used to gently bred females. Would she be terrified, as he'd heard some men tell? Would she lie beneath him and grit her teeth and do her duty? Or would she, as he hoped, throw herself into pleasure?

She pressed her palm against his chest. 'So soft, and yet so hard.'

His shaft jerked at her unintentionally salacious words. 'That's not all that is hard,' he murmured, trying not to laugh in case he hurt her feelings.

He guided her hand to his falls. Gently, hesitantly, but not at all unwilling, she gauged the shape of him with her fingers.

Too gentle. He wanted to grasp her hand and press it against his arousal. But that might make her afraid, and so he let her delicate fumbling drive his torment ever higher.

'Does it please you, princess?' he asked softly after a moment or two.

Even the cold moonlight could not hide the rush of blood to her face, or the way she snatched her hand back.

'Don't fear it,' he said. 'I promise I won't hurt you.' He bent his head and captured her mouth.

With one hand cradling her nape, Michael cupped her bottom with the other and pulled her hard against his groin. She gave a little wiggle, obviously feeling pleasure.

A groan of frustration clawed at his throat as her mound skimmed over his sensitive flesh beneath the cloth.

He deepened the kiss. Slowly he eased one thigh across her legs, while his free hand explored the graceful line of her throat, the rise of her breast, the tiny ripple of ribs beneath skin. The dance of her tongue against his and the rapid rise and fall of her chest and little purring sounds in her throat drove him towards the lovely female flesh between her thighs.

A light touch, a skim of fingers and palm revealed the heat and moisture of her desire.

He pressed down with the heel of his hand and she raised her hips, arching into his hand. So wonderfully responsive. He kissed her breasts, suckled, and she rocked against his palm.

He glanced down the length of her delectable body. In time he would know every inch, but right now she was gloriously aroused and ready for him. Triumph surged in his veins as her emboldened hands wandered down his shoulders and arms.

If he didn't get inside her soon, he feared he might not last. He pulled away. A small cry of disappointment from her lips jangled every nerve in his body. Hands trembling with the effort to maintain control, he unbuttoned his breeches and peeled them off.

She'd not be disappointed long.

He leaned over her and slid his knee between her legs. The silky soft skin of her upper thigh brushed the head of his shaft, a mere whisper of the pleasure ahead.

It took every ounce of his will not to drive himself home. With lust straining at a leash stretched beyond reason, he kissed the tip of her nose, her delicate cheekbone, dipped his tongue in the hollow of her ear and felt her skin's shiver of excitement with a deep sense of wonder.

His wife. Small, yet strong enough to fight him every inch of the way. He kissed her lips and her tongue probed his mouth greedily, searching out his tongue as if she couldn't get enough of the taste, her little gasping breaths and her fingers raking through his hair, enchanting and incredibly arousing.

Her legs came up around his hips and her heels

pressed against his buttocks, her tilted hips demanding what she wanted.

Not an innocent. Thank God. He'd never survive.

Bracing on one hand, he sought her hot centre. His questing fingers parted the delicate folds of skin, slid into her velvet depths and found her hot and slick and ready. He gently guided his shaft into her heat. So tight and wet and hot. She sighed. Ripples of pleasure coursed through his veins and he groaned deep in his throat.

Mindless, he drove into her.

He lifted her with one hand beneath her slender buttocks, opening her to him. She was just so damn tight. He wanted to feel the friction against his hard length, feel his testicles tight against her soft bottom.

He took a deep breath. If he lost control now, he'd be nothing more than a rutting beast. Her hands drifted lower, across his shoulders, sliding down his back. His muscles twitched and shivered beneath the light exploring touch.

She drew in a breath. 'Michael?' she whispered. 'What…?'

He stilled and swallowed a curse. Of course she'd feel the marks with her gentle healing hands.

What had he been thinking? He never bared himself in front of a woman. Not after the first time he'd seen a harlot's pity. He hadn't been thinking. He hadn't had a logical thought since he'd pictured her in his bed.

Breathing hard, he pulled away, rose up on arms trembling with the effort to remain in control. 'A scar,' he bit out.

'Does it hurt?' she asked softly, the pity in her voice stirring up memories of impotent helplessness.

What would she think when she realised he'd been beaten like a dog? Shame soured his gut. 'It's nothing,' he forced himself to say. He gentled his tone. 'An old injury. I don't like it touched.' He eased his weight on to one hand and brushed the hair back from her face, then dropped a kiss on her forehead. 'I'm sorry if I startled you.' He captured her small hand and placed it on his chest. 'I love the feel of your touch here.'

She blinked like a kitten gazing into the light. She nodded. 'I'll be careful.'

A pang speared his heart at the tenderness in her whisper. His eyes stung at the unexpected need to feel worthy of her kindness and knowing the one thing she would ask of him, he would not give. The best he could offer was the pleasure he could bring with his body. It would have to be enough. Slowly he began to move inside her.

Bliss, Alice thought as sensations rolled through her. This is what the word meant.

Against the glitter of night-sky through the skylight, his large male shape hung over her like a dark avenging angel. Her angel.

Pleasure increased tenfold as he thrust into her. She lifted her hips in time to his slow and powerful thrusts, smooth strokes that drove her wild. Her body clenched him tight within her and she reached for the stars outlined above his head.

He paused to kiss her mouth and throat and suckle at her breasts. She moaned and writhed as if a serpent had invaded her body, its flame-breath heating her blood, its coils tightening inside her until she cried out with the pain of too much pleasure. Thoughts refused to form.

Awed, she clung to the sweat-slick shoulders bunching beneath her fingers. She heard his ragged breath in her ear as he thrust deeper, faster. One hand reached between them, circling and rubbing, driving her higher amid waves of endless pleasure.

And then she flew apart. Scattered like ashes on the wind, burned by the fiery beast.

He pulled away, and his groan of completion mingled with her gasps of joy. Vaguely, she felt him draw her against his scorching body, stroking and petting, her hair, her breasts. He rained kisses on her face. She glowed like a smouldering ember, yet her limbs felt liquid.

Heavy lidded, she stared at his beautiful sensual face. 'That was…astonishing. Wonderful. I never—'

'I'm glad to hear it,' he said, his chest rising and falling, his voice full of laughter. He stilled, gazing at her for a long moment. His expression changed, hardened. She felt herself brace.

'Who was he?' he asked. 'Your first lover.'

She should have guessed he would ask. No sense in hiding the truth. 'My fiancé. Does it bother you?'

'The man was a cur.'

It bothered him. She opened her mouth to say more, but he pressed a finger against her lips. 'Rest, my sweet. There will be time for talk later.'

She didn't want to talk. Not of Andrew. So she smiled and nestled into the hollow of his warm broad shoulder. With limbs as heavy as lead, she let her eyelids fall closed. She lay in his embrace, his lips nuzzling her neck, his warm breath stirring her hair.

Tendrils of bliss ran through her veins. Married. To a pirate. Perhaps, given her nature, she'd made the right choice, even if it was for all the wrong reasons.

* * *

Michael strode up and down the deck above his stateroom clad only in his shirt and breeches, his teeth clamped on his cigar, his gaze constantly straying to the skylight overlooking the bed.

The early morning air did nothing to cool the heat running through his veins, while his mind reviewed the previous night in graphic detail and his body responded with vigorous enthusiasm.

The woman had courage. And passion. Bottomless passion. She'd been thoroughly delightful. Delicious. Responsive.

Not an innocent. Hah. She might as well have been a virgin for all she knew about the art of love. Clearly the fellow had fired her ardour and then debauched her without much thought to her pleasure. He'd probably broken her heart into the bargain. The bastard.

His fists clenched. And he was going to do the same. Hades. He wanted her again. Badly. More incredibly, he'd woken at dawn with her snuggled in his arms without a moment of his usual confusion. Only by exercising the greatest restraint had he been able to leave her to sleep. He wanted to please her, not wake her like some rutting animal. Because he wanted her to be happy.

A worrying thought.

He halted and leaned against the rail, staring down into a green ocean creaming away from the stern. How happy would she be when she realised the future he had planned?

A kind of madness seemed to have infected his brain. A desire to lead a normal life with Alice at his side. To forgo justice and be at peace.

He struck the bulwark with his fist.

How did one delightful night pay for the horrors inflicted by Fulton?

His gut churned. It couldn't. Nor did marrying the wench. A scant three years ago he'd learned of his past. Since then he'd lived only to see Fulton punished. Set his plan in motion. No matter what, he must see his vow through to the bitter end.

She'd hate him when she found out he'd tricked her.

Bitterness dried his tongue and the back of his throat. With a grimace, he tossed the cigar over the side.

If the future was as empty as his past, it was Alex Fulton's fault and Michael would take whatever scraps of joy the Fates offered in the here and the now.

He approached the skylight, leaned over, one bare foot on the sill. She stretched, the sheet slipped to her waist, exposing her tiny perfect breasts, taut and rose-tipped in the early morning sunlight. His blood thundered and his body hardened. He turned and leaped down to the main deck.

Wishart beside the helm caught his eye. Michael waved him off and entered his cabin, all thoughts focused on the woman in his bed.

She sat up when he burst through the door.

'Oh, it is you,' she said, colour flushing her cheeks, her gaze wary. 'I suppose it is time I arose.'

He knelt on the bed and took her face in his hands. She lowered her gaze, hiding her thoughts.

'Don't be in such a hurry, sweetheart,' he said.

The delightful shade of pink deepened to rose. Embarrassment? Shame? Had her enthusiasm been naught but a sham? A female wile?

'Shy today, love?' he said, trying to keep his suspicions from his voice.

She winced as if he'd caused her pain. Clumsy fool. He tipped her chin, brushed his mouth against hers, wooed her with flicks of his tongue.

After a moment of hesitation, she melted against him, her arms sliding around his neck, her body arching, her lips clinging.

Reluctantly he broke the kiss. 'I am here on Simpson's orders to say your bath is ready.'

She glanced around with a frown. 'A bath?'

He tried not to look overly smug, tried not to feel proud as he crossed the room. 'Through here.' He triggered the catch to the hidden door in the bulkhead and revealed his dressing room.

Rising from the bed, her hair around her shoulders in glorious disarray, she wrapped herself in the sheet and tiptoed past him to gaze through the door. Lit only by candles, the copper tub gleamed softly and scented steam filled the small space. 'Oh, my.'

He grinned. 'My one luxury.'

Clearly beguiled, she smiled, and his heart faltered at the beautiful sight of her pleasure.

Capturing her around the shoulders, he fastened his mouth to hers and kissed her deeply, drank of her gentle sweetness, pushing aside the future. For now she was his and perhaps he could bind her to him. If the Fates were kind.

With a swift kick of his heel, he pushed the door shut and pried the sheet from her fingers. It pooled at her feet with a rustle.

Her soft gasp of protest filled his mouth.

Slowly he released her and took her hand as if leading her into a ballroom. With a bow, he led her to the wooden stool before the steaming tub.

Skin, the colour of cream, untouched by cruel sunlight, stretched over fine bones he could snap in one hand. Small and firm, her breasts invited his large calloused hands, a sweet indent of waist, hips that were almost boy-slim, aroused a protective instinct he barely understood. Most of the women he had known could only be described as voluptuous. In hindsight they seemed vulgar, overblown, whereas once they had seemed exotic. The knowledge that this one was his alone was stronger than the most powerful of aphrodisiacs. He wanted her.

Her cheeks blazing, his not-so-virginal, but modest wife, stepped up and over the side of the bath, quickly immersing in fragrant water that hid little from his view. As a sop to her delightful modesty, he pretended not to look and went around behind her.

'I can manage,' she said, clutching her knees to her chest and hiding her face with the silken fall of her hair, while providing him with a lovely view of the curve of her slender back and the delicate roundness of buttocks below the water. A water sprite. An earth goddess, but no seductress, for all her brave words. Yet she pleased him enormously. More than he'd ever hoped.

Had he hoped?

For years he'd wallowed in the depths of a stinking navy ship. A rat below the waterline, fighting for scraps, friends like Simpson guarding his back when he awakened with terrified screams at nightmares he didn't understand. Every breath he'd taken had been about the next crumb, the next task, survival.

He'd dreamed of a simple life on shore. A family. Children.

Then he'd learned the truth.

Hope had no place in his life. Not until duty was done. Again he fought off a vague feeling of rocky shoals ahead. What the hell was the matter with him? He had his ship, a willing woman, and a fair wind for England. He also had the means to bring his enemy down. Everything had fallen into place.

The hair on the back of his neck rose. The Fates demanded payment for too much good fortune.

Enough. He'd worry about that later.

For now, Alice was his to enjoy.

He rolled up his shirtsleeves and gathered soap and towels from the washstand. He dipped one end of a towel into the water behind her back and worked up a lather. The scent of sandalwood perfumed the air. His scent. On her it smelled different. Intoxicating.

Gently he parted her hair to fall over her shoulders and breasts, leaving her nape and slender back a feast for his hungry gaze. He circled the soapy cloth over the smooth creamy skin with its dusting of tiny golden hairs, paying attention to each small nub of her spine and the delicate striation of ribs. Nothing marred her tender perfection.

She reminded him of a china doll. If he did not know better, he would have feared she would break.

His eager body stirred. He tamped down his desire. There was no need for haste. He would have many days to savour her delights, to get to know every inch of that delectable body before the world and its obligations intruded.

He ran his soapy hands down her softly rounded arms, then her shoulders, reaching under her arms to soap her breasts. She murmured a soft sound of approval. He adored her tiny body with his hands. She shivered as his slippery fingers skimmed her nipples. They hardened at his touch. He flicked them gently with his thumb and thrilled to her indrawn gasp of pleasure.

His penis jerked to attention.

The hairs on his chest brushed her back each time he leaned forwards. He felt her breathing pick up speed in response. He soaped her narrow ribcage. Wickedly, his index finger dipped inside her navel and she leaned back against his shoulder, eyes closed in dreamy passion.

Contentment glowed in a dark corner of his soul. A soft and gentle light. A mere flicker, not much more than an ember, but so precious he would guard it with his life.

With gentle strokes, he washed her flat belly, a soft plain of pure delight. He measured the span of her waist and traced the bones at her hips. He exulted in the feel of her silky skin beneath his rough and calloused hands.

'May I join you?' he whispered.

Her gaze fractured. 'What if I said no?'

'Then I would be sad, but you would have your way.' A reckless offer, but not one he couldn't keep. He nuzzled her ear. 'Sweet Alice, don't you want me in your bath?'

She let go a long sigh, as if she'd been fighting a battle in her head and had lost. 'I do,' she whispered. She turned her face and kissed his cheek.

'Then I'm pleased.' He stripped off his breeches and shirt and climbed in, saw her little jolt of awareness at the sight of his erection and resisted the urge to crow in triumph like a lad.

Instead, he settled into the water, thanking God he'd

insisted on a bath big enough for him to lie down in. With his legs cradling her hips and her feet draped over his thighs, there was more than enough room for them both. From this angle she looked glorious. Pink and soft and glowing. The damp ends of her hair clung to her breasts. Steam sheened her face with moisture. He wanted to lick it off her skin. Her modestly cast-down gaze drove him to distraction, because he could see her peeking at his body from beneath her lashes.

She wanted him.

He lifted her ankle, clasping her small foot. It barely filled his palm. He washed the sole, the heel and between each small toe, then massaged the arch.

She wriggled enchantingly, making tiny ripples in the water.

'Like that, do you?' he said, his voice a growl.

'Mmm,' she said.

'Good.' He moved the cloth up her shapely ankle. 'There's more.'

Alice watched his bronzed hands move over her white skin, her limbs melting as he caressed first her calf, and then her knee. She drew in a breath and glanced at his face softened by desire, intent on his task, his long black eyelashes veiling his eyes.

Dark and hard and ruthless as a general rule, at this moment he seemed almost tender. Yet this was all about money. And lust. Heaven help her, even knowing she'd had no choice in this marriage of theirs, she could not resist his allure. What kind of wicked woman was she?

Some might say it served her right, after what she'd done to Andrew. But they didn't know the truth. How he'd spoken of love, and lied.

And now she was lying to Lionhawk.

Her heart picked up speed. Fear. Fear of him and the spell he wove. Too much, she loved the feel of the slide of his hands over her skin, the temptations offered by his mouth.

She could not allow the temptation to be all one-sided. She grabbed at the washcloth.

Eyes smoky, he gazed at her. 'Had enough?'

The disappointment in his voice made her want to giggle. Nerves. And excitement. And a feeling of daring. She batted her lashes. 'My turn to wash you.'

His raised brows and the grin of surprised pleasure on his bearded face fired her confidence. A kind of feminine pride she'd not felt for a very long time.

She slid forwards, her calves around his waist so she could reach him.

'Very nice,' he said, looking down through the soapy water at the junction of her thighs.

Heat rushed to her face. 'You too,' she said, bravely indicating the male member jutting proudly from the water.

He laughed and pulled her against his arousal. Then, he leaned back against the edge of the tub and closed his eyes with a sigh. 'I'm all yours.'

He was. Hers. Her husband. The realisation jolted her stomach. If she brought him joy, mayhap he wouldn't care about her hiding the extent of Father's debts.

Drawing in a breath, she took the soap and lathered her hands. Where to start? His broad expanse of chest with its sprinklings of short black curls and smooth sculpted curve of muscle tempted her fingertips. Tentatively, she placed her hands flat on his chest. The feel of rough wet hair against her palms was wicked and delicious. Her insides clenched with a little thrill.

She stroked in slow circles as he had, raking her fingers through the hair on his chest, and massaging the hard muscle beneath.

The nub of his male nipples hardened against her palm. Fascinated, she tweaked one between her finger and thumb.

A groan rumbled up from his chest.

'I'm sorry,' she gasped, snatching her hand back.

He opened an eye. 'Oh, don't be sorry, sweet. Do it again. Harder.'

Her insides quivered at the rough note in his voice.

With a quick swallow to ease her dry throat, she grazed her nails across both of his nipples. His erection gave an odd little jump against her belly, the ridges of muscle beneath his ribs tightened and rippled. A beautiful sight. Pleasure sent spirals of heat up from her belly.

Apart from a small dark line of hair running from the centre of his chest down to his navel and disappearing into the thick thatch of curls at the base of his member, the skin on his stomach was smooth and tanned from the sun.

Whereas his shoulders were broad, his waist tapered down to narrow hips in a most interestingly enticing way.

She'd seen statues and men working in the fields with their shirts off in summer, and had her hands on Andrew in the dark, but nothing had prepared her for this vision of hard, lovely, male strength or the feel of his nakedness under her hands. She lathered the soap and set to work to wash his ribs and stomach, loving the feel of muscle and bone and sinew.

He let go a soft moan.

She scooped up handfuls of water and washed away

the bubbles and eyed his lower torso. She desperately wanted to touch him there, but lacked the courage.

Arms. First she should wash his arms. And his hands. A naughty drawing she'd seen once flashed into her mind.

She washed his hand, then rinsed it in the tub. She lifted it to her mouth and sucked each digit dry, including his thumb.

His eyes flew open. 'Do you have any idea how sensual that feels?'

Sensual. The word curled around her insides. 'I saw it in a book.' A dreadful, blood-stirring, shocking book she'd found in her father's library. Not that she could imagine her father ever reading such a naughty work. Or her mother.

'A book?' He chuckled. 'Alice, you are full of surprises.'

He must think her dreadfully bold. Andrew had. She'd shocked him to the core of his strict Scottish soul. 'I'm sorry.'

'Good God, don't be sorry. I love it.'

'Oh.' She leaned forwards and kissed his lips for those kind words. A quick brush and a little flick of her tongue, just to taste. Quick as a cat, he grabbed her nape in warm wet hands, holding her captive while he plundered her mouth. Her mind spun away in a current of pleasure.

Mindless, she sank into the bliss of his kiss, the strokes of his tongue on hers, the feel of strong firm lips, the tickle of his beard against her chin, his hardness probing her belly.

Her hands went around his neck and her breasts pressed against his hard wall of chest. Cupping his face in her hands, she came up on her knees.

Breathing hard, he broke away, the turquoise of his eyes glittering hotly. 'Is this your idea of torture?'

'Yes.'

He cracked a laugh of surprise.

She tilted her head, narrowed her eyes, and saw the muscles of his jaw flicker with tension. He wanted her.

And she wanted him. All of him.

But she couldn't let him see how weak he made her. He'd tormented and teased her body last night and now it was her turn. 'Lean forwards,' she demanded.

He did, his eyes closing as his mouth sought hers. She dodged his lips and reached over his shoulder, intending to soap his back.

He grabbed her arms. 'No.'

His lack of trust hurt more than his fingers digging into her flesh. 'Why not? I've seen scars before.' She pointed to the red line with its neat row of stitches on his arm, and then to the faint white line on his upper chest.

His expression tightened. 'Those are nothing.'

Her stomach dipped, her rapid pulse beat a warning. 'It can't be all that bad. And besides, we are married. I am going to see it sooner or later.'

He leaned forwards. 'Then look your fill, wife.' The bitterness in his tone gave her pause. She gathered her courage, took a deep breath and peeped over his shoulder.

Instead of a smooth plane of skin across the wide shoulders, the flesh was knotted and raised in a criss-cross of welts. Not one scar, but dozens. Hideous.

She stifled a gasp. Sensing his tension in his utter stillness, she sat back and stared into a face rigidly blank. 'Who did such a dreadful thing?'

The silence was palpable. His chest rose and fell as if

he had trouble speaking the words, but when he did, his voice was as flat and unemotional as his expression. 'The Royal Navy. The cat-o'-nine-tails is routine punishment.'

'What could you have done to deserve…?' She wanted to recall the words the moment they were out of her mouth. It didn't matter what he had done. Nothing deserved such abominable cruelty.

'I existed,' he said flatly. 'Have your delicate sensibilities suffered enough? Shall I put on my shirt?'

'It's horrible.'

He lowered his brows, his gaze avoiding hers, his lip curling as if he suddenly found the situation vastly amusing. 'I knew it would turn your stomach. I told you not to look.'

'I didn't mean you. I meant what they did. It's barbaric. Wrong.'

His forehead dropped to hers; he breathed hard for a moment or two as if he'd been running. Not fear. A bone-deep anger. 'It happens every day.' He raised his head. As his gaze met hers, she thought she saw traces of a shame that belonged to the perpetrator of this crime.

She slipped her hands beneath his arms and slowly stroked the irregular lumps and bumps, unable to imagine how much it must have hurt. 'It is wrong. Evil.'

'Yes,' he said his voice husky. 'It is wrong. It turns men into brutes. The punished and the punisher.' He sounded sad.

'But not you, Michael,' she whispered.

'Not me?' He stared at her, clearly dumbfounded. 'You don't know what you are talking about.'

Was that how he saw himself? As a brute? 'You've been nothing but kind to your prisoners. You provided medical care, you treated us with respect. You could have taken what you wanted without our marriage.'

'Don't think I didn't think of it.'

'But you didn't act on the thought.'

His jaw hardened. 'Don't make me out to be a hero, Alice. You don't know me well enough.'

She resumed her stroking and a groan rumbled up from his deep chest. She felt it all the way to her heart.

He pulled her close so she could reach farther. 'Your touch soothes me,' he said in her ear, his voice husky. 'It takes away the anger.' He rested his chin on her shoulder, relaxed, exposed.

Alice smiled, at his steady heartbeat against her breasts, his bold hardness pressing against her stomach. His vulnerability touched her more deeply than any of his charm. Coils of snaking pleasure unfurled deep within her being. Wanton that she was, she wanted him inside her again. She knelt, raising herself over him. He swiftly realised her intention.

'Hussy,' he said in tones so velvet her scalp tightened in anticipation.

'Rogue,' she replied, sinking slowly on to him.

Her breath caught as he slid inside. So deep, so hard, he filled her to her very core. His warm hands grasped the cheeks of her bottom and he helped her find the stroke and angle for greatest pleasure.

'You were right,' she murmured. 'I really had no idea this would be so good.'

'I'm glad you are pleased,' he said low in her ear, his heartbeat loud in her ears.

The water moved in waves to their languid rhythm. It cascaded over each end of the bath in a soapy waterfall she barely noticed. She only felt him deep inside her, pleasuring her with the sweetest of agony, his hands and mouth on her breasts, torturing her with delight, his heart and hers melting together through their skin, as water swirled around their joining.

'Now, Michael,' she demanded.

'Bossy little wench, aren't you?' he murmured and he thrust deeper and harder and his fingers sought the place that brought her to the peak of fulfilment.

For long sweet moments, he teased her with an exquisite agony of gentle rocking, then there was nothing except the spiralling pleasure of release.

Sated, they lay together in the cooling water, their limbs a tangle of creamy white and bronze. Her wet hair stuck to his chest, her arm, her cheek, his chin.

'Come, sweet Alice,' he whispered when their breathing steadied and their heartbeats returned to normal. He lifted her out of the tub, wrapped her in a towel and carried her to the bed. He lay her down as if she was made of spun sugar and patted her dry gently. When he was satisfied not a drop of moisture remained on her skin he covered her with the sheet and grabbed another towel. 'I'll send your friend to help you dress,' he said, as he dried himself before donning his clothes.

She hadn't expected a man of his ilk to be so thoughtful. It made her want to weep, she felt so treasured.

Because he only treasured her money.

When he discovered Father had no money, his attitude would surely change. The deck seemed to tilt, causing a nauseous feeling.

Chapter Eleven

'Michael?'

She stared at the strong features softened by love-making and took a swift heartening breath. 'About Fulton's. My father really does only have the *Conchita* left.'

'I see.' His expression became carefully blank, shuttering his thoughts on the matter. Yet she didn't think he was displeased. Perhaps because she'd told him the truth right from the beginning?

'I hope you are not too disappointed.'

He raised her hand to his lips. He turned it over and kissed her palm, his lips warm and dry, his gaze on her face. 'How can I be disappointed when I have you?'

A soft velvet touch. A shiver ran down her spine. Her body tightened with yearning. She fought the insidious longing, forced her mind to ignore the clamouring of her body for his touch. He still didn't know about the debts. But those were Father's and not hers to discuss. 'I will do everything I can to help restore the business.'

Regret flickered in his eyes. 'It doesn't matter.'

But it did, she could see that it did in the way his gaze seemed to turn in on itself. 'Your entry into society is assured,' she said almost wildly.

A knock sounded at the door. 'Cap'n? Mr Wishart needs you on deck.'

He glanced over his shoulder at the door, then back to her.

'Cap'n.' Simpson again. 'Mr Wishart says it's urgent.'

'Blast,' he said and rushed out of the door.

Bugger Wishart, Michael thought, closing the cabin door. Surely he didn't need Michael's help at every turn? He glanced at Simpson's oddly serious face. 'What is it?'

The ship yawed beneath his feet. A quick glance up revealed the men scrambling aloft to make more sail. Hell.

'Simpson, ask Lady Selina to help Miss…my wife dress.'

'Aye, aye, Cap'n,' the little man said. 'And, Cap'n?'

Michael raised a brow.

Simpson grinned. 'Congratulations. She's a fine young lady.'

Lady. Aye. Therein lay the problem. The lady had been honourable to a fault, leaving him feeling like the worst of curs. 'Stir your stumps.' He headed for a frowning Wishart beside the helmsman.

'About time,' David said.

'What blows?'

'The wind backed around an hour since, we've barely made any headway.'

Wishart should have let him know, but Michael appreciated his friend's forbearance.

'What's our heading?'

'North by nor'west. But that's not the problem.' He gestured over Michael's shoulder. 'We've got company. Kale, blast his eyes, said he didn't see it.'

Michael cursed. He strode to the bulwark and Wishart handed him a glass.

The sail was low on the horizon, but even so, Michael knew in his gut what sort of ship he would see. He climbed the ratlines, hooked one foot in the ropes and looked again.

'Ship of the line,' he muttered. 'Seventy-four guns.'

'Altering course,' the lookout sang out from his perch on the yard. 'She's seen us.'

'Hurry up, you bastards,' Michael yelled. 'Unfurl those sails. Wishart, bring her round. Let's get the wind at our backs.'

Silence rang in Alice's ears. The shots followed by crashes and the trembling of the ship like some startled filly had ceased as suddenly as they began. 'What is happening?'

Anderson pressed his ear to the door of their prison, then shook his head. 'I do believe we are heaved to.'

When Michael had rushed her down here, he'd said nothing except not to mention their wedding. Not to anyone. When she'd tried to ask why, he'd cut her off and asked her to do his bidding. His gaze had asked her to trust him, although he hadn't said the words.

So she'd said nothing and had quelled Selina's questions upon her arrival in the gown she'd worn last night with a cool look and a glance at her brother. But she couldn't help wondering. Couldn't help going over the marriage ceremony and wondering if it had been real.

Richard, who'd also been forced to join them in the hold, had expressed confidence that the *Gryphon* would easily outrun the naval frigate. Then the cannon fire had started. And none of them had said a word about anything.

Selina uncovered her ears and placed her hands flat on the table. 'What is going to become of us?' Her voice quivered with tears. 'They'll leave us here to die.'

'Rubbish,' Richard declared, putting his eye to the crack in the door. 'The fighting is over. Someone will be along in a moment.'

If Alice hadn't been quite so worried, she might have laughed at how disconsolate he sounded. She could not help but be glad that Michael had not permitted him to take part in whatever battle had taken place above their heads. She just wished she knew who had won. Hopefully Michael.

But the sounds above their heads, the shudders of the ship left her fearing the worst. She put an arm around her trembling friend. 'Richard is right. Someone is sure to be along in a moment. Captain Lionhawk won't let any harm come to us.' Did she really believe that?

The sound of marching feet thumped overhead. Minutes later a key rattled in the lock and the light from several torches spilled into the hold like dawn into a cave. She blinked to clear her vision. Red jackets adorned with white piping of Royal Navy Marines poured into their prison, their boots clattering on the bare planks.

'British lobsters,' Richard shouted, his face full of excitement. 'Hooray.'

Alice's stomach plummeted as the red-and-white tide formed a line. Michael had lost. An American privateer was unlikely to receive a warm reception from the Royal Navy. Was this his reason for asking her not to speak of their marriage? Knowing they might be captured, had he feared they'd treat her badly as his wife?

Or had the wedding been a sham after all? There it was. Out in the bright daylight. The fear that once again she'd been played for a fool. The worst part was the hope she was wrong.

A mist blurred her vision and prickled hot behind her nose. She sniffed and inhaled a deep gasping breath. They'd made a bargain. Until she was proved wrong, she would trust him to stand by his word. And in the meantime, she'd say nothing.

An officer, a young man with red cheeks and a magnificent moustache, saluted. 'Lieutenant Liversedge at your service, ladies and gentlemen.' He bowed. 'Captain's compliments. You are to board the *Essex*.'

Alice took a deep breath. 'Thank you, Lieutenant. I am Alice Fulton. This is Lady Selina Albright, my brother, Richard Fulton, and Mr Anderson, the Fulton business agent.'

'The *Essex*?' Richard said, pushing forwards, his face alight. 'Wasn't she at Trafalgar? Do you think I can look around?'

The officer's jaw slackened. 'I...er...I am sure it can be arranged, sir. Now, if your party would follow us, we'll get you transferred.'

Mr Anderson urged Selina and Alice forwards. Richard sidled up to the lieutenant, plying him with questions. The troop of soldiers fell in behind.

Up on deck in harsh sunlight, the ravages of the fighting made her heart ache. The aft stateroom where she had spent her wedding night was naught but a splintered wreck. The mainmast trailed in the sea like a broken wing. The smell of gunpowder lingered on the warm breeze flapping the idle sails on the remaining mast. Beside the smaller *Gryphon*, his Majesty's *Essex* sat fat and wide, like a huge goose next to a wounded seagull. At the stern, ten or so redcoats encircled the dispirited crew. With his blond hair and massive height, Wishart stood head and shoulders above his comrades, but where was their captain? Where was Michael? Alice craned her neck to see around her accompanying guard. There. Smeared with soot, a livid bruise on his forehead, hair wild around his shoulders, he was kneeling beside a man stretched out on the deck.

'Someone is injured.' She pushed forwards. A marine barred her path with his musket. 'Stay away from the prisoners, miss.'

'They'll be cared for, Miss Fulton,' Liversedge said at her elbow. She didn't believe him. There was too much indifference in his voice.

A marine prodded the clearly furious Michael to his feet with the point of a bayonet. One of the soldiers shoved him into line, locking his wrists and ankles into manacles joined by chains to Wishart and the others.

Bile rose in her throat. She couldn't bear to look and yet she couldn't look away. Don't argue, she wanted to call out. Please don't. You'll only antagonise them.

The marines closed ranks, blocking her view.

'Over the side, ladies and gentlemen,' Liversedge said. 'The sergeant and his men will help you into the longboat. If you'll excuse me, I have prisoners requiring my attention.' He saluted and marched off.

Feeling rather like an ewe being worried by a collie,

Alice allowed the sergeant to chivvy their little party to
the side of the ship. She looked back for Michael and
saw that Kale had been pulled out of the line of prisoners and was in deep conversation with Liversedge.
Every now and then the lieutenant's gaze shot to
Michael.

Kale meant no good, she was sure. Anxiety gnawed
at her stomach.

'I can't,' Selina wailed, bringing Alice's attention
back to her own party.

'Sorry, miss,' the sergeant said. 'It's the only way.'

Below them, a very long way below them, four
sailors worked their oars to keep the waiting launch
steady, while a midshipman in the stern directed their
efforts.

The marine hoisted himself over the side, climbed
nimbly down the rope ladder and jumped into the bobbing
boat. He steadied himself, then held the ladder taut.

Alice recalled with fondness the bo'sun's chair
Michael had provided to get her from the *Conchita* to
the *Gryphon*. It began to look luxurious compared to
the swinging ropes against the side of the ship.

'Over you go, miss,' said the soldier at her side.

Alice smiled at Selina through gritted teeth. 'We
have no choice.'

Selina shuddered. 'Why can't I just go home on this
ship?'

'It's a piece of cake,' Richard said, grinning. 'I'll go
first and make sure you don't fall.'

'Buck up, Selina, it's quite safe,' Alice said, with
more bravado than her pitching stomach warranted. The
sooner she was on the other ship, the sooner she could
find out what would happen to Michael and his crew.

Selina peered down at Richard below, shrugged, and let the sergeant help her over the side. To Alice's amazement, she climbed down as if she'd been doing it all her life, despite her hampering skirts. Richard, young gentleman that he was, kept his gaze firmly fixed on the planks in the bottom of the boat.

If Selina could do it, there were no excuses for her. The sergeant gripped her arm. 'That's it, miss. Don't look down and you will be all right.'

Wonderful. The ladder swung with the rhythm of the ship on the swell. Alice bit down hard on the little scream in the back of her throat. Her stomach knotted. She couldn't do it. She hated heights. She took a deep breath. Then another. This was no different to mounting a horse or climbing up a set of stairs. Calm good sense and a careful approach were all she needed. Tell that to her pounding heart.

Gritting her teeth, she found the first rung with her foot and staring at the hull in front of her nose, her trembling legs worked their way down rung by rung. The side of the *Gryphon* soon towered over her head and Richard's hands were around her waist helping her to a seat in the boat.

She let go an unsteady breath and collapsed on the bench beside Selina. The launch pushed off. She gazed across the water to a similar boat departing from the stern. Michael caught her eyes and stood and bowed with a devil-may-care smile. His men laughed.

One of the soldiers swung out with his rifle stock. Michael crashed to his knees.

Alice bit back her cry of outrage. How could they be so brutal to a man in chains? Anger rushed hot through her veins. She wasn't sure who annoyed her most, the brutal soldier, or Michael and his ridiculous gallantry.

'What will happen to them?' she asked the sergeant seated on the facing bench.

He grinned. 'Don't worry about that lot. The navy always needs experienced sailors. Of course, they'll try the ringleaders the moment we reaches port,' the man continued with far too much glee in his voice. 'Bleedin' pirates they are. Begging your pardon, miss. They'll hang 'em fer sure.'

Nausea filled her throat. Her stomach heaved. The gentle sea seemed to pitch the boat like a cork. She swallowed hard.

This was not the time for a fit of the vapours.

Alice and Selina stared at each other from their respective bunks in the cramped officers' cabin.

'Nothing but excitement on Fulton Shipping Lines,' Selina said in a dry little voice. 'Remind me to travel with you again.'

'Perhaps we should start a new venture—adventures on the high seas, battles included,' Alice replied in kind. Anything to take her mind off what might be happening to Michael and his crew.

Selina laughed. 'Gentlemen walk the plank at sword point, while the ladies are seduced by the handsome captain.' She sobered. 'Talking of handsome captains, you were gone all night. *Did* he seduce you?'

She stared at her friend's concerned face. Selina had proved herself a true friend over Andrew. Having discovered from his brother Andrew's plan of seduction to keep her from crying off, she saved Alice before she made the worst mistake of her life. The seduction was done. But she'd cried off anyway. She might have stayed the course, if she hadn't learned the poor boy loved his childhood sweetheart, but was prepared to make the sacrifice to save his family.

When she'd confronted him and returned his ring, he'd been scathing about the way she'd thrown herself at him, and there had been some gossip. Selina had stood by her.

Would Selina be as supportive now, if she thought Alice had made the same mistake with Michael? 'I married him.'

'What?' Only Selina could make one quiet word sound like a shriek.

'There was a ceremony conducted by Mr Bones, last night. I signed a document. Michael told me not to speak of it, but I had to tell someone. Promise you won't tell anyone.'

'But why marry him?'

'He wouldn't agree to forgo the ransom without a contract. There's nothing more binding than marriage.' She couldn't help the doubt creeping into her voice at her friend's worried expression. She winced and put her fear into words. 'I'm not even sure it was a proper wedding.'

Selina's jaw dropped. 'But that means…Alice, you spent the night with him.'

A blissful night. Her body warmed. Her face felt hot, all the way to her hairline.

'Alice,' Selina said, her eyes popping open, 'you look…besotted.'

No hiding things of that nature from Selina. She lifted her chin. 'It was lovely.'

'So, you hope you are married.'

'Yes.' She pressed cool palms to hot cheeks. 'But please say nothing until I've spoken to him.'

Selina's fair brow wrinkled. For a stomach-clenching moment, Alice thought she'd balk.

'Oh, very well,' Selina said. 'I don't quite see where all this is leading, but you can trust me to follow along.'

There weren't many true friends in a life and Selina was one. But even friends had lines beyond which they would not pass. And this was asking a lot. Alice reached out and took her hands. 'Thank you.'

'So now what do you plan to do?'

'First I want to find the surgeon.' At least one of Michael's men had been injured in the fighting and she wasn't sure the navy would bother to provide medical attention. Then she needed a word with the captain of the *Essex*.

Selina swung her legs up on the bunk and put her hands behind her head. 'Liversedge said we weren't to leave here without an escort. For our own safety.' She mimicked the fussy voice of the lieutenant. 'Why not speak to the surgeon when we dine with the officers?' She sounded as if she felt it was the right thing to say, even if she knew it was hopeless.

'If I wait, it might be too late. I don't trust the lieu-tenant.'

'I agree. There is something about him one cannot quite like.'

Selina's instincts about men were infallible. The echo of her own feelings about the lieutenant served to deepen her fears. Alice kept her face cheerful. 'I won't be gone long.'

'Perhaps I ought to come with you. As a chaperon.'

'No.'

Selina's elegant brows rose at her abruptness.

'You wandering around the ship is sure to attract attention. No one will notice me.'

Selina grimaced. 'Be careful, Alice. You don't want to make things worse than they are for Captain Lionhawk.'

Alice drew in a deep breath. 'I know. But I can't sit here not knowing if he is all right.'

'Ah, now we get to the heart of the matter. After all your talk of bargains, you've fallen for the man.' Selina tapped her lip with her forefinger. 'Tell me, was it love at first sight?'

Alice couldn't restrain her grin. 'You are impossibly romantic.'

'Me? Not likely. Find your pirate. But, Alice, don't let him break your heart.'

Hearts were not involved. Definitely not. She was just worried about his health and that of his men.

She opened the cabin door and peered out. The stink of pitch and the smoke from lanterns along the length of the dim passageway filled her nostrils. No one in sight. At least Liversedge hadn't placed a guard at their door. Why would he? In his view, they were guests, not prisoners.

With a quick wave to Selina, Alice closed the door. Surgeons usually operated their sick berth on the gun deck, which meant she had to go down. She took a few hesitant steps in the direction of the bow. Where was Richard when she needed him? Having a good time following a new captain around, no doubt. No confined-to-quarters order for him. Because he was male.

'Pardon me, ma'am'

Heart in her mouth, Alice spun around to face a red-haired boy of about Richard's age in the uniform of a midshipman.

He saluted smartly. 'Permission to pass you, ma'am?'

Ma'am. She must have the appearance of some ancient crone to this youth. She stepped back. He ducked his head and hurried past.

'Wait,' Alice said.

He halted and turned.

'Can you direct me to the infirmary?' she asked, smiling.

'Seasick, miss?' The boy's squeaking adolescent voice held sympathy.

Memory of Michael saying much the same thing only two days before struck a painful nerve. She shook her head. 'Can you point me in the right direction?'

'Aye, miss.' He pointed back the way she came. 'If you take the first turn to starboard, go down the last companionway before you reach the stern, then two turns to port and one to starboard, you will find Mr Smollet's surgery.'

Alice must have shown her instant confusion because he grinned. 'May I escort you, ma'am?'

'Thank you.'

The boy squeezed passed her and trotted ahead.

'Have you met my brother, Richard?'

'The civilian? He's berthing with the middys. Seems like a good sort. Of course, he's under the care of one of the older men.'

'And the prisoners?'

'They got them safely in irons.'

Alice held her impatience in check and kept her voice light and easy. 'I'm glad to hear it. And just where would they be?'

'Just below the marines' wardroom. They mount a

guard day and night.' He dived into a companionway. 'This way,' he called back. When she reached the bottom step, he jerked his thumb over his shoulder. 'The lobsters' berth is that way.'

Men's voices and laughter emanated from an open door. 'They ain't got nothing to do all day except play cards.'

'And guard the prisoners.'

'Hah. They're all locked up. They only need one man down there. Get off with it light, they do.' He forged ahead.

Alice followed him. Away from the marines and away from Michael. Alice glanced over her shoulder, trying to memorise the wardroom's location.

The midshipman knocked on a door and opened it. 'Visitor, sir.'

A tallish man with thinning sandy hair swung around, wiping his hands on his bloody apron. His gaunt long face set in a frown, he glared at the intruders over his eyeglasses. 'Shut the bloody door, Mr Tib.'

'Aye, aye, sir,' Tib replied, ushering Alice in.

Tib saluted. 'I'll be off now then, sir.'

'Damn your eyes, boy. You're here and here you'll stay until I'm done with you.'

'Aye, aye, sir, but Mr Meadows wants me on deck.'

'I'll deal with Meadows,' Smollet muttered. He turned to Alice. 'I lost my middy over the side last week and didn't bother to replace him.' He picked up a bottle from amongst his bloody instruments and took a deep swallow then squeezed his eyes shut before giving Alice a sharp look. 'Now, young lady. What brings you to my corner of the *Essex*?'

She smiled. 'I came to ask about Mr Anderson, my father's employee.'

The doctor shook his head.

'He had a broken arm.'

'Oh, aye. I remember him. He didn't need my attention. Whoever did the work on him did a good job. As good as I could do, if not better. He's berthed with the officers.'

Alice's gaze skimmed over the bloody plank table behind him. 'Were a great many men wounded in the fighting yesterday?'

'Five. A cannon broke loose. Curse it.'

'At least one of the men of the *Gryphon* was also injured.'

Smollet grimaced, the lines on his face deepening. 'I don't know anything about the prisoners. Only when I have finished attending to every sailor on the *Essex* will I spend my time assisting a bunch of cutthroats.'

Alice swallowed the angry reply that raced to her lips. Honey, not vinegar, she reminded herself. 'They do have their own doctor. He was the one who set Mr Anderson's arm. Perhaps I could take him some supplies?' She held her gaze steady with the brown eyes observing her. The man looked exhausted.

'I could come back and give you some help,' she added, sensing a refusal on the tip of his tongue.

'I don't need females fainting all over my surgery, thank you kindly.'

Alice glanced down at his apron. 'I don't faint at the sight of blood, I assure you.'

'All right,' Smollet said in grudging tones, 'if you help me here, I'll give you some supplies for the blasted prisoners.'

Alice nodded. 'Agreed.'

'Here.' Smollet turned and pulled bandages from a

cupboard. 'I'll spare what I can. But, young lady, I warn you, be very careful. Those men are cornered and dangerous.'

'I understand.'

'Do you? Then you are more intelligent than most females I know.' Smollet hauled out a couple of blankets and spread them on the floor. He dropped bandages and swabs in the centre and added basilica powder, unguent, needles and thread to the pile. He tied the four corners. 'That should do.'

'I'll take some of that rum,' Alice said, pointing at the row of flasks on the bottom shelf.

'You drive a hard bargain, Miss Fulton.'

Alice smiled. 'So do you, Dr Smollet. Thank you.'

'Hmmph. Tib, take Miss Fulton to the prisoners.'

Tib, who had watched the exchange with a rather bemused expression, snapped to attention. 'Aye, aye, sir.'

'I want you back here on the double. No lolly-gagging with the prisoners, boy.'

'I'll have to ask Lieutenant Liversedge for the key, sir,' Tib said a mite anxiously.

'Nonsense,' Smollet said. 'Get the key from the wardroom. They've a spare. Look smart, boy. Don't stand there or I'll put you on a charge.'

A flush stained the lad's cheeks. 'Aye, aye, sir.' He dashed out of the door with the bundle in his arms. Alice hurried after him.

'Miss Fulton, take this.' She looked back to see Smollet holding out a battered leather bag. 'Some spare surgical instruments. If he's got shot to deal with, he'll need it.'

Clearly Smollet's bark was far worse than his bite. She smiled her thanks and hustled after Mr Tib. She didn't dare lose sight of the boy. She'd never find her way through this rabbit warren of timber.

At the end of the passage, Tib dived into the wardroom. The smoke of strong-smelling cigars curled out of the door along with the noise of men in a rollicking mood. Tib ducked out a second later, gleefully holding a key aloft like a prize. 'Got it,' he whispered.

'Where was it?' she whispered back.

Tib jerked his head. 'Hanging on the wall just inside the door. They never even looked up.' He grinned. 'They'll never notice it's missing.'

Alice peeped through the door at the group of men engrossed in a game of dice at a large wooden table. At the other end of the room a series of hammocks were slung between upright posts. 'Surely it is better to seek permission if Dr Smollet gave instructions?'

The boy glowered. 'He might outrank Liversedge, but the lieutenant's a stickler for the rules. No one crosses him. Not if he knows what's good for him. Come on, miss, or the old sawbones'll be after my hide.'

Tib lit a torch and plunged ahead.

Chapter Twelve

'**D**amnation!' Wishart threw his cards down. His manacles clanked against the battered table, punctuating his disgust.

Michael grinned and scooped up the neat row of straws in the centre of the table. 'That's one year's prize money you owe me.'

Wishart grimaced. 'If I live to collect it.'

Michael shook his head in warning. He didn't want the men to lose heart. He glanced at the group of six conspirators whispering in the corner out of sight of their guard. Men who'd been with him since he had bought the *Gryphon*. They'd bring their plan to him when they had worked it through. Trouble was, there really was no way off this hulk, not with a wounded man. Still, it kept them busy and hopeful. The rest of his twenty-five crew were doing their best to ensure the guard didn't notice the plotters, singing, playing dice. At least they'd put them all together in one big cell, rather than locking them up in small cages.

Bones, his face more craggy than usual in the flickering light of the lamp Jacko held, was doing what he could to staunch the bleeding in Simpson's shoulder.

Michael took a deep breath. He stifled a gasp. Damn Liversedge and his sergeant's hobnailed boots. He had at least one broken rib. The bastards.

Wishart glanced up. 'Where's Jacko with the water?'

'Leave the boy, he's helping Bones. Deal again.'

Wishart stiffened, a look of shock on his face as he stared beyond Michael's shoulder.

Michael braced himself to stand whatever nasty surprise Liversedge had planned next and swivelled in his seat.

'Bloody hell.' For a moment, he thought he was delusional, that his mind had tipped over the brink of madness after the blow to his head, but Wishart obviously saw her too.

Alice, her face pale and her eyes huge, was peering through the bars as if they were wild animals.

Careful to show none of the pain ripping through his battered chest, Michael eased to his feet and gathered his chains in his arms.

'Michael,' Wishart said with a warning in his voice.

Michael brushed it off with a brief shake of his head. Wishart knew better than to betray Michael's weakness. He shuffled to the iron bars of their cage, calling on all of his will-power not to lean against them for support.

'Michael. Thank God. Are you all right?'

Her fear for him was water to a parched soul. He stood in a hold stinking of unwashed men and blood and sickness and drank her in. Until this moment, he hadn't realised how much she'd come to mean. If Liversedge learned of her visit, there would be hell to pay. Worse if he learned they had wed.

'You shouldn't be here.'

She frowned. 'I heard some of your men were injured. I brought medical supplies.' Her gaze dropped to his arm where the blood had soaked through. 'You've opened the cut.'

Liversedge's work. 'It's nothing. Bones will take care of it.'

Bones reached Michael's side. 'Did I hear someone mention supplies?'

Drunk or sober, the man had ears like a hawk when it came to his calling.

'There are bandages and ointments and some surgical tools. Mr Tib, if you please.' While she looked calm enough, her hand trembled as she gestured to the midshipman at her side.

Michael clenched his hand around the cold metal bar to stop from reaching out to hold that shaking hand in his.

'Step back, you!' The guard shoved his bayonet in Michael's face. 'That 'un's dangerous, miss.'

Fury rose in Michael's gullet and he all but snatched the weapon and turned it on the soldier. He dragged in a breath and stepped away. He wouldn't risk harm to Alice. Or his men.

'Be calm, friend,' he said softly.

The marine jerked his weapon. 'Stay back from the lady. I ain't your friend, neither.' Michael took another pace back, wincing at the knife-edge of pain.

The young middy unlocked the cell, tossed the supplies to Bones and banged the gate shut again.

Alice was staring at him, her face anxious. 'Are you hurt?'

He forced his lips to smile and felt the stiffness in

his cheeks and wondered if it looked as bad as it felt. 'I'm enjoying my vacation. Thank you for the supplies, Miss Fulton.'

She glanced at the middy. 'M—Captain Lionhawk?'

Even his false name sounded as sweet as honey on her lips. He fought the insidious longing. She had almost given herself away. He didn't want Liversedge using Alice against him. He didn't want the lieutenant anywhere near her.

'Miss, we gotta go,' the middy said.

'Yes,' Michael said. 'Go. Your friend with the musket looks nervous.'

'Wait a moment.' She gestured for the lad to move back and lowered her voice to barely a whisper. 'Listen, Michael—' her low tone contained urgency '—I will speak to the captain. Tell him that you are a half owner in the *Conchita* and haven't committed any crime.'

His chest contracted, the pain far more intense than that from his broken ribs. If she knew what he'd planned for her father, she'd dance for joy at his execution. 'I don't want you involved in my affairs.'

Something shimmered in her eyes. Her small laugh sounded husky. 'I am involved. We are married.'

He shot a look at the marine and the midshipman lingering behind her. 'Are you?'

Doubt crossed her face. 'Michael?'

He wanted to swear and curse. He kept his face blank, unmoved. And yet the thought of letting her go held him in irons far stronger than those on his limbs.

She must have seen something in his face because she stepped closer to the bars with a frown. 'Michael, what is happening?'

'Miss.' The marine cocked his weapon.

'Your hand,' Michael whispered. 'Quickly.' He tossed the small gold circlet. 'Keep it for luck,' he said, his voice rough and hoarse around the odd dry lump in his throat. It spun, catching the light for a second before landing in her palm.

The signet ring was the only thing he'd owned when he came to his senses on board his first ship. He'd taken his name from the figure carved on its face. He'd intended it for Jaimie, but now he wanted her to have something of his.

He gave a black laugh at the way she closed her hand tight around it. 'Call it payment for our time together,' he added cruelly. Even if it only reminded her how much she hated him, at least he wouldn't be forgotten.

For a moment he thought she'd throw it back in his face, half-wished she would in some perverse desire to sever the bond. But then she pressed it to her breast and he almost broke. Almost said something he would regret.

The midshipman nudged her elbow. 'Come on, miss. You'll get me into trouble.'

Her eyes were misty as she turned away.

Michael cursed and stepped closer to the bars.

The marine thrust the stock of his weapon at him through the bars. 'Get back. You'll get it when I tell the lieutenant.'

'Don't come back, Miss Fulton,' Michael shouted after her. 'Your charity is not welcome here.' Because whatever happened tomorrow, he didn't want Alice to see.

He closed his eyes briefly, focusing on the pain in his ribs, a pain he knew how to deal with, then turned to face his men.

'Martin, where's that whistle of yours?' he called out. 'Let's show these navy bastards how real sailors dance a hornpipe. Jacko, let's see you pick up those fairy feet of yours.'

Hoots and laughter filled the cell.

Chapter Thirteen

Alice tied off the bandage around Gridge's stump of a thigh.

'You've a talent for this work,' Smollet said over her shoulder

Intent on her work, she hadn't heard the surgeon's approach. She kept her hands steady and her gaze fixed on her task. Any sudden movement would cause the poor man agonising pain. 'Thank you.'

'When you are done there, join me for a cup of tea,' Smollett said. He squeezed between the row of hammocks, peering at his patients over the top of his glasses.

Alice pulled the blanket up over the laudanum-infused Gridge. 'He'll need water when he wakes,' she said to the man in the opposite hammock, who was lucky enough to have received only a broken collarbone when their gun broke loose. The sailor grinned, exposing a lack of front teeth. 'Aye, aye, miss.' He had the accent of a Yorkshireman. 'Sight for sore eyes, you are.'

She grinned back and made her way to Smollet's surgery, where she found him behind a china teapot and a set of mismatched cups and saucers laid out on the operating table. Tired from being on her feet since first light, she sank on to a stool.

'Rare to find a woman with skills such as yours, Miss Fulton,' the surgeon said, dropping lumps of sugar into the cups.

'Because we are not given the chance.'

'Hmmph. Where did you learn?'

'When I travelled with my father to India as a child the only person doing anything interesting was the surgeon. Much to his annoyance, I followed him around. More recently I've helped where permitted at St Thomas's Hospital.' She sighed. 'Bringing soup to patients. Rolling bandages. Raising money.'

He poured the tea and gave her a sharp look. 'You know, it's interesting, but the men behave better with a woman around. They rest easier too.'

'Perhaps on those grounds women should be accepted into medical circles. The Ladies of Charity do wonderful work for the poor in Paris.'

He sucked in his cheeks. 'Nuns. I don't doubt they are capable, but the work is too hard for most women. Too bloody. Look at you. Already worn to the bone.'

Lack of sleep worrying about Michael's rejection of her help, not the work for the doctor, had her exhausted. The cruelty of his words when he'd sent her away made her think he'd lost hope.

She touched the ribbon around her neck. If they weren't married, why had he given her his ring?

'I've been trying to see the captain since yesterday,' she said. 'He didn't come to dinner with the other officers. Every time I ask, I'm told to wait. You wouldn't know where I can find him?'

'Busy man,' Smollet said. 'We can't make sail until the ship they took yesterday is repaired. He's overseeing the work. Won't want to lose a valuable prize. Drink your tea. It will put colour in your cheeks.'

She sipped at the steaming brew and found it strong and sweet. 'The marines won't let me up on deck.'

'Well, they won't be stopping you this morning,' he said. 'They've other duties on their minds.'

She raised a brow.

He grimaced. 'Punishment.' He chuckled grimly. 'Then it'll be up to me to repair the damage.'

'It's cruel.'

'It is the law. Take my advice, Miss Fulton, don't go up there. It's more than the strongest stomach can stand.' He took a swig from his flask and began gathering up the tea things. 'Now if you'll excuse me, duty calls.' He glanced upwards. 'I suggest you return to your cabin and rest. I'll see you tomorrow.'

Dismissed, she could do nothing but leave.

Resting was not an option. She must see the captain. Pausing to get her bearings, she realised she was outside the marines' wardroom. They would be able to direct her. She peeked inside.

Empty and as neat as a pin.

Three keys hung on the wall beside the door. One of them she recognized. The key to the prison below. Her heart stilled. She shouldn't.

She glanced up and down the passageway.

A breath caught in her throat. Her stomach flipped. Every muscle in her body tightened. She snatched the key. Tucked it up her sleeve, cold against the inside of her wrist.

Breathing hard, she sauntered out of the door on

legs as stiff as boards. Inside, her body shook, her heart pounded with the urge to run.

No challenge rang out, no cry of alarm. She kept walking and her heartbeat slowly subsided, but the key felt as big as a house brick against her skin. A large visible lump.

She glanced down. It was barely noticeable. And she wouldn't dare use it. Would she?

She headed for the lower deck.

Pain bit into Michael's ribs and bruised temple as Liversedge's men slammed him, spread-eagled, against the grating on the *Essex*'s main deck. He bit back a curse of protest.

They'd come early, the bastards. Brought him up on deck for questioning, wanting him to give up other supposed deserters.

An excuse for the marine officer to lay on the cane.

A drummer gave a few practice riffles on his drum. Sweet saints! Michael had thought he was done with the Navy and its love of the lash.

Liversedge yanked his head back by his hair. Pain seared his chest. His eyes watered. He inhaled sour breath and stale cigar as Liversedge glared into his face.

'One last chance, Lionhawk. Admit to piracy and spare yourself a flogging. You'll hang, but it'll be a quick death.'

For a heartbeat, Michael considered the offer. He stared into Liversedge's cunning eyes and saw the blood-lust. Liversedge wouldn't forgo his pleasure, whatever Michael told him. Navy law required seventy-two lashes and Liversedge would see it carried out. Now or later.

'Go to hell,' he said.

His cheekbone crashed back against the grating, and

along with the dull pain, Michael tasted the copper of blood. Through his blurred vision, he glared at the stiff marine. 'Die, you bastard.'

The tinny drumbeat beat out the call. All hands on deck.

The *Gryphon*'s men were slumped against the walls or stretched out on the floor, their faces sullen. Wishart came to the bars, carrying his chains, his fair beard-stubbled face looking grim. He leaned close with one eye on the guard who remained watchful at the door. 'Michael doesn't want you here.'

She eased the key from her sleeve and held it through the bars, careful to shield it from the guard's view. She glanced down. 'Leave tonight. It's your only chance. The *Gryphon* will cast off tomorrow with a prize crew aboard. But tell Michael, whatever he does, he is not to hurt anyone when he leaves.'

The blond giant grabbed the key and shoved it in his pocket. 'Michael won't be going anywhere.'

She stared at him. A strange feeling clawed at her chest. 'Why not?'

He grimaced. 'They took him up on deck a few minutes ago.' Wishart struck the bars with the flat of his hand, sending dull reverberations through the hold. 'Seventy-two lashes for desertion.'

It was as if a rock had dropped from the sky and knocked the bottom out of her stomach. She couldn't move. Bile rose in her throat. 'He's a deserter?'

'No. But his word counts for naught against Kale's accusations. The lousy rotten bastards pressed him as a boy and now they've got him again. There'll be no escape.'

She grasped at a sick kind of hope. 'He's been through it before and survived.'

'Aye. But Bones says the skin is too thin. If the pain doesn't do him in, he'll bleed to death. I've seen it before.'

'There must be proof.'

Frustration etched lines in his face. His hands balled into fists. 'At the Admiralty, but they'll not wait. We should never have taken prisoners. Women on board ship are bad luck.'

The anger in his gaze landed so heavily on her shoulders she wanted to sink to the floor. 'What can I do?'

'Hear that?' Wishart cocked his head. The faint steady beat of drums sounded above them. 'They're assembling the crew.'

Clamminess cooled her skin, dampened her palms. She clutched the bars, fearing she would fall if she didn't hold on to something solid in a world shifting beneath her feet. Why hadn't she forced her way in to the captain, instead of waiting for permission?

A scalding sensation behind her eyes and in the back of her throat thickened her voice. 'I'll speak to the captain.'

The drumming stopped.

'You're too late.' Wishart said. 'They've begun.'

Lifting her skirts, she fled for the deck.

The midday heat beat down on Michael's shoulders. Sweat trickled down his back, soaking his shirt. Fulton would never know how close he'd come to paying for his crimes.

Michael wanted to hate Alice for diverting him from his purpose, but he only hated his own weakness, his cowardice, because something deep inside him felt glad Alice would never know.

A seaman slopped two buckets of salt water beside Michael's bare feet—to bring him round when he passed out, so he wouldn't miss a moment of excruciating agony.

The bo'sun sliced Michael's shirt through with his knife, exposing his naked back. A mutter ran through the assembled men. Michael could smell their lust for blood on the breeze, and the stink of his own sweat and dirt.

'You've been here before, mate,' the bo'sun said.

Michael relaxed the muscles across his shoulders to minimise the pain and braced his legs. He forced himself to empty his mind, willing himself not to cry out, determined to deny Liversedge the satisfaction, to defeat the bastard with silence.

Liversedge counted out the drums' first beat. 'One.'

The blow stung like raking claws. Michael's breath hissed between his clenched teeth. The bo'sun clearly knew his business.

'You're a pixie,' Michael gritted out. 'My old mother could do better.' The angrier the bo'sun got, the harder his strokes would fall and the sooner Michael wouldn't feel it at all.

The man grunted and drew his arm back. 'You'll be talking out of the other side of your mouth by the time I've finished with you, lad.'

'Two.'

Searing pain. The knotted ends scored the sensitive flesh of his side. 'A maid could lay it on harder,' he taunted. 'You must have lost your strength arse-licking the lieutenant.'

Trickles of warmth ran down his back. Blood. Too much blood for so few blows.

'Well, what do we have here?' a light female voice said from behind him. His gut tightened, the pain from his back screamed into his conscious mind as he fought the gut-wrenching horror. She'd come to witness his punishment. He tried to see behind him. All he could see were the nearest men, their mouths open in shock, their eyes avid. The thought of her standing there behind him, looking at the ruined flesh and the blood filled him with helpless fury. His fists opened and closed against ropes that bit into his wrists.

'What the deuce?' Liversedge muttered.

From the corner of his eye, Michael saw a red flush rising up the lieutentant's neck.

'I heard the drums,' she said.

'You have no business here, Miss Fulton,' Liversedge choked out as if his collar was cutting off the air from his windpipe. If things hadn't been quite so unpleasant, Michael would have laughed at the man's discomfort.

'This is a Navy matter,' the lieutenant said. 'Please be so good as to go below.'

Alice strolled into Michael's line of sight. She looked pale and calm. Too calm for the feverish glitter in her eyes. 'Why?' Her gaze swept the deck. 'Isn't this a public event?'

Michael cursed. 'Get her out of here, Liversedge. Aren't you in charge?'

'Silence!' Liversedge roared. 'Sergeant, escort the lady back to her cabin.'

Alice crossed her arms over her chest and tapped a foot. She looked so damned small beside the bulky officer, Michael feared for her safety. The man had no control on his temper, which was the reason why

Michael's cheek was laid open and he could only see out of one eye.

'I am not under your orders, sir,' she said. 'I would like to know why this man is being punished. That is not too much to ask, is it?'

'He's a deserter,' Liversedge said. 'Articles of War require a minimum seventy-two lashes at the mast.'

'How do you know?'

He looked blank. 'It is in the book.'

'I didn't mean the rules,' she said, as if speaking to a rather dull child. 'I mean, how do you know he is guilty?'

A couple of men snickered. Liversedge glared. He tugged at his collar. Trickles of sweat ran from the hair at his temples down the side of his face. 'I can assure you the proper inquiries have been made and the verdict rendered. I really must insist you leave.'

The captain's word was law. There was nothing anyone could do, least of all a civilian and a woman to boot. Worst of all, she was defending a man who'd had every intention of ending her father's life and ruining hers.

Damn it all. He'd sworn that if by some miracle he got out of this alive he'd pursue his justice to the bitter end. If she knew, she'd cast him into the sea.

'Get the woman out of here,' he ground out.

Eyes cold, she stared at him. 'You, sir, are a thorn in my side.'

Perhaps he had it wrong. Perhaps she'd come to enjoy his punishment. Perhaps she really was her father's daughter. His gut roiled at the thought.

Liversedge bared his teeth in a triumphant smile. 'Seems like the lady doesn't care for you any more than I do. Why don't I take you below deck, Miss Fulton?' The man tucked her hand under his arm.

At the sight of the lieutenant's hand on her, rage consumed Michael, blinded him, shut out reason and logic with an urgent need to take the smirk off the other man's face. 'She liked me enough to bed me.'

She stiffened.

Liversedge's eyes widened.

'Wishful thinking,' she scoffed with a brittle laugh. She turned to the lieutenant. 'He's nothing but a common sailor.'

The scornful curl to her lip felt like a sabre going right through Michael's heart. But she was right to deny it. He should have kept silent.

'I'm glad to see you are not one of those foolish women who fall for a rogue's silver tongue, Miss Fulton. Now, my dear...' he patted her hand '...we must continue on with this unfortunate business. I really must request that you leave.'

Liversedge preened as she smiled brightly up at him. Michael wanted to punch him in the face. Instead he slumped against the grating and closed his eyes. Go, Alice. And good riddance.

'But, Lieutenant, I don't quite understand,' she was saying as they walked away. 'Much as I dislike him and his common ways, he isn't a deserter. I've seen his discharge papers. You can't flog an innocent man, can you? Wouldn't you get into some sort of trouble?'

Don't do it, Alice, Michael wanted to shout. You will only regret it. The words burned in his throat, but he held them behind his teeth, clung to them with the same thread of hope he'd felt as a child that whoever had lost him would find him and take him away from the misery of his life. A futile hope.

Thanks to Alex Fulton.

'What did you say?' Liversedge's voice carried across the deck, high-pitched and horrified.

'You are making a mistake,' she said. 'If you wait until we reach port, you will have your proof. If you continue with this—' her friendly tone hardened '—then the consequences might be dire. After all, he is a partner in Fulton's Shipping.'

Good God. Was she actually going to carry this off? The faint hope in his chest grew too wide to contain. He opened his good eye. Liversedge's complexion had drained of colour. He was staring at Alice with fear on his face. Damnation, the woman had nerves of steel.

A disturbance, feet shuffling, men mumbling sounded at his back. Liversedge heard it too and swung around. He snapped a salute. 'Captain Halworth.'

Alice smiled at the newcomer whom Michael couldn't see. 'Captain. I've been trying to see you all morning.'

A white-haired, beetle-browed captain resplendent in gold braid hauled into view. 'What is going on here, Lieutenant? Explain yourself.' The captain's tone was full of distaste. 'Why is the punishment not proceeding as ordered?' He frowned. 'Why is this lady on deck? I ordered them kept to their cabin.'

Rigid with fury, Liversedge stared straight ahead. 'Miss Fulton has brought new evidence to light, sir.'

Saving his own neck by hiding behind a woman's skirts, the cur. This was better than a farce at the playhouse.

'New evidence?' the captain said. He strode up to Alice, his weather-beaten face full of concern. 'What sort of evidence?'

'He is not a deserter. My father would never have

taken him on as a partner if he was. He saw proof of his discharge.'

The captain stroked his chin while he gazed at Liversedge. 'It seems you acted with undue haste, Lieutenant.'

Michael's breath stopped. His heart no longer seemed capable of beating. His throat closed. The sweat running down his face felt cold on his cheek, fear for Alice knotting his stomach. If Liversedge suspected her of complicity, he'd have her clapped in irons.

Liversedge's complexion turned purple. 'But, sir, you heard the evidence. How do we know Miss Fulton is speaking the truth?'

'A common sailor's word against this lady's, sir?' The captain's voice had a gloating note. 'I say the matter warrants further investigation. Cut the man down at once.'

Dear God. Michael went limp against his ropes. She'd actually done it.

'Aye, aye, sir.' Rigid, Liversedge gave the necessary orders to his men. Bracing against the pain, Michael straightened his shoulders and looked over at Alice. She met his gaze with a tiny raise of her brows

Brave-hearted woman. His wife. Courageous. God, what he'd give to be someone else. Despair grabbed him by the throat. He owed her his life, but the one thing he knew she'd ask in exchange, he could not give.

The unfairness of it scoured the vast empty place in his chest.

The Portsmouth jetty loomed out of the drizzle. The sailors at the oars of the *Essex*'s launch pulled hard against the wind-whipped waves.

'You look as if you didn't get a wink of sleep last night,' Selina said from beneath her borrowed oilskin. 'If I had known those dreadful pirates were loose, I wouldn't have closed my eyes either.'

'Privateers,' Alice muttered. Selina was right. She'd lain awake all night, every nerve of her body alive with fear in case Michael and his crew were caught. Then she'd worried they hadn't left until news of their daring escape reached the passengers at breakfast.

'Look at poor old Liversedge,' Richard said, thrusting his wet face between them from the bench behind and pointing to the quay.

Water dripping from his bare head, the grim-faced lieutenant was being marched off, chin high, in the middle of his marines. A prisoner. He'd been blamed for the midnight escape of the *Gryphon* and her crew. He'd been arrested first thing this morning and was being hauled off to answer for dereliction of duty. Beside him shambled a disconsolate-looking Kale. 'It really wasn't the lieutenant's fault.'

'Of course it was,' Richard said. 'He was in charge of the prisoners. I'm glad to see they have Kale, too. I heard that if it wasn't for him, the *Gryphon* would have shown a clean pair of heels. He cut the mainsail rigging.'

So that was why Michael had been caught. Kale. While Liversedge was an unpleasant bully of a man, he'd been doing his duty. Kale had betrayed his captain. Well, she would use what little influence she had to make sure the lieutenant wasn't too badly treated.

The sailors tossed their oars and the launch tied up to an iron ring beside the jetty steps. Richard and Anderson helped her and Selina up the steps covered in long strands of dripping brown seaweed and green slime.

Glad to have her feet on dry land, Alice fixed her face towards the shore. England. Home. She ought to feel glad, but her thoughts kept returning to Michael. An escaped prisoner, wanted by the navy, he'd never set foot on these shores. She'd likely never see him again.

Her throat felt tight, her chest felt tight, her stomach felt tight and if she didn't keep it that way, she would start to cry. And she feared if she did, she might never stop.

Dash it all, she wasn't even sure they were married. She touched the ring through the fabric of her cloak. She did not want to believe he had played her false.

If she had any sense at all, she'd be content with a safe arrival home. But being sensible and happiness seemed mutually exclusive.

Chapter Fourteen

'It is so unfair.' Selina paced from the window to the marble fireplace and struck an elegant pose. Her pale green spencer over a light walking gown of sprigged muslin showed her curves to full advantage. Her straw bonnet framed her pretty face, now set in a frown. 'Can you believe it? While I'm getting kidnapped by pirates, Father gets betrothed to a woman five years my senior. It really is disgusting.'

'Privateers,' Alice said.

Selina waved a dismissive hand. 'The thing is, while he's off to Scotland displaying the family pile to her nearest and dearest, I'm left here with Aunt Gadridge, the old dragon, and confined to afternoon visits to Hookham's and walking Pip.' She glowered at the dog curled up on Alice's sofa. The pug raised an eyelid, revealing one very bulbous eye. They glared at each other. The pug yawned and returned to its nap.

'Ugh,' Selina said. 'Three weeks and I just cannot endure another minute.'

Alice pursed her lips. 'Well, if you hadn't left your chaperon in Lisbon—'

'Pooh,' Selina said. 'A mere formality. Besides, I was with you.' She frowned and looked around. 'Why is there so little furniture in here?'

'We are moving back to Oxford. The town house is sold. I need to get Father away from London for the sake of his health.' Keep him away from the clubs and the dangers of brandy.

Anxiety crossed Selina's pretty face. She floated across the room and grasped Alice's hands. 'You are leaving me to deal with Aunt Gadridge alone?' Tears welled in her green eyes.

'This isn't about you, Selina. If we don't go now, the bailiffs will be at the door.'

The pout disappeared. An expression of genuine concern crossed her friend's face. 'Are things really that bad?'

'Not yet. But they will be when the loss of the *Conchita* becomes known to our investors. We must find a way to pay them back and we can no longer afford to maintain a house in town and keep Westerly.'

'What of your agreement with Lionhawk? Does it still stand?'

Michael. Her chest squeezed painfully. It did that every time she thought about him and she'd grown accustomed to keeping her face expressionless. This time she smiled at her friend. 'An American privateer? He won't come to England. Not unless he wants to get himself arrested.'

Against all logic, she had hoped he'd find a way to return for her. She'd told herself it was impossible, but a little voice kept whispering that Michael would do anything he pleased, should he want it enough.

Selina grasped her hands. 'I'm going to miss you. We will write often.' She resumed her pacing, then paused at the window, swinging about in a swirl of skirts, her face hopeful. 'Or can I come with you? To Oxford?'

Alice pictured her friend in the bare rooms at Westerly. 'I'm sorry, but it will be a while before we are able to entertain. Besides, your father wouldn't allow it.' He'd been furious that his daughter had boarded the *Conchita* in the first place and blamed Alice.

'Oh, while we are on the topic of furious men,' Selina said, 'I had a word with my uncle, the admiral, about Liversedge.'

'Was he able to do anything?'

'After a few tears and some handwringing by me, he found him a berth on a ship bound for the West Indies. They demoted him, I'm afraid, but he will have a chance at promotion as time goes on.'

It was fair. Liversedge deserved some punishment for his cruelty, but not for Michael's escape. 'Thank you.'

A crash sounded above their heads. Alice shot to her feet. Drat it, now what had they broken? 'I hope you don't mind, but I really am dreadfully occupied with our move.'

Selina was staring down into the street. She pulled back the curtain. 'Oh, my,' she breathed.

Alice crossed to her side. All she saw was a beautiful, shiny black phaeton and a pair of ebony horses at the curb. 'It must be someone for next door.'

A rap of the knocker reverberated through the house.

'Apparently not,' Selina said.

'Blast. It is probably one of Father's investors wanting to know when he will get his money.'

Selina winced. 'Oh, dear.'

Alice nodded. 'I think you should leave. Your father would be furious if your reputation was dragged into our mire.'

Selina's shoulder straightened. 'If you think I would abandon a friend—'

'I don't think so.' Alice smiled. 'But it won't do us a scrap of good if we add your father to a long list of complainants. I really think it would be better if we didn't see each other for a while.'

Footsteps echoed in the hall, all the more noticeable for the lack of carpet. Father's voice floated down the hallway. 'This is most unexpected, my lord.' He sounded tremulous.

Alice whipped open the door and glimpsed the back of a pair of broad shoulders encased in a snug-fitting blue coat beneath a head of dark wavy hair disappearing into Father's study.

Her stomach gave an odd little lurch. Her skin prickled with a sense of recognition. Michael? There she was again, letting her hopes override common sense. Not even Michael would risk a hanging.

Just the thought of it made her feel cold.

Whoever it was, she hoped Father remembered to say nothing about the *Conchita*.

'Who is it?' Selina said from behind her.

She closed the door. 'I didn't see. I'm sorry to rush you, but I really must oversee the rest of the packing; besides, if you don't arrive home soon your aunt will send out a search party.'

Selina groaned and picked up the dog's leash. 'You

had to remind me. Come on, you horrid little beast.' The pug rose on its spindly legs, shook from stem to stern and leaped to the floor.

Alice saw them out of the front door and watched her friend trip down the street with the little dog prancing ahead and her maid behind. A couple of gentlemen stopped to watch her saunter by with mouths open in awe.

As usual, Selina didn't give them a second glance. Alice was going to miss her friend. The scraping noise across the floor above ended in a loud bump. She gathered her skirts and ran for the stairs.

Three long years Michael had bided his time waiting to meet his family's murderer. Bided his time until he had sufficient resources to strike. The monster of his imaginings had looked nothing like the bleary-eyed, balding, middle-aged man across the desk from him. Fulton looked pathetically confused.

'Hawkhurst?' Fulton was saying. 'The son? Everyone said you were no more.'

You hoped, Michael thought viciously. He gripped the chair arms to stop himself from leaping across the desk to throttle the old man. He forced himself to smile. 'They were wrong. My petition awaits confirmation by the Lords, but there is no doubt they will give it.'

'Good. Good. Your note said you had some matter you wished to discuss?' He eyed Michael warily.

Had he guessed what Michael had come for? His body tightened like the string of a bow ready to loose an arrow. He leaned back, kept his expression guileless. 'I do. Something to advantage us both.'

Fulton's tongue flickered over his dry lips. His

glance slid to the brandy bottle on the corner of the desk. 'Can I offer you a drink?'

Clearly the man had something to hide. It was too late. Michael had turned over the rock and now had the maggot exposed and ready to crush beneath his heel. 'Nothing for me, but feel free.' He waved a languid hand at the decanter.

Fulton's hand shook as he splashed the honey-coloured liquid into a glass. Drops splashed on the desk and the old man looked as if he'd like to lick them up. He raised the glass to his lips and took a swallow. The brandy seemed to give him strength; he sat up straighter, his gaze sharpened. He grimaced at his glass. 'Promised my daughter I wouldn't.'

Alice. A tingle across Michael's skin had warned him of Alice's presence the moment he had entered the house. He could almost taste her on his tongue, smell her in each breath he drew. These past few weeks free of her temptation had given him time to think, to plan, to regain his purpose.

Yet an urge to see her pulled at his muscles.

He would face her soon. When his business with her father was concluded, he would protect her from her father's calumny, if she'd let him, and her brother too. It was the best he could do in exchange for his life.

Fulton took a long pull from his glass. 'Tell me how I can be of service, my lord.'

'I've been absent from England for years.' He shrugged diffidently. 'I understand you and my father did business together.'

Fulton shifted in his chair as if the cushion was spiked, his gaze became wary. 'Many years ago now.'

'My man of business has made all kinds of suggestions of how I might invest my fortune, but he also advises that there are many unscrupulous men in the City waiting to pluck a fat pigeon, as he put it.' Michael curled his lip, as if the idea was ridiculous. 'I would not be surprised to find he is one of them. My father trusted you. I will too. I want to invest in Fulton's.'

The sunken chest swelled. 'I would be pleased to help my old friend's son.'

Friend. A bitter laugh filled his chest. The vengeful arrow strained for release against his grip. He smiled.

The old man shook his head. 'Shipping is not what it was. The war has ruined it.' His lips twisted. 'And the ravaging of privateers.'

Not the answer he'd expected. Was this some ploy to increase the price? 'Are you turning me down?'

'No. Not at all, dear boy.'

Michael forced himself not to stiffen at the endearment, although blood ran ice cold through his veins. He eyed his target calmly. 'I'm glad to hear it.'

'What were you thinking?'

'A half-share in Fulton's Shipping. I am sure we can arrive at a fair price. The only trouble is, my funds are tied up in land long neglected.'

Fulton's disappointment was palpable. 'Oh, dear.'

'But I understand you have a daughter of marriageable age. A link between our families would not do your credit any harm and your first grandson would be a peer of the realm.'

Fulton looked bewildered, then his eyes gleamed as the merchant in him saw the possibility Michael dangled before him. As he saw the way to pluck the pigeon. As he calculated on losing nothing, since it would be Alice's half of Fulton's Michael would receive.

Michael raised a brow and waited.

'You wish to marry my Alice?' Fulton said.

Michael wanted to smash his fist in her father's incredulous expression. Didn't he know Alice's worth? He let his arrow fly. 'I'm in need of a wife who knows the ropes, who can ease my way into polite society. What better way to seal our agreement? Once our families are united and funds start to flow from my lands again, Fulton's could rival the East India Company.' His jaw ached from smiling. 'I am also hoping you will do your part. Introduce me around town. Propose me to White's.'

Fulton didn't know he'd been hit. He rubbed his hands together. 'My dear boy, what can I say? How can I refuse the son of an old friend?'

Michael swallowed the nausea pressing up in his throat. He stood. 'When may I have the privilege of meeting my future wife?'

Fulton shot to his feet. 'No time like the present.'

Alice. God. If she knew what he was about. No time for regrets. The die was cast and he'd thrown a main.

A meagre few boxes crowded the hallway awaiting shipment to Westerly. Personal items. The furniture would be auctioned off as soon as they vacated the premises. Only Father's study remained unpacked and infuriatingly the door remained closed

The longer the low rumble of their visitor's voice continued, the more sure Alice became that it was Michael closeted with her father. Reason bade her dismiss the idea out of hand as wishful thinking. Her foolish heart continued to beat a little too fast.

With no choice but to wait, Alice padded up and down

the drawing room, much like their visitor's horses walked up and down the street outside. If it was Michael, he was taking a terrible risk. And what on earth would he say to Father? She'd said nothing about their marriage to anyone.

Hope and fear hopped around in her stomach.

The door along the corridor opened. Voices echoed off the bare walls. She ran to the sofa and perched on its edge. From here she could see the visitor pass and finally set her mind to rest. Her heart picked up speed. Her breathing came in short little spurts.

She clenched her hands in her lap to still their tremble. It was not Michael. Could not be.

Father appeared in the doorway. Beaming. Looking like a man who had lost a crown and found a pot of gold. 'I've someone here who wishes to meet you, my dear.'

Alice stared at the gentleman behind Father. Dark-haired, clean-shaven, and elegant, he looked like any other English gentlemen, but there was no mistaking those gleaming turquoise eyes. Michael. He looked more handsome, more delicious, dressed as a gentleman than he had on board ship. Her skin warmed

Her heart leaped forwards in greeting.

A smile on her lips, she started to rise. His gaze issued a warning. He shook his head.

She sank into the cushions, unable to take her gaze from his face.

Father gestured for Michael to enter. 'Alice, this is Lord Hawkhurst.'

Lord Hawkhurst? Her indrawn gasp sounded loud in the quiet room.

Michael's eyebrow shot up, giving him a quizzical

expression. The corner of his mouth twitched. Fortunately, Father seemed oblivious to her response.

Knees shaky, she rose and dipped a curtsy. 'My lord.'

'Miss Fulton,' he said with a clipped formal bow, so unlike his sweeping courtesy on board ship. 'I am pleased to make your acquaintance.' He took her hand. He squeezed her fingers lightly. She gathered some strength from the small connection.

The wretch winked, a mere flick of one eyelid. He was laughing at her. She frowned. His smiled broadened. 'Your father has been extolling your many accomplishments.'

She shot a bemused gaze at Father, who rubbed his hands together. 'Good news, daughter.'

'What may that be, pray?'

'His lordship has asked for your hand.'

'H-he has?' Then the wedding on shipboard was not a true marriage after all? Why was she not surprised?

But then—why was he here?

He bowed with all the grace of the lord he was pretending to be. 'Indeed. I would be honoured, Miss Fulton, if you would consent to be my wife.'

A glance passed between Michael and her father. There was more.

Father cleared his throat. 'As part of the settlement, Viscount Hawkhurst will become a partner in Fulton Shipping.'

He already was. Unless they weren't married.

Father shot her a warning glance. Oh dear, he was up to something. And Michael? Viscount Hawkhurst, no less, the rogue. What was he about?

Michael was watching her expectantly. Father had a similar expression. She was beginning to feel a bit like a carcass about to be shared between two wolves. She didn't like it.

'Come,' Michael said, flashing his pirate smile, all teeth and charm, and definitely wolfish. 'What do you say, Miss Fulton?'

In spite of her misgivings, the urge to say yes trembled on her tongue. She glanced over at her father. A groove formed between his grey brows. His eyes warned. Something was wrong.

'It is all rather sudden, my lord. I should like some time to think about your kind offer.'

'I have already accepted on your behalf,' Father said, sharply. 'It is your duty.'

'I know my duty, Father.'

'Perhaps Miss Fulton and I should spend a few moments alone,' Michael proposed, the airy wave of the dandy quite spoiled by the bunching of powerful muscle beneath the tight fabric of his elegant coat. 'Get to know each other.'

'Yes,' Father said, before she could speak. 'Take all the time you need. I'll be in my study.' He turned and bustled out of the door.

A *fait accompli*.

Michael sat down beside her on the sofa. Heat radiated from his body. Sandalwood wrapped around her like familiar arms. She straightened her shoulders and half-turned so she could see his expression. 'What are you about, Michael?'

He took her hand, brushed his lips against her knuckles, his gaze fixed on her face. 'Claiming my wife.'

She fought the trickle of heat low in her stomach. 'Disguised as a lord? Do you want to be hung?'

His face grew serious. 'There is no risk, Alice. This

is who I am. Michael Preston, Viscount Hawkhurst. The confirmation a mere formality in the House of Lords.'

She tried to pull her hand away. He held it fast, covered it with his other hand. She read the truth in his eyes.

'And Lionhawk?'

'Is no more.'

'What if someone recognises you?'

'I was a privateer, but I worked for England against France.'

'But you took my father's ship. An English ship.'

'A ship flying Spanish colours. I had reason to suspect she was not all she seemed.'

'You flew an Americaan flag.'

He winced. 'A mistake. I've already explained it to the Admiralty. And now I am here to claim what is mine.'

Her insides clenched, the betrayal of desire. Yet her mind wasn't quite turned to mush and something didn't ring true. Or was it that she couldn't believe he was here, that he wanted her?

She stared down at her hand and forced herself to voice her doubts. 'You don't have to marry me. I'll freely give you my half of Fulton's.'

'Sweet Alice,' he murmured, 'I am afraid we are already married. There is no going back.'

She raised her face, searching his face for the truth. His expression seemed carefully neutral. 'Then why the denial on the *Essex*?' A denial that had cut her to the quick.

He flashed her a wicked smile. 'If you recall, I asked you if *you* were sure.'

'Yes, you asked. But in such a way as to make me think we were not married. And if we are, then why make an offer for my hand now?'

A smile flickered across his lips. 'You returned to England as Miss Fulton. It would look rather odd if we announced a secret wedding. I thought to save you embarrassment.'

There was something he wasn't telling her. She saw it in the way he shuttered his gaze. Dash it. What was the matter with her? It wasn't as if theirs was a love match. If her body would recognise that fact, then they might rub along quite well.

Father clearly wanted the connection. What did she have to lose? She took a deep breath. 'As you wish.'

He took her other hand, and she gazed into his eyes, melting at the heat of his fingers grasped around hers.

'I have a special licence for tomorrow,' he said. 'I apologise for the haste, but I have to go north right away, to visit my cousin. He is ill. I want him to meet you. The trip will serve as our honeymoon.'

Days and nights of wedded bliss instead of being alone. Anticipation ran hot in her blood, her skin glowed, her pulse raced. The longing she'd tried to ignore consumed her, made her weak.

'Tomorrow is all right.' She laughed, casting her doubts aside with abandon. 'Today would be better. I am already packed.'

He touched her cheek with his fingertips. A gentle brush. A promise of nights in his arms. 'I will see you in the morning. In the meantime, I will arrange rooms for your father here in town. He tells me this house is sold.'

Father. She'd forgotten about his part in all this. 'Father isn't well. He really should retire to Westerly.'

'I need his help with the business.' His voice took on a cold edge.

A trickle of unease stirred in her stomach. Trust, her heart whispered. If this marriage is going to work, you have to trust him.

She nodded.

He rose to his feet. 'Until tomorrow then.'

Chapter Fifteen

The second day on the road after their wedding proceeded very much as the first. Michael had begged her indulgence, citing a horror of enclosed spaces and had ridden his horse in spite of the rain.

Unlike Selina, Alice didn't despise her own company. Never had. She'd brought along a book and some needlework to while away the hours. She'd been less indulgent about his disappearance into his own room at the inn last night. He'd pleaded a headache. A little nagging doubt made her think he might be avoiding her.

She sighed. There she was again, worrying without cause. Dash it, had her brush with Andrew made it impossible to trust even her husband? It had been she who had forced him to admit to feeling under the weather. His grim refusal of her offer of help had hurt a little, but he had apologised for being the worst of bridegrooms before he went off to find Simpson and left her to spend the night of her second wedding alone.

At breakfast this morning he'd looked pale and drawn and disinclined to speak. When he'd helped her into the carriage with a rueful smile, he informed her they would arrive at his cousin's house for luncheon.

It was now well past one o'clock.

The carriage lurched. Looking out of the window, she saw they had turned on to a drive. Drips from the over-arching trees drummed on the roof of the carriage. She pressed her cheek against the glass in the door, and made out the house ahead. A lovely old building of Palladian proportions, with walls the colour of wet sand.

Thank God. Food at last.

Michael came to help her down. From the colour in his face the fresh air had done him some good. 'How are you?' she asked.

He smiled and her stomach gave its usual flutter of appreciation. 'Better, thank you.'

She glanced up at the house. 'Your cousin must be a great man?'

'I apologise, I should have told you about him last night. He is the Earl of Sandford. He eagerly awaits to welcome you into the family.' He hesitated. 'You might find his ways a little odd. He's been an invalid since childhood.'

'Oh, I am sorry. What ails him?'

Michael tucked her hand under his arm and started towards the front door. 'The doctors really aren't sure. Some sort of wasting disease. I just wish they could get him to eat. It is almost as if he doesn't want to get well.'

A butler stood ready at the open door. 'Lunch is ready, my lord, but Lord Sandford hopes you will join him in the garden room first?'

'Of course,' Michael said. 'I am sure my wife would like to freshen up?' There was a proprietorial note to his voice that made her stomach jolt.

'Yes, please,' she said.

The butler organised the housekeeper to take her to an upstairs chamber where she found a bowl of hot water, a towel, soap and a maid.

The young woman set to work to make her presentable.

'Whenever you are ready, my lady,' the housekeeper said a few minutes later. 'I am to take you to the garden room.'

Alice gazed at the wrinkles in her gown and smiled at the maid. 'That's the best we can do, I think.'

She followed the woman downstairs and along a corridor to the back of the house. A pair of glass double-doors opened into what indeed looked like a garden, with box hedges and roses, and small trees, but a roof covered it all. Along one wall an open bank of windows brought in a breeze and sunlight. It reminded her of the orangery at Kensington Palace

Along with the smell of greenery, a sweetish, pungent scent drifted on the air. Curls of smoke hung over the plants as if someone had lit a fire.

'You'll find the master at the end of this walk, my lady,' the housekeeper said, bobbing a curtsy and leaving Alice to find the rest of the way alone.

Male voices rumbled off in the distance. They seemed to be engaged in some sort of heated discussion. She followed the sound.

Where the hedge-lined walkway ended, a scene out of the Arabian nights opened up. A colourful swathe of fabric draped down from the ceiling. A curtained canopy, beneath which, stretched out on piles of cushions, a man in a peacock-blue banyan and a turban of gold-and-blue silk smoked a long wooden pipe with a silver bowl.

The source of the smoke.

Cross-legged beside him among the brightly coloured silks, Michael looked distinctly out of place in his dark coat, doeskin breeches and dust-coated Hessians.

Both men stopped talking and looked up. The man sprawled on the cushions looked very much like Michael, but finer boned and darker eyed. His paper-white skin clung to his cheekbones and jaw as if no flesh lay beneath. His dark eyes, rimmed with long black lashes, were huge.

Michael rose to his feet with all the grace of a large cat and the frown on his brow disappeared as he smiled warmly. 'My dear, I would like you to meet my cousin, Sandford. Jaimie, this is Alice.'

She dipped a curtsy.

'Forgive me if I don't get up,' Sandford said in a soft dreamy voice, casting a rather sly smile at Michael. He reached out a languid hand, the skin so translucent every blue vein was clearly visible.

Alice took his hand and found it cool and dry. She gazed into huge black pupils surrounded by warm brown. 'I am very pleased to meet you, my lord.'

'Call me Jaimie,' he said, collapsing back against the cushions. 'Do sit down, please. Michael, make your lady comfortable. It is giving me an ache in my neck looking up at you both. I swear, Coz, you get taller each time I see you.'

Michael grimaced. 'You are equally as tall, if you'd bother to stand up.'

'Too tiring,' Sandford said.

When in Rome. Alice crossed her ankles and dropped to the carpeted floor beneath the canopy. Michael arranged some cushions at her back. Despite his cheerfulness, she sensed an underlying worry about his cousin.

He dropped down beside her with a cocky grin. 'What do you think, Jaimie?'

The pale young man regarded her intently, his dark gaze sweeping every inch of her. She felt her skin grow hot beneath his gaze.

'Not your usual bill of fare, if your stories are true.'

'Sailors' talk. Mind your manners, whelp,' Michael said in a growl.

Jaimie laughed. 'Please excuse me, my lady. Michael is so easy to tease, but I mean no disrespect. I must thank you for bringing Hawkhurst's prodigal son home to his family.' He gazed at her from half-lidded eyes. 'The question is, are you granite or sandstone?'

'I'm sorry, I do not take you meaning?' she said.

Michael lifted a hand in warning.

The young lord didn't seem to notice. He gave her a sweet smile. 'It takes granite to bend a river in full flood. It cuts straight through weaker rock.'

'Jaimie,' Michael said, 'don't talk in riddles.'

A gentle smile curved the young man's lips. 'I think I am sandstone. Take after my name. I would wish you both well, if I thought it would do any good.'

She glanced over at Michael, who frowned and shook his head at his cousin.

There were secrets between these two men. And an undercurrent of the argument she'd interrupted remained in the air. It made her feel itchy and uncomfortable, and definitely unwelcome.

Once more she became aware of those huge dark eyes on her face. This time, they held regret. 'Ring the bell for champagne, Michael,' Jaimie said. 'I will drink a toast to the bride and groom. Then you will partake of luncheon.'

Food. The thought of it made her stomach gurgle. Both men pretended not to notice, while her face went as red as the silk of the cushion against which her host reclined.

The butler must have expected the call, because he appeared almost immediately with a silver tray and three glasses. He handed them around and departed on slippered feet.

Alice couldn't help but stare at the embroidered footwear.

'I don't like noise,' Jaimie said, following the direction of her gaze. A small smile curved his full sensual mouth, and he looked more like Michael than ever. Michael the privateer, not the English lord with his neat hair and careful manners.

'To health and happiness,' Jaimie said.

'And yours,' Michael said, in an oddly strained voice. They drank.

'About that offer of lunch?' Michael said, rising and pulling Alice to her feet.

'Waiting in the dining room,' Jaimie said. 'I won't join you. I ate earlier.'

'I wished I believed you,' Michael said, frowning as Jaimie picked his pipe.

'Don't worry,' Jaimie said with a smile. 'Cynthia makes sure I eat.'

Michael cursed under his breath, but seemed disinclined to argue since he placed Alice's hand on his sleeve. 'Will we see you later?'

'Perhaps not.' Jaimie inhaled deeply and gave Michael a meaning-filled look. 'I think you and I need to talk, though, Michael. Soon. In private.'

'Certainly,' Michael said, sounding more than a little irritated. 'I'll call back the first chance I get.'

His mood infected his stride; his steps were so long she felt like a colt galloping to keep up with its trotting mother. 'Slow down,' she said.

He winced. 'I'm sorry. My mind was elsewhere.' He adjusted his steps to hers. He clearly knew his way around the house, because after passing a dizzying number of doors along a hallway, he marched into the dining room where a buffet was laid out on a sideboard. Two places were set at a long table, which also bore a decanter of red wine, another of lemonade and two glasses.

Michael handed her a plate and proceeded to fill it with slices of shaved ham, a portion of pie and some slices of chicken. He added some asparagus shoots.

'Enough, thank you,' she said and took her plate to the table while he filled a plate for himself.

He sat down and gestured to the decanters.

'Lemonade, please,' she said.

He filled his own glass with red wine and attacked his pie with obvious relish. She did the same with hers. Sandford might eat little, but he had an excellent chef.

'What did your cousin mean when he said it wouldn't do any good to wish us well? He doesn't like me, does he?'

Michael put down his knife and fork and picked up his glass. 'I apologise for Jaimie. He thinks I'm making a mistake.'

That hurt. More than she liked to admit. She hoped her expression didn't show her feelings. 'Why?'

He shrugged. 'He is not always easy to understand. It could be fear I'll spend less time with him. It could be the smoke.'

Jealousy. It did strange things to people. 'Surely smoking that…stuff isn't good for him?'

He took a deep swallow of wine, then stared into what remained in his glass. 'Probably not.'

'Then shouldn't you try to stop him?'

'It is not always possible to repair things, Alice. He's happy.' His mouth tightened. 'Or he says he is. I'm sorry if you don't approve. He is the only family I have left. Eat up, for we must be on our way.'

The deliberate change of topic made her feel like an unwelcome intrusion in his life. It stopped her from questioning him further.

'I am ready to leave whenever you are,' she said.

The bleakness in his gaze disappeared. He smiled and she felt her breath catch at the sheer glory of the sight. 'Excellent,' he said. 'I want to be there by night-fall.'

'Where is there?'

'You'll see.'

His eyes held a promise and she felt hot and breath-less, as if the room had grown over-warm.

Nightfall seemed far too far away.

Chapter Sixteen

The rain had stopped while they were at lunch and the sun still lingered well above the horizon when the carriage halted in front of a small stone cottage located behind the break in an ivy-covered granite wall. A gate-house from all appearances, without any gates. An avenue of beech trees led away from the opening, but wild grasses covered any sign of the drive.

The carriage rocked, signalling Simpson's descent. He pulled open the door with a grin and a wink.

'Where are we, Simpson?' she asked as he let down the step.

'Not sure, my lady. I've been following the Cap'n.' He jerked his thumb towards Michael tying his horse to a post near the front door of the small stone house. Simpson handed her down and went to his horses' heads.

Alice forged through the damp grass to join her husband, who was jerking his crop through his gloved hand.

She quickened her steps. 'What is this place?'

His brows lowered, his eyes full of shadows and not quite meeting her gaze. Yet he held out his hand. 'I want you to see something.'

Wherever this was, it was not a happy place for him. When she took his hand, he drew her close to his side and she felt stronger, ready to face what lay ahead.

Side by side they walked through knee-deep grasses that rippled like a troubled ocean with each puff of breeze. Her skirt hem quickly became sodden. The beech trees linked above their heads and splattered rain on their shoulders. The scent of clover and damp vegetation filled the air.

If it wasn't for the tension she felt radiating from Michael, she would have felt thoroughly content with her hand tucked beneath her husband's arm.

'Are you going to tell me what this place is?' she asked.

'In a moment.' The rough quality of his voice forestalled her questions yet again. She bit back a sharp retort. Time. They both needed time to become used to the married state.

They rounded the curve of the avenue. A crumbling relic of what had once been a grand house overlooking a magnificent sweep of countryside came into view.

Time and nature had softened the outline of broken walls rising two storeys in some places and completely gone in others. A chimneystack emerged from the ruins, pointing skywards like an accusing finger.

'Oh, my,' she whispered.

'Hawkhurst Place,' he said with soft reverence, one hand shading his eyes against the dying sun.

'Your family house?'

'Yes. It burned down.' His voice lowered to a murmur. 'This is the first time I've been here since…'

Shadows carved deep hollows beneath the high, stark planes of his cheekbones. Mouth etched into a hard painful line, he stared at the ruin. Bleakness hung about him like a cloak, isolating and cold.

Awkward and sad, Alice waited quietly at his side. To break in on his reverie felt invasive.

He took a deep breath, straightened his shoulders and set off towards the house. His long stride ate up the ground, leaving her to follow in his wake.

The longing to comfort was an empty place in her chest and an ache in her arms. He did not seem to want her sympathy. She tramped in his trail of bent and broken stalks.

In the dying light, with grasses bending before him, she had an image of a lonely rock jutting from unfriendly seas. He halted and as she reached his side, he waved an arm to encompass the whole. 'Not much left.'

The carefully matter-of-fact tone sounded painful to her ears, but she took a deep breath and responded in kind. 'It must have been lovely.'

How shallow the words sounded in the face of such devastation.

He pointed with his riding crop to the shield engraved on the arch above what once would have been the entrance. Lichen marred the weathered crest. 'The Gryphon,' he said softly. 'The family crest.'

'Hence the name of your ship.' And the symbol of the ring he had tossed at her so casually. She fingered the ribbon at her throat, wondering whether to ask him about it, but he caught her hand. She curled her fingers around his and realised they trembled. For all his stoicism, he was in the grip of strong emotion.

Without understanding what had happened, all she could offer was silent support.

Together, they mounted the shallow steps. Inside the walls, the air seemed to hold its mouldy breath. Shadows threw up barriers after the bright daylight outside. Cold and damp and dark prowled in the corners. It was like entering a cathedral, or a crypt. She shivered.

Slowly, her eyes became accustomed to the gloom. Ivy-strangled beams lay at crazed angles. Moss smothered charred yellow brick. Creepers and nettles carpeted uneven flagstones. If it wasn't impossible, she could have sworn the faint smell of smoke invaded her lungs.

He led her over fallen rubble, past brambles whose thorns snagged her skirts. A pigeon up among the jagged chimney pots softly cooed a warning.

At last he stopped before the remains of a blackened hearth. 'This was the library,' he murmured. 'My father had a wonderful collection of books and manuscripts. I think I remember learning to play chess in this room.' His voice was raw with pain. She wanted to say something, but he was already moving on, turning to help her over a beam before peering into a room with a magnificent view of the park. Great oaks cast shadows over unkempt lawns and overgrown gardens. 'The drawing room. My mother took afternoon tea there, according to Jaimie.'

His gaze followed the column of lone chimney up into the deepening blue. 'Up there was the nursery where Meg slept.' His tone remained horrifyingly conversational, his body tightly controlled, so rigid, Alice feared that at any moment he might snap in two.

He vaulted a beam and, putting his hands around her waist, lifted her over. 'This was the ballroom. The fire started here. The house was full of people.'

'How awful,' she whispered.

He stared out between piers of brick, which once must have supported a bank of windows leading out to a veranda, from the looks of the stone balustrade. A shudder shook his frame. 'I should never have come here.'

He turned away, headed for the front door, leaving her to follow as best she could. She clambered over the bricks and the beams, all the while wishing she had comfort to offer instead of platitudes.

At the front step he seemed to remember her presence and stopped, staring off into the distance. He looked so alone.

She touched his arm. 'I'm so sorry, Michael.' She slipped an arm around his waist.

His eyes when he looked at her were fractured, glittering, his expression full of loneliness. 'I didn't think coming back would be so hard. Not after all this time.'

She could only imagine how such a tragic loss would feel. 'Sit for a while,' she said. 'Catch your breath.'

He sank on to the step. Elbows on his thighs, he clutched his hair in raking fingers as if fighting the images in his head.

With nothing but her presence to offer, she remained silent. When he spoke his voice was low and raw. 'Meg was in bed.' He gulped a breath, staring at the tufts of grass between his feet. 'I should have saved her.'

She laid a hand flat on his back. 'You were just a boy.'

He turned his head and gazed at her with anguish. 'I was out on the veranda peeping in through the window, when I should have been upstairs asleep.'

He covered his eyes with a shaking hand, but not before she saw the sheen of threatening tears.

'I saw flames and ran inside, looking for my parents. I remember the screams. And the heat. I remember…' His mouth twisted. He shook his head as if to shake the sights from his mind.

She slipped an arm around his back, pulled his head down, pillowed it against her shoulder. Patted his back. 'Hush.'

He buried his face in the crook of her neck, breathing hard, a painful, raw sound. After a moment or two he started speaking again. 'Somehow I ended up outside. On the lawn.' He swallowed. 'Meggie called from a window. Someone behind her broke the glass. The next second she was falling. Screaming. Her nightdress in flames. I looked away.' He pinched the bridge of his nose, squeezed his eyes closed. 'For years I saw her in my dreams not knowing who she was. Always running to catch her, but my feet won't move. I want to catch her, but I can't. I let her fall to her death.'

'It was not your fault.'

He raised his head, staring at her, his eyes dry and empty. 'If I'd been where I was supposed to be, I would have saved Meg. My parents would not have tried to go up there to find us.' He groaned. A deep awful sound from low in his chest. 'Father told me to remain in my room. I disobeyed.'

'Perhaps you would have died too. Do you think they would have wanted that?'

He exhaled a short breath, closed his eyes, lifted his face to the heavens, anguished. He swallowed. 'It's odd. Sometimes I see them out of the corner of my eye, but when I turn to look, there's no one there.' His voice cracked. 'I'm alone.'

A chord twisted in her heart. Tears for his pain clogged her throat. 'Not alone, Michael. You have me,' she whispered. 'And Jaimie.'

Lost too deep in his memories, he didn't seem to hear. 'I've seen portraits of them. It is like looking at strangers. No matter how hard I try, I can't recall their faces as part of my life.'

'Perhaps if you don't try so hard…'

'God, if only it was possible.' He swiped at his face with the heel of his hand and drew in a shuddering breath. 'I was ten. Meg was five. My parents were in the prime of life. They didn't deserve such a fate.' Anger coloured the grief.

'Michael, it was a terrible accident. No one was to blame, least of all a small boy.'

His face hardened, the furrow in his brow deepening. 'The fire was deliberately set.'

Her stomach gave a sickening lurch. 'Who would do such an awful thing?'

'An evil man.'

'Do the authorities know?'

'The magistrate? The local constable?' He barked a short hard laugh, full of bitterness. His fingers clenched convulsively on her shoulders, biting into her flesh. 'They refused to do anything.'

Something about the way he was looking at her caused her heart to jolt. Her stomach clenched with a sudden surge of fear she couldn't explain. She drew in a rasping breath of realisation. 'You know who it is, but you don't have proof.'

'I have all the proof I need.' His gaze darkened,

fixed on her face intently. 'What would you do if it was your family? Wouldn't you do all in your power to seek justice?'

The weight of the question pressed against her chest. The intensity with which he awaited her answer burned in his gaze. She thought about her father, her brother, how she would feel if someone hurt them so cruelly. 'It would be hard to forgive such a terrible act.'

He let go a long breath, as if she'd lifted a great burden from his shoulders.

The hairs on the back of her neck rose in warning. 'Michael. Don't set yourself above the law. Nothing good can come of it.'

Had he even heard? He looked to be in a whole other world, his expression cold and hard.

'Michael?'

He came back to her with a blink and heartbreaking sadness in his smile. He bent his head and touched his lips to hers. 'Thank you,' he whispered.

She caught his nape, pressed her mouth to his, as if she could somehow absorb his pain, make it less hard to bear. He relaxed in her arms. She rocked her body against his, kissing, stroking, until he slowly pulled away and tucked her head beneath his chin.

'I'm sorry,' he said softly. 'I should not have burdened you so.'

'I'm glad you did.' He'd shared such an important part of himself. She felt closer to him than ever before. They sat in companionable silence watching the shadows grow.

'How were you pressed into the navy?' she asked.

His chest rose and fell on a deep inhale. 'I don't know. I must have taken a blow to the head.' He rubbed his hand over his chin. 'My first memory for years was coming to my senses on board a frigate bound for the West Indies. I had no idea who I was or where I had come from.'

Her chest squeezed in fear for the ten-year-old boy he'd been. 'Oh, no.'

He stroked her cheek with his thumb. 'The navy thought I was a slow top. They told me they were doing me a favour by giving me a trade and a home.'

'Dear Lord,' she whispered. She'd seen patients in St Thomas's Hospital who had lost all recollection, confused, anxious and often angry. A child would be terrified. 'But your memories eventually returned?'

He gave a soft little chuckle. 'Came as quite a shock, let me tell you. I'd just left the navy and purchased the *Gryphon*. I'd named it after the design on the only thing I owned when I came to. The Hawkhurst heir's ring, though I didn't know it at the time. We were in port. A runaway block clouted me on the head and shook some memories loose. After that, I looked up the insignia in a library, wrote to people in England, found Jaimie and learned the whole story.'

It ought to be a happy ending, yet he sounded strangely sad. 'Jaimie must have been glad to see you?'

He smiled down at her. 'That he was. And I was glad to see him.' He raised her hand to his lips, pressed a gentle kiss to her wrist. She felt the scrape of his stubble across the tender skin. 'Thank you for listening.'

She kissed his cheek. 'Thank you for sharing your memories.'

A shadow passed across his face, leaving her feeling there were things he had not revealed. Darker things.

The connection between them dissipated on the cool evening breeze. She shivered.

'Come,' he said. 'You are cold. We must return, before it is too dark to see our way. There are plans we must make.' His voice had a determined ring, as if he had news she might not like. Whatever it was, the future could not be as bad as his past. She let him haul her to her feet and arm in arm they set off for the gatehouse.

'Do you think you could bear to live here again?' she asked after a moment or two. 'Rebuild the house?'

'I don't know.' He turned to look at her, his cheek-bones as stark as axe blades in the dying light, his eyes deep in shadow. 'Hawkhursts have lived on this land for centuries.' He circled her waist with his arm. 'Jaimie says my father would want that. He remembers him better than I do.' There was an ocean of emptiness in the soft spoken words. 'I'm not sure.'

He'd lost so much. His family. A good part of his childhood. 'Is it your head injury that causes your head-aches?'

'The doctors aren't sure. They were worse before my memory returned. During bad spells, the bo'sun would lock me in irons, I was so wild. Jaimie says it was the memories trying to get out. Dark and quiet helps. Simpson knows what to do.'

'Is that what happened that first night on board the *Gryphon*? And last night?'

'It was.'

They were almost at the gatehouse. Alice stared at the carriage in surprise. Simpson was nowhere in sight, but he had unloaded the luggage from the carriage's boot and must have taken it into the house. 'We are staying here?'

'This is your new home,' Michael said.

At first she didn't quite take in his meaning. 'You mean us to live here?'

He nodded. 'For now.'

The remoteness in his gaze caused her a moment of panic. 'Why here? Why not go to Oxfordshire?'

Simpson emerged from the cottage. 'Goodnight, my lord, my lady.' He headed for the waiting carriage and swung up on to the box.

'Where is he going?' Alice asked.

'The carriage is Jaimie's. I borrowed it before I came to London. There is nowhere here to keep it.' He grasped her shoulders, looking down into her face. 'Go inside, while I stable my horse. See what you can find for supper.'

Dismay twisted her stomach in a knot. What was the matter with her? It didn't matter where they lived provided they were together.

She pushed open the little house's front door and immediately stepped into a parlour. Small, clean, furnished with a sofa and a chair, a faded but serviceable rug covering the flagstone floor. A table and two chairs sat in front of the diamond-paned, leaded window looking out over the stone gateposts. Whoever lived here would have had a good view of visitors coming or going to the great house beyond.

Opposite the front door a low passageway led past a winding set of stairs. Wondering what she might find, she wandered through to a tiny kitchen, with a scrubbed pine wood table and a dresser against one wall. Beyond the small window, a walled garden, long overgrown, contained an apple tree and a small wooden shed nestled against the stone wall.

A pocket-handkerchief of a house. Very humble, but clean, and with quite enough room for two. Spending her honeymoon here with Michael, far from the tumult of London, might not be so bad. An optimist might even call it rustically romantic. They could spend time getting to know each other here before returning to the business of saving Fulton's. Perhaps it would give Michael a chance to come to terms with his past.

She opened the pantry and found it stocked with eggs, butter and milk and some sort of meat pie beneath a muslin cloth. There was a cask of small beer tucked in one corner beneath the shelves.

Enough food to keep them going until the morning.

How long would he want to stay? A week? More? They would need to hire some sort of servant. Or might he have already done so, since clearly someone had prepared the house for their arrival?

Most importantly, they needed wood for the fire if they were to make a cup of tea or warm up the pie. Thank goodness she wasn't expected to cook a meal.

At the sound of the front door opening and closing, she returned to the parlour to find Michael removing his coat. He hung it on a hook behind the door, picked up an armful of logs he must have set down when he entered.

'You must have read my mind.' At his enquiring look, she smiled. 'About the logs.'

He grinned, looking comfortingly like her handsome pirate for the first time since he'd arrived in London. 'This will get us started. I will cut some more after supper.'

Her heart lifted. Whatever the future brought, they would face it together.

Chapter Seventeen

Shadows filled the corners of the room, the glow of the fire their only light. Supper over, Alice smiled at him over the tea tray.

'Good lord, it's dark in here,' he said and crossed to the hearth, lit a spill and held it to the candles on the mantel. He brought one back and placed it in the middle of the table. The glare captured a bitter twist to his lips, but it was only a trick of the shadows, because when the flame steadied his expression was utterly calm.

'Simpson won't return until tomorrow,' he said, going to the door and shrugging into his coat. 'I'll chop some wood for the morning.'

'I'll wash the dishes.'

Her shadow flitted back and forth. Washing the dishes. If he listened, he could hear the sound of crockery in the sink and her humming through the casement. The sounds the wife of an ordinary man would make in her kitchen after supper. The kind of life he'd dreamed of before his memory returned and with it the burden of duty.

He hefted the axe-head in his palm. Caught in the light, the blade flashed a fiery reminder. He didn't want to go, he realised with savage sadness. Duty didn't stop him from wanting her the way a man dying of thirst wanted water. That's why he'd stayed tonight, when he should have left with Simpson. For one night, he wanted to sink into her warmth, immerse himself in her calm spirit, and ease the constant ache in his chest. It was wrong, given his intentions, but he couldn't resist.

Michael slammed the axe into the log. The blow sent vibrations up his arm and into his shoulder.

Hell. He felt like a bastard.

He should never have taken her on his ship. Never have let her get beneath his skin. Now he couldn't let her go.

Another blow of the axe jarred his spine. The log split in half. He hacked it into kindling, woodchips flying.

She didn't need to know. Didn't need her illusions about her father destroyed. She'd be all right here. Safe.

It wasn't cowardly to protect her from her father's crimes, from seeing him pay the price. The sins of the father need not be visited upon the child.

Goddamn it. She loved her father. Whatever happened, she'd be hurt. Just thinking about the pain he would cause her weakened his resolve.

Which was why she had to remain here, out of his sight, so he wouldn't be tempted to forgo his justice.

Bloody Jaimie hadn't helped him feel any better by begging him to give the whole thing up. They'd argued for the first time since their reunion two years ago.

Tell her, Jaimie had said. Explain.

Time enough to tell her when it was all over, then she must understand. She was his wife.

And if she didn't? He pushed the thought aside.

Forwards. He could only go on. There was never any going back. He raised his arms, tensed his shoulders, gathering his strength for the next blow. He'd tell her he was leaving in the morning. Tonight he'd bind her close.

Crack. The log shattered in tune with something inside his chest.

All of the downstairs rooms were dark when Michael entered the cottage. She'd retired for the night. Gone up to the small room at the top of the stairs. Tucked into bed below the eaves. Waiting. Hot blood streamed through his veins.

If he was any kind of gentleman, he'd make his bed down here, pretend to have one of his headaches, instead of enjoying her favours knowing full well he intended to betray her trust.

He hung up his coat, untied his cravat and left it hanging loose. The stairs creaked under his weight. She'd hear. Know he was on his way. Would she welcome him as warmly as the yearning in her eyes had suggested? A lump of anticipation lodged in his throat.

A sliver of light surrounded the slightly ajar door. A good sign, surely? His heart drummed in his chest as if he was some callow youth on the trail of a chambermaid, instead of a man bent on seducing his wife. A push with his fingertips swung the door back.

Hair around her shoulders, a virginal white gown tied low across the rise of her breasts, she gazed at him, eyes wide. She snatched the sheet up to her throat. Delicious colour rushed up her face. She laughed, an awkward little chuckle, and let the sheet fall.

'I'm sorry to keep you waiting, my lady,' he murmured, making no attempt to hide from her gaze the beat of lust in his blood.

Her breasts rose with her quick intake of breath. Anticipation was not at all one-sided.

She primmed her mouth. 'You will be suitably punished for your lateness, sir.' Laughter sparkled amid the brown-green velvet of her eyes. 'I have been waiting since yesterday.'

He found himself smiling like a besotted fool. 'Would you berate a man for his illness?'

'On his honeymoon? Yes.'

'Demanding wench.' He unbuttoned his waistcoat and tossed it aside. 'Believe me, I have every intention of making up for lost time.'

'Good. I shall hold you to that promise.' Smiling saucily, she rose up on her knees, affording him a glimpse of the valley between her pert breasts. He had no doubt from her smile that she did it on purpose. Fire rushed through his veins in a torrent of desire.

He tossed his cravat over the bedstead and she set to work on his shirt buttons with nimble fingers. Grasping her shoulders, he inhaled the scent of her hair, rubbed his cheek against its silken strands. A sense of deep familiar contentment, as if he'd sailed into a well-remembered port, enveloped him. A coming home.

'I missed you,' he murmured into those silky tresses. He pressed his lips to the pulse below her ear, felt its rapid beat beneath the sensitive skin.

The top button popped free.

'I thought I'd never see you again,' she said, her voice rough, her fingers busy with the next button. 'I didn't dare believe you'd risk coming to England. Not for me.' There was pain in her voice. It caught him by surprise. He captured her chin, turned her face until he could see her expression. A shimmer of tears glistened in her eyes.

'There was never any danger,' he murmured. 'You knew I'd come for you.'

'I hoped. Oh, Michael, I did hope. But how could I be sure? After what you said.'

Damn, he felt like a cur. He thumbed away the trail of tears on her cheek. 'No tears. Not tonight.'

'No,' she said gravely. 'I want this night to be one we will remember.'

So did he, for both their sakes. He broke away. Ripped the shirt off over his head and let it fall to the floor. Her gaze ran over his body, avid, greedy, scorching. It roused him harder than ever before.

How did an English primrose go from shy to siren in the space of a minute? The seduced becoming the seducer. However she did it, he would not rush this, no matter how much she tempted. He would make every moment count. It might be weeks before he was with her again.

If ever, the small doubting voice whispered. A voice he refused to acknowledge.

'Alice,' he murmured. 'Lay back, my lovely,' he whispered close to her pretty ear. He blew a breath on her tender column of neck.

She shivered.

His groin tightened at the feminine sign of arousal. Gently he eased her on to the sheets and let his gaze rove her body. 'Let a pirate show you what he does with his most precious treasure.'

Her lips curved in a smile. 'I'd rather know what a privateer does with his captive.'

'Would you, indeed?'

She bit her lower lip, clearly trying to keep from laughing. 'I would.'

'Then you shall.' He bent his head, his lips so close to hers, their breaths mingled. 'First there are kisses.' He brushed his mouth across hers, once, twice, thrice, a whisper of kisses. She moaned for more. He melded his mouth to hers, wooing, seeking entry. Her hands flew to his shoulders, pulling him close, her open mouth all fire and passion.

No maidenly reserve from Alice, thank the gods.

He swirled her mouth with his tongue, tasting sweetness and heat. He cupped her small breast, felt the nipple bead against his palm. Her hips rose eagerly against his thigh.

Slowly he drew away, looking at the full rosiness of her lips now pouting in disappointment. But this was her fantasy and he would not disappoint.

'Then I bare my captive to my gaze.'

Her indrawn gasp of sweet longing hit him hard in the groin, urging him on to ravish and plunder. Not yet.

Gaze fixed on her face, he untied the tapes of her bodice, slipped the filmy garment over her shoulders and down to her waist. Her eyes widened. Her lips curved. Her lashes lowered in invitation.

He allowed his gaze to wander down her delicious length. High small breasts with peaks puckered and hard begged for his touch. He took them in his hands, stroked and caressed, remembering their shape in exquisite detail, their fit in his palms, their weight. A dreamy expression crossed her face, her ribcage rising and falling with deep, even breaths. He ached to be inside her. Not yet.

Reluctantly, he returned to his task, sliding the wisp

of fabric under her lovely curved bottom, over the gentle swell of her hips and past the triangle of soft-brown feminine curls. He trailed it down her thighs and calves and whisked it over her shapely feet.

Bare. Gloriously naked. He gazed on her loveliness, breathing hard. A raging beast barely leashed.

Her eyes popped open. 'What now, wicked privateer?'

For a moment the words made no sense, he was all feeling, all bone and straining sinew, hot blood and rigid phallus. He inhaled. 'Then I feast.' How he would feast. But not yet.

'Unfair,' she said, her eyes laughing. 'You are still clothed.' Her husky murmur strummed every nerve until his body hummed.

'All part of the torture,' he said, with a wicked-pirate grin.

She curled her fingers into a fist and punched his shoulder. 'Take that, you brute.'

Quick as a flash, he manacled her wrist, pressed her hand into the pillow above her head. Felt her soft breasts rise against his chest. 'Fight me, will you, fair maiden?' he growled.

Her lovely eyes blinked slowly, slumberously, her lips turned sultry. 'Probably not.'

The prosaic tone hit him low in the gut. It was the sexiest thing he'd ever heard. He laughed and leaned in to reward her with a kiss.

In one swift move, her leg pushed up between his, rubbing with delicious pressure against his groin. Amazingly wicked. He leaned forwards to allow her better access. A quick twist and she pushed him off balance. He fell to the side to avoid crushing her beneath his weight. She flung herself across his body.

He looked up into her triumphant face and raised a brow.

'The wicked privateer needs to keep better watch on his prisoner,' she said.

With her knees either side of his waist and her damp quim pressed against his belly, her breasts hovered a tongue-length from his mouth, like peaches on a low-hanging branch, impossibly tempting, soft and mouth-watering. He licked a tightly budded nipple.

She moaned.

The temptation to retake control, to assert his ascendancy, surged like a tidal bore in his ears. He clenched his jaw. 'So…my prisoner has escaped. What will she do now?' In truth, he couldn't help but wonder what she would dare, now she had him at her mercy.

She pursed her lips. 'A little torture of my own.' She snatched his cravat from the bed-head. 'Give me your hand.'

'What are you about, lass?'

A small forefinger tapped his lips. 'Silence, prisoner.'

He watched as she tied the cravat around one wrist and passed it though the bars of the iron frame behind him. She grabbed his other wrist.

His body clenched. A pulse beat hard in his temple. 'No.' He jerked out of her grasp. And saw the dismay in her eyes. He forced a smile. 'You don't need to bind me to have your way,' he said, hoping he sounded a whole lot less panicked that he felt.

She tilted her head in question. 'But you are my captive. You must do as I say.' She waggled her brows.

He laughed. Let go his breath. He trusted her. An odd feeling, when he'd only ever trusted himself. 'Do your worst, then, fair maid.'

A breathy laugh tickled his wrist as she tied off the second knot. 'Oh, I will.'

She slid off the bed to admire her handiwork, naked, lovely, a tormenting smile on her lips. He wanted to feel her beneath him. He tested the fabric holding his wrists. It would be an easy thing to slip his hands free, if he wished.

Ah, hell, she trusted him not to.

She pointed to his breeches. 'First off with these, I think.' With some fumbling and laughing and some help from him, she undid his falls and pulled his breeches over his hips. A gasp when his erection sprang free only served to make him harder. From the look on her face, she was pleased with what she saw.

A feeling of pride made him swell all the more.

A small pink tongue flickered over her lips, her eyes turned smoky, like heather-clad hills in the dusk. 'You are a naughty privateer, all ready for plunder.'

A growl rose in his throat. Damnation, this was torture of the most salacious kind. 'Come here, you little witch.' He jerked against the ties. 'I'll show you how I plunder sweet maidens.'

'Oh no, sir,' she said sweetly, pressing the back of her hand to her forehead dramatically, unconsciously lifting those wonderful breasts high. 'I couldn't possibly let you go. Not yet.'

'Blazes, woman,' he said, wrenching at the binding. 'Come here.'

She knelt over him, gave him a swift kiss on the lips, and drew back to smile into his face, saucy and teasing. 'I'm not finished.' On those words, she gathered up a swathe of her hair and drew it across his chest, feathering across his nipples. They beaded. His muscles danced and shivered, his groin grew heavy and unbearably tight. He fought for control.

The feather-light touch traced the outline of every hill and valley of his chest, ribs and stomach. Unbearably soft. A tickle. A tingle. His flesh quivered with delight and agony. She lingered at his navel, swirling the soft living brush into the indentation. He raised his head, gaze fixed on her progress, unutterably aroused. Would she…?

The lock of hair floated down the dark line of hair on his belly, and circled the head of his shaft.

He hissed in a breath and collapsed against the pillow, eyes closed as he absorbed the pleasure and the pain of wanting her.

'How,' he grated out between pants for air, 'did you learn such a trick?'

The torture stopped. 'Is it not right for a wife to…pleasure her husband?'

'For pity's sake,' he ground out, 'don't stop.'

She took him at his word. A toffee-coloured strand wound around his yard, constricting and releasing, sliding around his flesh like a silken chord. Too tight. Too loose. Then she kissed the sensitive tip.

His hips shot of the bed. He tore one hand free and flipped her over on her back. 'Oh, madam, you will pay for that in kind.'

She grinned. 'I hope so.'

Fates help him. He adored her. He wanted to lay his life, his whole being, at her feet. Slow and sure he slipped the head of his shaft inside her wet, welcoming heat.

Pleasure gripped him hard.

'Oh, yes, my wicked privateer,' she whispered, 'yes.'

Blind with lust, drawing every nuance from her slight body's response, he rode her with long slow strokes. Her legs rose up to cradle his hips in softness, her hands clinging to his shoulders, her nails a sweet pain on his bunching muscles. He lowered his head, took her breast in his mouth. Inner muscles gripped him and her soft cry assaulted his ears.

Her hips slammed against his groin, encouraged him deeper, harder. Their bodies clashed in a battle of pleasure, and then there was nothing in his mind but the urge to conquer and succumb, to challenge and submit. He pounded faster and harder and she rewarded him with guttural cries that rang in his ears.

'Michael,' she cried out.

Consumed by the fire of her body, he brought her legs over his shoulders, opened her fully, groin to groin. He rocked against her sweet flesh, felt the trembles, the rush of her heat and drove home to the hilt.

The dark turned blinding white. Her climax sparked his, tipped him into liquid heat, and he poured forth his essence and his very being.

Languid, her arms lay around his neck, her body a cradle as the spasms went on and on. At last he collapsed beside her, drew her into the circle of his arms, held her close, breathed in their mingled scents, embraced in peace.

Her face turned into his neck, she kissed his jaw, his cheek. 'My husband,' she whispered. 'My love.'

Her breathing slowed with sleep.

Rigid beneath her limp delicate form, he stared at the ceiling. *My love.* He'd forgone all thoughts of love.

A dawning realisation washed through him. If hope shone in her eyes in the morning and she asked him to stay, he might just forget about duty. As surely as she'd tied him with a strip of cloth, she had bound him to her, body and soul.

A strong sense of foreboding closed his throat.

Early the next morning, he poured her a cup of coffee in their little kitchen. 'I'm leaving for London,' he coolly announced, handing her the cup.

Seeing him gone from the bed this morning, she'd come down to find him dressed and already breakfasted.

She frowned. 'If we are not staying, why did you send Simpson away with the carriage?'

He glanced up then, and she saw guilt pulling at his mouth. 'You are staying. I am not.'

Prickles of unease darted across her shoulders. 'You intend to leave me here alone?'

'Alone? No. Simpson will return tomorrow. He has a room in the village. He will come each day, light the fires, run errands.'

A horrible writhing sense of unreality twisted in her stomach. A sense of dread. 'Was it something I said? Something I did?' Had her behaviour last night disgusted him?

He reached across the table and grasped her hand. 'Listen. I will invest every penny in Fulton's, but I won't risk my ship to an unknown captain.'

'You are going to sea?'

A sharp jerk of his chin signified *yes*. 'Your father will work with my man of business in my absence.'

'Father isn't well. He…' She twisted her hands together under the table, hating to make public what she'd tried to keep hidden for so long. 'His health is poor. I can help. I know the merchants, their reputations. What they buy.' The begging note in her voice stopped her from saying more.

'Your father's a drunkard.' Michael looked her in the eye. 'But he's promised to lay off the bottle. Your place is here.'

She looked around the cottage and back to Michael's face. 'There is nothing for me to do here. Why not rent a house in London?'

'My home isn't good enough for you?'

The edge in his voice gave her pause. Men were strangely sensitive about their ability to provide. She chose her words carefully, kept her face and voice cheerful. 'It is a lovely house, but it is miles from anywhere. And from Father and Richard. In London I could continue my work at the hospital. Wait for your return.'

'I can't afford the expense. To be truthful I don't want you in that den of iniquity. I've seen the fops who inhabit ladies' drawing rooms with nothing better to do than flirt. I don't like it. I won't have them simpering over my wife in my absence.'

He was jealous? She didn't know whether to be pleased or angry. 'Don't you trust me?'

He narrowed his eyes. 'I don't know how long I will be gone. You are a passionate woman, Alice.' His voice roughened. 'Men sense that. They take advantage.'

'And it has happened before,' she said coldly. 'You think I won't be faithful.'

'I—no. I trust you, Alice. It's them I don't trust.'

He brought her hand to his lips, kissed each knuckle in turn, the brush of his mouth velvet soft, his gaze a flare of heat. 'Won't you trust me to care for you, Alice?'

Her stomach settled, then warmed. And Lord help her, her insides stirred and fluttered. She had no resistance when it came to this man. And yet something jarred, some underlying note sounded off key and alerted suspicion born of experience. Pushed and pulled. Torn in two directions.

She took a deep breath. 'I trust you.'

He patted her hand. 'Thank you.'

If she trusted him, why did she see guilt in his eyes?

Chapter Eighteen

The rumble of male voices in the great subscription room of White's was not unlike the sound of idlers below deck on a frigate. The dim lighting and wood panelling felt comfortably familiar to Michael. Only the comfortable chairs and fine brandy at his elbow and the attentive servants were different.

That and the four finely clothed gentlemen around the table. Three peers of the realm and Fulton.

The pile of guineas and vowels at his elbow were evidence of smiling fortune. Michael scooped the pot towards him. 'Thank you, gentlemen.'

'That's me done for the night.' Cargrew, a lanky viscount with fine light-brown receding hair, stretched and pushed to his feet. 'I've a session to attend in the Lords tomorrow. Congratulations, Hawkhurst, on your call to the House, by the way.'

Michael nodded his thanks.

The brawny Sir Paxton also rose. 'If I stay any longer I'll be signing away my firstborn's inheritance and my wife will have my head. You are a lucky bastard, Hawkhurst.'

The other men laughed.

'Then we'll call it a night.' The dandified Lord Dalrymple had almost as big a pile of winnings as Michael. 'Will I see you at Lady Brandon's rout tomorrow?'

Michael flicked a glance at the sweating Fulton and shook his head. 'I have to go out of town for a while.' His plans were set. The executioner's axe would fall tonight, and Jaimie must be told.

And besides, he did not want to run into Lady Selina again. The woman was worse than the Spanish Inquisition with her questions.

Fulton reached for his glass, his hand shaking wildly. He forced a smile, a baring of teeth. 'I bid you goodnight, gentlemen.'

The three men bowed their farewells and walked off arm in arm.

Fulton drained his glass. He gazed at the pile of vowels, most of them his. 'It is time I left also.'

'Not yet,' Michael said. 'There is something we need to discuss. In private.' He signalled to a waiter. 'A private room, if you please.'

The man gestured them to a room across the hallway. Michael palmed him a guinea.

'Too generous, my boy,' Fulton said as he went ahead into the small antechamber. He must have caught the flash of gold. 'I told you, servants need only be given silver.'

Fulton had taken Michael's introduction to society very seriously, everything from proposing him for membership in White's to finding him a dancing master.

The servant followed them in with the brandy decanter and the two glasses on a silver tray. When he left, Michael dumped the vowels on the table.

Fulton eyed them askance when Michael added a pile from previous evenings' play. He swallowed. 'Not all mine, surely?'

A week. It had taken a week of playing the dutiful but green-as-grass son-in-law to bring Fulton to this point, to put him completely at Michael's mercy.

Deep in drink most of the time, the old man hadn't seen it coming.

Fulton wiped the sweat from his brow and grabbed for a glass. His skin had a liverish cast, a yellow tinge that had nothing to do with the lamplight. The man was drinking himself to an early grave without Alice to keep an eye on him.

Michael didn't want him to die. Not yet. Not before he received his full measure of punishment.

Michael leaned forwards and twisted the glass from Fulton's weak grasp. 'You've had enough, old man.'

'What! A little more respect, if you please.' He lunged for the glass.

Michael held it out of reach. 'We need to talk.'

'I've told you everything about the business. What more do you need to know?'

Michael rose, turned the key in the lock and pocketed it. 'I want to know when you are going to pay your debts. All of them.'

'W-what?' Fulton choked out and tugged at his collar. 'We are family, dear boy. We don't dun family members.'

Michael watched the old man squirm in his seat with savage pleasure.

He let his face show puzzlement. 'I thought it was a debt of honour?'

'Well, yes, of course. But—but…' He spluttered into silence, staring at the brandy decanter.

'Tell me about the night of the fire.'

Fulton raised his gaze, a blank look in his eyes. He was so far gone, he was barely processing Michael's words.

'The night my family died,' Michael enunciated slowly. *The night you murdered them, you bastard.* He held the accusation inside him. It would be too easy for a simple denial.

The bleary eyes misted. 'It was so long ago. I don't remember much. I'd been drinking.'

No excuse for murder. Michael's stomach churned. He kept his expression calm, his voice cool. 'You and my father argued that night. Over money. You were heard.'

Fulton squeezed his eyes shut. 'I don't recall. Doesn't matter now anyway,' he mumbled.

'You did get your money, though, didn't you? From the estate?'

'I…' He tugged at his collar. 'My claim was proven, yes.'

'Some say you were the only one who profited from the fire. And rightly so, of course. It was your money, after all.'

'It was all done through the courts,' Fulton said, gripping his hands together. 'All legal.' His gaze shifted away, but not before Michael saw shame and guilt.

'There was no one left to contest the claim.'

Indignation shone through the bleariness. 'What are you suggesting?'

'Nothing,' Michael said. 'I don't need to suggest anything. You were seen.'

'What? Yes. I was there.' The confusion was back.

'You left the ballroom with a lad under your arm.'

Fulton frowned. 'The little boy,' he said. Gnarled fingers rubbed at the back of his neck. 'Yes. Yes. I took him away.'

The admission, so callous and uncaring, hit Michael like a blow to the kidneys. Excruciating pain. Nausea. The faint hope he'd harboured of Fulton's innocence, for Alice's sake, winked out. Cold fury filled his veins as he stared at the shrunken old man. No longer could he bear to be in the same room and not kill the murdering bastard who had callously left him at the dockside in the hands of the press gang. There was a time he'd have gladly hanged to see the light go from Fulton's eyes, but now Michael wanted the life Fulton had stolen. The last night he spent with Alice had made him realise he wanted a home and a wife. He wanted Alice and he'd never be able to face her with her father's blood on his hands.

He dropped his gaze to the table. 'About these debts.'

'You have to give me time. The *Conchita* is still in Lisbon, before the prize courts. Once it is established that there was no reason for that cursed privateer to take her, I'll be dibs in tune.'

Fulton had no idea Michael was the privateer to whom he referred. 'And if the prize court doesn't find in your favour?'

'It will.' He swallowed. 'It has to.'

'I need the money now,' Michael said, his voice cold. Implacable.

Fulton rubbed a finger across his lips, staring at the pile. 'How much is it?' he croaked.

'After tonight? A cool five thousand.'

'So much? Surely you can wait a week or two?' He

poked one finger under his cravat and tugged, stretching his neck like a turtle.

'You play deep, old man.' Michael pursed his lips and furrowed his brow, pretending to think it over, when all the time his blood beat in time to the words *You are mine.* Finally, he met Fulton's hopeful gaze. 'I'd be willing to take the other half of Fulton's in lieu.'

Fulton shifted back in his chair, opened his mouth to accept, knowing full well it was worth nowhere near that amount.

'And the house in Oxford.'

The old man recoiled. 'That is my son's inheritance.'

'All he will inherit is a pile of debts the sale of the house won't cover. Come now, Fulton. This is a generous offer. More than you deserve. If you weren't family, believe me, I would see you in the Fleet, along with that boy of yours.'

'Richard?' His jaw dropped. 'I can't give up Westerly,' Fulton wailed and shook his head. 'Without the revenues, I can't pay for Richard to remain at school. I've already let the town house go. Where will I live? You are a member of this family now. You can't do this.'

Michael watched the man disintegrate before his eyes. It was what he had always wanted for this man. A living death.

The same as he'd given to Michael and Jaimie.

'As a family member,' he said, not hiding the sneer in his voice, 'I'm willing to pay for your son's education and give him a place in the business.'

Fulton slumped in the chair; he seemed to age twenty years. His skin turned the colour of parchment. Michael found himself feeling sorry for the old man. Something he hadn't expected. Didn't want.

He snatched the agreement from the pocket inside his coat. 'Sign here, and no more will be said about the debt.'

'Please,' Fulton said. 'I don't understand.'

'Sign,' Michael shouted, clenching his fists, 'or face the consequences.'

Fulton's chin bobbled. 'I don't have a pen.'

Silently, coldly, Michael strode to the writing desk and brought back a pen and inkwell. He unrolled the document, holding it flat. 'Sign it and I'll tear up the vowels. You'll owe me nothing and your daughter and son will be cared for. Sign it and no one else need know.' Alice need not know.

Fulton looked confused and fearful. In his drunken panic, he read not one word of the confession Michael had drawn up. Hand shaking and tears bright in his eyes, he simply scrawled his name.

Michael had seen the signature often enough over the past two weeks to know he'd signed true. He blew the ink dry and rolled document in hand, headed for the door.

Fulton was finished. Not dead. Worse than dead. Living in hell. He'd never see either of his children again, unless he wanted to end upon the gallows.

He had expected triumph, perhaps even joy, but instead he felt empty. Joyless.

'What about me?' Fulton croaked. 'Where shall I go?'

'I'd leave town if I were you, before I change my mind,' Michael said cruelly. 'Before your other debtors find you've nothing left.'

The old man gasped. 'You devil.'

Michael smiled. 'No more devil than you.'

'Alice. I should go to Alice. She'll advise me.'

He delivered the final blow without emotion. 'Alice is where you will never find her. I'll make sure you never see her again. Or your son. You've brought them nothing but shame.'

Fulton let out a strangled cry, but Michael could see his acceptance in the way he crumpled.

He unlocked the door.

'What have you done with Alice?' Fulton whispered. He spoke her name like an invocation to a goddess. But the goddess was Michael's now.

And if she ever learned what he'd done, she'd never forgive him.

He hesitated. For some reason he couldn't quite fathom, he reached into his pocket. 'Go to the Mermaid in Portsmouth. There's a man there, name of Bones. He'll give you a berth, some work at the inn if you mention my name.' He tossed Fulton a half-guinea. 'Use this for the stage. But mark my words well, never let me catch you in town, or anywhere near Alice, or your life won't be worth living.'

Alice looked up from her weeding. Almost midday and still no sign of Simpson. He'd be too late to go to the post office if he didn't come soon. After three weeks, she was sure there would be a letter today.

Out of sight, out of mind.

No. Selina had promised to write and Alice had walked to the post office in the village the day Michael left and sent word of her address. There had to be a reply soon. She rose to her feet, feeling the pull of muscles and the stiffness in her legs and back. A walk would be good after working in the garden all morning. With no hospital nearby and nothing else to keep her mind off worrying about Michael, the overgrown garden had become her project. The neat rows of herbs, parsley, rosemary, thyme and sage, mint and hissop, gave her a feeling of something accomplished, as well as some supplies for her medicine chest. The fruit from the apple tree would make wonderful pies in the autumn and go with the blackberries on the brambles hanging over the wall.

It wasn't much, but it would help save a few pennies on food. She pressed her fingers into the centre of her back and stretched. After lunch, she usually walked up to the derelict house. Pulling weeds up there seemed almost futile, yet she felt it brought Michael closer for all that it was a mere drop in a gargantuan bucket. And she'd found a few treasures amid the debris. A child's coloured marble that might have belonged to him as a lad. A statue of Venus, with only one small chip. She was keeping them as a surprise.

She opened the gate and stared down the road. Where was Simpson? No sense in waiting any longer for luncheon. She went inside, cut some bread and a hunk of cheese and, as she munched, watched rain clouds gather. No weeding up at Hawkhurst Place today. But a little bit of rain needn't prevent her from walking to the post office. She cleared the table, put on her coat and picked up her umbrella. She tucked the letter for Selina in her reticule.

The two-mile walk to the village took close to an hour and because Simpson had taken a room above the stables at the local inn, he'd taken to bringing all their needed supplies each morning. Every day he'd also checked for letters.

Today he had gone further afield, to the market in the nearest town, because Alice had decided she needed fabric for chair cushions. He hadn't been very happy about going, but in the end he'd agreed.

Sometimes Simpson had a mind of his own.

The post office, a charming thatched cottage in the middle of a row of three, sat at the edge of the village. Farther along, beside the village green, lay the King's Arms where Simpson boarded and on the other side of the green the village shop, which fulfilled most of their day-to-day needs.

She pushed open the post-office door. A bell tinkled above her head. A grey-haired woman of about fifty, with gimlet eyes and spectacles on the end of a sharp nose, looked up from behind the official-looking counter. 'Lady Hawkhurst.' She dipped a curtsy. 'May I help you?'

'Good day,' Alice said with a smile, fearing she looked more like a vagrant than a peer's wife with dust on her shoes and clinging to her hem. 'Do you have any post for me today?'

The woman made a show of checking an array of five pigeonholes behind her. 'Not today, my lady,' she said brightly. 'Unusual for you not to have a letter or two.'

A tremble started low in Alice's stomach, an odd little quiver. She swallowed. 'Have there been letters for me over the past few weeks?'

The woman's iron grey brows drew together. 'Your man picked them up. He brought a letter from his lordship giving him permission.'

The woman must be confused. 'But none addressed to me personally?'

The red in the woman's cheeks deepened. 'Do you mean that man of yours hasn't been giving you your post?'

Apparently so. A hot buzz sounded in her ears. Anger. She took a deep calming breath and smiled at the woman. 'Mr Simpson is sometimes forgetful. May I borrow a letter opener, and a pen? I have just thought of a postscript I wish to add to my missive.'

The postmistress proferred a pen and sealing wax. Alice took them to a table against the wall and pulled out the note for Selina. She dashed off a few lines across those already written and returned to the now very suspicious woman.

Pretending unconcern, despite the hot fury in her veins, she handed over the letter and the woman dropped it into a canvas bag at her feet. 'Please keep any post addressed to me here until I call for it personally,' Alice said.

The woman sniffed. 'Interfering with other people's post. Ain't right.' She pressed her thin lips together, as if to keep from saying more.

Alice gave her what she hoped was a not-to-worry smile and headed for the door. 'I am sure it is a simple mistake.'

The woman jerked a disapproving chin. 'As you wish, my lady.'

Outside, low clouds now covered the sky, releasing their burden in the form of a light drizzle. Alice put up her umbrella. Her gaze lingered on the inn just a few yards down the road. Might Simpson be there? He had some explaining to do. And she wanted her letters.

She set her steps for the inn, avoiding the puddles that were already forming in the rutted lane. The cottages on either side of the road hunched beneath their sodden thatch with nary a sign of their occupants. At the green, she glanced up at the sign, the King's Arms, an overly grand name for a one-storey thatched and half-timbered building boasting one taproom.

The idea of bearding Simpson in his den no longer

seemed quite so attractive. After a moment's hesitation, she straightened her spine and marched around the back to the stables.

A down-at-heel groom forking hay looked up at her entry.

'Is Mr Simpson here?' she asked, closing her umbrella and giving it a shake.

His eyebrows shot up. 'Mr Simpson, is it?' He chewed on the straw sticking out of his mouth.

'George,' she said, remembering. She smiled. 'He's expecting me.'

'Aaar,' he said, somewhat mysteriously. 'He's not in.'

She gulped a quick breath. 'He said to wait.'

He chewed his straw, then jerked his head to the back wall. 'Up them stairs, then. Key's under the mat. Don't steal ought or he'll have your guts. Not a man to cross, our Mr Simpson.'

Apparently female visitors were not an unusual occurrence for Simpson. Lucky for her. She climbed the wooden steps to the landing, a half-loft really, found the key and opened the door. The smell of stale smoke hit the back of her throat.

Simpson's quarters were spartan. A hammock hung across one corner, a neatly made cot against one wall and a table and chair beneath the window. A row of hooks held two shirts and an overcoat behind the door. Breathless, not from climbing the stairs, but from the press of her rapidly beating heart against her lungs, Alice ran to the window. She peered up and down what little she could see of the lane. A workman hurried past on foot. A woman scurried along beneath her umbrella. No Simpson.

But he could return at any moment.

She whirled around. If he had stolen her letters, would he keep them or destroy them?

Only a pipe in a stand inhabited the rough wooden table. A sea chest had been pushed beneath the cot. She dragged it out. Dash it. It was locked.

She lifted the ticking mattress. A document fluttered to the floor. A letter. She lifted the mattress higher and discovered another caught in the bedropes. She scooped them up and walked to the window. Each was addressed to her. Both from Selina.

She wasn't forgotten.

She glanced outside. The inn courtyard was empty.

She opened the one dated first. 'Glad to get your note…Mrs Bixby's rout a disaster…Father still absent from town…'

The second was along the same lines, but began with a querulous question about why there had been no reply to her last missive. And then Michael's name jumped off the page. '…taken London by storm. There are even whispers of his adventures at sea…ladies swooning at his every glance.'

She frowned. Michael? In London? There had to be some mistake. He was at sea repairing their fortunes.

Alice's hand shook.

She steadied the paper and continued reading. 'They say he's won a fortune at White's. When I saw him in Bond Street and asked after you, he said you preferred the country and, if I may say so, was really quite rude, wandering off while I was speaking. Now I hear he has left town to visit a cousin. I made enquiries about your father, but no one has seen him recently.'

She couldn't breathe. It was as if some great weight had landed on her chest and was restricting the air.

Michael was in London, enjoying himself. And Father had disappeared?

Surely not.

She pressed her fingertips to her temples and gazed unseeing out of the window.

Michael had lied about going to sea.

The bottom fell out of her stomach and it hit the ground with a sickening jolt.

She'd trusted him and he'd lied.

An ache in her chest rose up in a hot hard lump to scour her throat and scald the backs of her eyes. She clutched her arms around her waist. Something tender and small, the seedling of hope she'd nurtured after their last night together, a hope for more than a marriage of convenience, seemed to wither inside her.

No. She would not believe the worst of him, not without proof. She'd been sure he meant to treat her honestly. So hopeful for the future. But the recollection of the way he'd left ground away at her defences.

And where was Father?

A cold chill ran down her back.

Only Michael could explain. And she needed to tell him about Simpson's odd behavior. She skimmed Selina's note. Michael had left town to visit a cousin. Jaimie. Then why would he not have come to Hawkhurst Place only a few miles away? She forced the nagging question aside. She would have her answers directly from Michael, not spend time in useless conjecture.

The distance to Sandford's was less than ten miles. The letter was dated three days ago. Michael might still be there. If not, she would travel to London.

Michael. How could you? The thought whirled

around in her head. A maelstrom of emotions. Hurt. Anger. Worry. Fear that she'd trusted the wrong man. Again. Let her passions rule her head. She felt sick.

She took a deep breath. And another. If she left now she could be with Sandford before dark.

And Simpson? Let him worry when he found her gone, the rotten thief.

She stuffed Selina's letters into her reticule, made sure everything looked undisturbed and deposited the key back under the mat. If she was lucky, Simpson wouldn't realise where she'd gone until it was far too late to follow.

Michael handed his hat and gloves to the Sandford butler and raised a brow. 'Garden room?'

The butler must have seen something of his mood in his face because he stepped back smartly. 'Yes, my lord. You know your way.'

Michael strode for the back of the house. This interview with Jaimie was not the triumphant homecoming he'd planned. The weight of the world bore down on his shoulders as he contemplated his news.

The farther he'd driven from London with the news, the stronger the realisation had become. Alice would never forgive him for what he'd done to her father. Even if he hadn't physically harmed the man. Even if Fulton was safe with Bones.

If she found out…

How would she not? He was going to have to tell her. He couldn't pretend he didn't know what had happened, or why. She'd never stop looking for the old man.

The only reason she'd married him in the first place was to save him from financial ruin. She'd sacrificed herself and then she'd trusted Michael to help him out of his difficulties. When she found out the truth, she'd never trust Michael again. He'd never hear her say *I love you* again, because she wouldn't.

He couldn't go through with it. Not while there was still time to salvage something of his marriage.

As usual, Jaimie lay among his cushions, his gaze hazy from smoke. Michael's fingers tingled with the desire to knock some sense into his cousin. But brute force never did any good. Either Jaimie would come to it on his own, or he'd fade away to nothing.

'I have bad news,' Michael said.

Jaimie paled. The blue of his veins stood out on his pallid face like rivers drawn on parchment. 'What has happened? Did something happen to Alice?'

'No. It's not that. I just came from utterly ruining Fulton—he's destitute. On the street with nothing to his name, not even his children know where he is, but...' Chest tight, he dropped to his knees beside his cousin. 'Jaimie, I'm sorry. I can't go through with it. I know I swore revenge for the sake of our families, but I can't do it. I'll lose Alice. I have to go straight back to London and sort it out.'

Jaimie laughed. High-pitched and hoarse, he sounded hysterical. 'Why didn't you come before this? I wrote to you twenty times this past fortnight.' He sounded so strained, Michael stilled.

'I told you, I had something to tell you.'

Michael had a strange sinking feeling in the pit of his stomach. 'What is it?'

'About the fire,' Jaimie whispered. 'About what happened.' His eyes misted.

Michael reached out and clasped his cousin's thin

shoulders. 'It's all right. You don't have to talk about it. I know how it pains you.'

Jaimie shook the hand off, his face agonised. 'You don't understand. I did it. I caused the fire.'

The words hung in the air, pungent, hot, dizzying, like opium smoke. Michael shook his head to clear it. 'No.' It was the only word he could think of.

Jaimie covered his face with his hands. His bowed shoulders shook. 'I killed all those people. It was an accident.' The words frothed forth like wine from a bottle of champagne, except this brew tasted bitter.

Horror erupted in Michael's chest. 'You lie,' he roared. Yet he knew. He'd broken Alice's trust for a lie.

'It was l-late.' Jaimie spoke dully, as if by rote. 'I could hear music. People laughing and talking. I—I wanted to see the fun. I saw you weren't in your bed and I thought they'd fetched you down and left me. I crept downstairs and into the ballroom.' He choked on a sob.

Michael could only stare. Numbed by denial. He'd planned to forgive Fulton and tell Alice what he'd done. She might have forgiven him then, but this? 'Oh God, Jaimie.'

Jaimie inhaled a shuddering breath and began again. 'There were so many people. Someone knocked the candle out of my hand. It must have rolled beneath the curtain. I saw smoke. No one else noticed. I ran away.'

'Are you sure?' Michael said. 'This is too important for one of your opium tales.'

Jaimie pressed his shaking hands over his ears. 'Let me finish.' His voice dropped to a grating whisper. 'When I looked back flames were licking up the curtains, spreading across the floor. I couldn't move. I knew what I had done and I froze. If I had shouted, anything…'

Michael couldn't look at him. He stared up at the reds and blues of the canopy, unable to watch the agony on his cousin's face, unable to bear the heavy beating of his own heart, or the taste of bile in his mouth. But he couldn't stop the words from pounding into his head.

'All hell broke loose, Michael. Fire raced across the floor. Furniture. Pictures. It took seconds. And hours. I was rooted to the spot. People yelling. Heat.' His voice broke. He shuddered for a long moment. 'Someone tossed me over their shoulder. I hid my face. I couldn't watch.'

Sick, numb, legs as heavy as lead, Michael sank back on the cushions. He felt empty. Sucked dry.

The tears running down his cousin's face were real. There was no doubt this was the truth.

Dear God. What had he done?

He fought to regain his senses. 'Why, for God's sake, didn't you tell me?' His voice was rough, as if scarred by the long-ago fire.

Jaimie's huge brown eyes pleaded for understanding. 'How could I? For years, I thought you were dead. I'd lived with the guilt, knowing what I'd done and wanting to die. You appeared out of nowhere. A miracle.' He cracked a bitter laugh. 'An absolution of sorts. And when we talked about it and you named Fulton, I grabbed for salvation. You were terrifying, Michael. So angry. So hurt. I feared I'd lose you.'

Instead, it was Michael who would lose everything—again.

Jaimie stared at the brightly patterned rug, avoiding Michael's gaze. 'You were so angry, Michael. I knew you would never forgive me. Hell, I couldn't forgive myself.'

It would be hard to forgive, after all this time. Alice's voice breathed in his inner ear. *Vengeance is mine, sayeth the Lord*, a harsh voice followed up with a rather grim chuckle. His own voice. Oh, the Fates had played him cruelly. Made him blind to everything except his self-righteous anger.

Dazed, he stared down at the bowed head with its carefully ordered brown curls. His only living blood. 'Oh God. If you had only told me last time I visited,' he whispered.

His cousin lifted his head, the despair in his face painful to see. 'I wanted to. I saw how you looked at her, Michael, that day after your wedding. I'd never seen such happiness in your eyes. God help me. I wanted to tell you. Before you did anything. I swear it. Why didn't you come back? I sent messages. Every day. But you never came.'

Michael remembered the messages. But he'd been far too busy destroying Alex Fulton to heed his cousin's pleas for a visit.

'Michael, there's more.'

A cold chill settled in his gut at the fear on Jaimie's face. 'Tell me.'

'It was Fulton who carried me out of the house.' He hesitated, bit his lip. 'And you. He carried us both out of the fire and collapsed on the grass. I lay down beside him, but you—you disappeared.'

'Are you telling me Fulton saved my life?'

Jaimie collapsed and buried his face in the cushions. 'I should have told you.'

A low ache started at the base of Michael's skull. He cradled his head in his hands. 'Then how the hell did I get taken by a press gang?'

'I don't know.' His hoarse voice was muffled. 'You—you disappeared. People thought you went back inside.'

Bright light speared the backs of Michael's eyes. The old visions of flames danced in his brain. He squeezed his eyes tight, in an effort to remember. There was nothing there. Nothing but the horrific images he wanted to forget. 'What are you saying?'

Jaimie looked up then, his eyes and nose red, his cheeks tearstained. 'Oh God, Michael. I've thought and I've thought ever since you came back. I think you must have run away.'

'Like a coward.'

A boy scared witless. It made terrible sense. Somehow he'd ended up at the docks, either carried there by a stranger who found him on the road, or on his own two feet.

He groaned. He should have known the Fates would play him false, that they'd find a way to punish him for seeing a happiness he didn't deserve.

Alice had given up her life for him. Given him her trust. Opened her generous heart. And he'd betrayed her.

She'd hate him. She couldn't hate him worse than he hated himself. Because if he'd not left his room, the fire would never have happened.

He deserved to lose Alice.

The emptiness in his soul deepened into a vast cold wasteland.

'Can you ever forgive me?' Jaimie asked, his head bowed.

A shudder ran down his spine. He couldn't forgive himself.

He placed a hand on Jaimie's shoulder, felt fine

bones beneath the silky fabric. 'There is nothing to forgive. It was an accident.'

'I should have told you the day you came here with her,' Jaimie wailed. 'I'm such a bloody coward.'

A pain, bright and white, stabbed Michael behind the eyes.

The walk in the rain suited Alice's black mood. By the time she reached Sandford House, she was saturated from hem to knee, and furious. She banged on the front door.

The butler's jaw dropped.

'Lady Hawkhurst to see Lord Sandford,' she said and pushed past him.

'If you'd care to wait in the drawing room, my lady, I will see if his lordship is at home.'

Alice stripped off her damp gloves. 'I do not care to wait. Please conduct me to his lordship now.'

The man looked startled, then shrugged. 'As you wish, my lady,' he said in one of those on-your-head-be-it tones butlers practised in off-duty hours. He led the way towards the back of the house.

'Is he in the garden room?' she asked.

'Yes, my lady.'

'Then there is no need to announce me. I know the way.' She brushed passed him and picked up her pace. She heard him follow for a few steps and then stop with a muffled exclamation. Good. The element of surprise was on her side.

As before, the sound of male voices led her to the far end of the conservatory. As before, two men occupied the cushions, but Michael was bent over his cousin, who seemed to be ill.

The suspicion that her husband had no intention of paying her a visit rose up to choke her. She swallowed her rage and disappointment and put her hands on her hips. 'Well, here's a pretty sight. And you told me you were going to sea.'

Michael's expression of ludicrous shock and horror was almost worth the pain in her chest.

'Alice?' He leaped to his feet.

An ashen-faced Jaimie lifted his head. His eyes darted to Michael. 'Bloody hell.'

Alice shot him a look designed to freeze. She turned her attention to Michael. 'What are you doing here, Michael? And why is your henchman stealing my letters? More to the point, where are my father and my brother?' Her voice rose with each question, because all she could see on his face was guilt.

'Why are you soaked through?' he asked.

'It was raining. Don't change the subject.'

Jaimie stared at her. 'Don't tell me you walked here, Lady Hawkhurst?'

'All right,' she said. 'I won't.'

'You and I need a private discussion,' Michael said grimly.

'Take her to the guest room in the east wing,' Jaimie said. 'You'll find some of Cynthia's clothes there.'

Michael cast his cousin a pained look and took her arm.

As they drew away, Jaimie called out 'Michael. Please. I'm so sorry.'

While Michael's touch was gentle, it was clear he would brook no argument about going upstairs. 'What was Simpson thinking?' he asked as soon as they were out of earshot of his cousin.

Her anger was the only thing keeping her upright. She clung to its support since she had no intention of collapsing in a heap of tears. 'Forget Simpson. You owe me an explanation.'

'We'll talk upstairs.' His voice sounded strange, as if he laboured under some strong emotion and was trying to keep it hidden. But what?

'You need to get out of those wet clothes, first,' he said. 'Up you go, unless you want me to carry you.'

Her stomach gave a little jolt. Anger, not desire. It had to be anger. She wouldn't tolerate anything else. 'I prefer my own feet.' Aware of the damp squelching in her shoes, she mounted the stairs with her back rigid and her gaze fixed firmly ahead.

'This way,' he said at the top, reaching out to guide her. She shrugged him off. With a sigh he preceded her down the corridor and flung open a door at the far end of the corridor.

She passed by him, aware of his height, his heat. She inhaled a quick breath, sandalwood mixed with sweet smoke and cigars. He must have been here quite some time.

She swung around and lifted her chin, taking note of his frown and his worried gaze. He wrenched open the clothes press and pulled out a towel. 'Here. Use this.'

She glared at him. 'I want to know what is going on. I've had no word from you and then I find you here!'

He squeezed his eyes shut for a second. 'There has been a mistake. A misunderstanding.'

'What are you talking about?'

He rubbed the back of his neck. 'Perhaps we can talk about this in the morning, when my head is better.'

'What mistake, Michael?'

An odd expression passed across his face, as if he were being tortured. 'I was coming to see you.' He turned away, striding to the window to look out into the evening sky, his profile a beautiful mask.

He must think her such a weak fool. 'Where is my father?'

He remained silent, still staring out of the window, clearly gathering his thoughts. Planning his lies. The suspicion writhing in her stomach, the fear stabbing at her heart, finally found a voice. 'Is it another woman?' She barely got the words through her clenched jaw.

'You heard from Selina.'

He sounded so calm. So uninvolved. She wanted to claw his face. Make him feel her pain. 'I found her letters under your henchman's mattress.'

'Very enterprising of you, my dear. I hope my *henchman* wasn't in it at the time.'

'Damn you, Michael.'

He cursed vilely and swung around. 'I didn't mean that. This has all happened so fast. I don't know what I am saying. God. I don't know where to start.'

She sank down on the bed. 'The beginning is often the best place.'

He cracked a miserable laugh and ran his hands through his hair. 'I suppose there is no way of keeping it from you.' He sighed. 'I hoped to undo the damage before it came to your ears.'

His face was full of resignation. And regret. The dread of what she would learn held her breath captive in her throat. She sat stiffly, ready to spring up and leave if she thought for a moment he was fabricating a tale.

'I wanted justice for my family,' he said in a low, hoarse voice.

She stared at him, confused, taken aback.

'I believed your father burned my family to death.'

The words fell from his mouth like drops of acid. Her ears sizzled, her heart stopped beating. 'My father would never do such a thing.' A wave of fear surged through her veins. 'He wouldn't.'

'I know.' He stared at her. 'Now, I know.'

'Now?'

'My memories of that night are faulty at best.' He passed his hand over his eyes. 'I needed someone to blame. Something someone said made me think the fire was deliberately set.'

'Something Jaimie said?' she asked, remembering his cousin's parting words.

'He was mistaken.'

'Did you ask my father?'

'I broached it. He said something damning and I took it for an admission of guilt.'

Her mind raced. 'You knew this when you captured the *Conchita*. It had nothing to do with you being a privateer.' Panic tightened her throat. 'Where is my father? Where is Richard?'

He held out his hand, palm up. 'Your brother is all right. He's with Wishart on the *Gryphon*.'

She glared at him. 'And Father? Did you kill him?'

'God, no!' He shook his head, but his eyes told another story.

'Where is he?' She narrowed her eyes. 'What have you done?'

'I did nothing.'

'Liar!'

'A week ago, he lost Fulton's to me at cards. That is the last time I saw him. Alice, I'm sorry. I'll find him.' He touched her shoulder. Just that light touch was like a lightning bolt through her body. She could not let him do that to her. She shrugged him off.

He pressed his fingers to his temples. 'Moments before you arrived, Jaimie told me the truth. I was about to go looking for your father. I'm so sorry.'

He looked sorry. He looked pale and ill. His hand went up to shade his eyes, as if the light pained him.

'Why did Sandford say nothing of this before?'

He groaned. A terrible sound in the small room, full of self-blame. 'He was afraid. Afraid of me. Afraid of what I would do.'

Slowly another thought filtered through her pain. 'You married me to get to my father.' The realisation was a stab to her heart. It wept the blood of betrayal.

'No!' He grimaced. 'At least, perhaps at first. I wanted information. I wanted justice. I wanted to see him hanged. Don't you see? He had to be punished. But I couldn't do it, because of you. I decided he would know the hell of never seeing his family again. It was only fair.'

'But he didn't do it,' she said coldly. 'He is innocent. Have you no idea where he is?'

'I last saw him at White's.'

This cave she found herself in was a cold, echoing, empty place. 'You married me for revenge.'

He stared at her, his face beautiful and hard and full of shadows. 'Yes.' He reached out. 'Only at first. Not—'

'How can I believe you?' she cried out as her heart collapsed in on itself. 'You've done nothing but lie.'

'Alice, please.' He covered his eyes. 'Can we talk about this in the morning? I can't do it now.'

'What is it, Michael?' she said, her voice rising in pitch, disgust dripping from her tongue. 'Is your conscience giving you a headache? Go, then. But I never want to see your face again.'

He stared at her for a long moment, his eyes narrowed, lines of pain around his mouth. 'Please, Alice. You are not thinking clearly. Get dry. We'll talk in the morning when we are both more rational. I will find your father. You'll see.' He stepped outside and closed the door behind him. The key turned in the lock.

She flew across the room and pulled on the handle. Futile. Damn him. He expected her to sit here and wait for him like an unwanted parcel, while her father was God knew where?

What a fool she'd been. He'd gulled her every step of the way with his charming lies. Tears spilled over as misery enveloped her soul.

She let them flow unchecked.

Slowly, a blanket of cold settled over her. Accept it, Alice. Their marriage meant nothing.

She was no more to him than a means to an end.

And if she let herself feel, it would hurt past bearing.

She dried her tears on her handkerchief and marched to the casement window. Directly below her chamber lay a square courtyard. A series of slate roofs angled downwards below her window like an uneven staircase of wide, sloped steps, slick with rain, the last of them at least six feet from the ground.

A sickening height from which to fall. Well, she'd managed the rope ladder off the *Gryphon*. She would manage this. First, dry clothes. And after?

No doubt, there were horses in the stable.

* * *

'Gone?' A pale Jaimie looked up from his pile of cushions. He looked worse than usual; the shadows around his eyes were purple bruises, his skin tinged grey.

'Out of the bloody window.' Michael ground his teeth until they threatened to crack in order to hold back his desire to smash everything in sight. 'According to your groom, she took a horse.'

Trust Alice to see her chance the moment he was laid low. He should have known she'd take matters into her own small hands. Michael cursed vilely and struck out at the wooden pole supporting the canopy. The structure wobbled. He grabbed the pole and steadied it.

He huffed out a breath. 'A woman alone, riding around the countryside in the middle of the night? Anything could happen. I have to go after her.' The little fool. He should have tied her to the bed.

The thought sent a jolt of lust to his groin.

God. These past weeks without her had been hell. He'd missed her. Up there in the bedroom he'd wanted to take her in his arms, kiss her silent, worship her with his body, bend her to his will. Make her forgive him.

Knowing Alice, she would, too. Kind-hearted to a fault, generous, she'd take pity on him. She might, given enough time, learn to love him again. Longing kicked him in the chest with the force of an iron-shod hoof.

He curled his lip.

His parents had loved him and, but for him, they would still be alive. He didn't want love. It brought too much responsibility, too much pain.

Like the pain gnawing a hole in his chest.

He only wanted to reunite the Fultons, as they deserved. Let them be a family again.

Jaimie observed him from beneath his lashes, his face full of regret. 'Where would she go?'

'London. To her friend, no doubt. She'll be looking for her father. I'm going to try to catch her before she reaches town.' At least he hadn't sent her on a wild chase to Portsmouth. He had no idea if Fulton had followed his suggestion, but he would do everything in his power to find the man and return him safely to his daughter.

'You will come back?' Jaimie whispered. 'I will see you again?'

He bent and squeezed the bony shoulder. 'I will.' Once he was sure Alice was safe. 'Will you do something for me?' He looked at the pipe clutched in Jaimie's fist. 'Give it up.'

A wry smile twisted Jaimie's lips. 'I wish it was that easy.'

'Nothing is easy, Jaimie.' What he had to do now would be the hardest thing of his life. He would put things right and let Alice go before he did her any more damage.

Chapter Nineteen

A week had passed since Alice had left Sandford House and landed on Selina's doorstep. Yesterday she'd received a cheerful note from her father. He'd sent it to Selina hoping she would know Alice's whereabouts. He was in Portsmouth staying with a friend. His note said he'd been ill, but was making steady progress and in a few days he'd be ready for a visit. He'd failed to provide his precise direction, which was why Alice was not on her way to the coast.

Father's note had been followed by a terse missive from Michael requesting an interview. So she sat perched on a sofa in Selina's drawing room with her friend beside her for moral support. Waiting. Feeling hollow and sick. 'I should have refused to see him.'

'You can't,' Selina said. 'He's your husband. If he made a fuss, Father would insist. And besides, he has your father's address.'

'He could have put it in his note.'

Selina patted her hand. Selina. She'd been so kind.

So understanding. 'I expect he wants to talk to you,' she said gently.

Alice bit the inside of her cheek. All morning long she'd vacillated from wanting to see him and wanting to flee. She'd said harsh things when they last met. Things he deserved, but knowing she was right wasn't making her happy. Indeed, she'd never felt so miserable in her life.

Her heart pounded uncomfortably against her ribs. 'He's late. He's not coming.' She started to rise.

Selina gripped her fingers. 'It is not yet four o'clock.'

The case clock in the hall gave her the lie. A knock sounded on the door. It swung back.

'Lord Hawkhurst to see you, my lady,' the butler said.

She observed him as if from a great distance.

At Jaimie's house, she'd put his pallor down to his new style of living, his weeks in London after years at sea. Now, he invaded the cheerful room like an impenetrable shadow. He looked positively gaunt.

He bowed. 'Lady Selina. Alice.' His deep voice vibrated a chord low in her belly. Sensual longings she could no more resist than she could resist taking a breath rippled through her veins. Desire. How she hated what his allure did to her.

She and Selina rose, curtsied and sat down side by side on the sofa in perfect synchronicity. Farcical amid the dark currents disturbing the air.

'Tea will be here in a moment, Lord Hawkhurst,' Selina said. 'Please, won't you sit down?'

He chose a chair as far away from them as possible, his body tense, his expression a mask of politeness.

'I wonder if we could discuss what I have to say in private?' He looked at Selina, who shot to her feet with an apologetic smile. 'I'll just go and see what is keeping the tea.' She skittered out of the room, careful not to catch Alice's eye.

The wretch. But it was probably for the best. This way she could unburden her mind.

Anxious to be rid of him and the flutters in her stomach, Alice plunged in. 'You have arrangements to discuss, you said, and an address to provide.' How remote her voice sounded. How still she was inside. How cold.

'Don't worry, Alice, I'm not here for any nefarious purpose,' he said.

Nefarious wasn't her greatest terror. She feared the way her heart leaped towards him every time her glance fell on his stark, beautiful face. Feared the ache in her chest and the longing of her wanton body.

'Here is the address.' He rose and handed her a small square of paper.

Somehow their hands touched. The spark she dreaded travelled up her arm, tingling and seductive. She felt ashamed of her reaction in the face of his calm.

He nodded at the paper. 'He was a very ill man, Alice. You will find him much improved.'

She stared at the writing. The Mermaid Inn, Portsmouth. 'An inn?' She could only imagine the depths of drink to which he'd sunk, despite Michael's assurance. 'I must go at once.'

He shrugged. 'I have purchased a town house in Grosvenor Square. You and your father are free to move in there whenever you wish.' His deep voice sounded lifeless. As if none of this mattered. 'The deed is in your name, settled on you. As is the deed for Westerly. My man of business will deliver them this afternoon. Have your lawyer look over the documents. I have issued orders that Richard is to return home, though I doubt he will be pleased.'

'He is too young for a life at sea.'

A wry smile twisted his lips. 'As you say. The titles to both houses are free and clear. An allowance will be deposited to an account in your name each month. There will be more than enough funds to endow that hospital of yours.'

His gaze, so steady as it met hers, held neither regret nor guilt. His eyes were blank. Empty mirrors. 'Our separation will begin immediately.'

'Our separation?' She was right. He regretted their marriage and without his revenge found no reason to continue the charade. The cold around her heart solidified to ice.

'You are free to do exactly as you please, Alice. You will hear no complaints from me.'

Permission to take other men to her bed, she presumed. A death blow to her heart.

Pride held her steady. She inclined her head. 'You are most generous, sir. Yet still we are tied.'

He sent her a bleak look. 'There is nothing I can do to end our marriage that would not cause you harm. You will never have to see me again.'

Her own words thrown back in her face. 'Good.'

An expression flickered across his face—a wince of pain? Unlikely.

He rose from the chair, looming large in the small room. She shrank back against the cushions.

His lips twisted wryly. 'Don't worry, I'm not going to inflict my person on you.' He moved to the window, gazed down into the street.

Clearly he had something to say that made it difficult for him to face her. She stared at the delicately patterned wallpaper wavering in and out of focus and held herself rigid, braced to withstand his next blow.

He straightened his shoulders, his face a mask of decision. 'I am going to sea. I don't expect to return.'

She blinked back the prickle behind her eyelids and, despite the stiffness of her lips, managed a cool smile. 'I understand.'

For a moment he stared at her, longing leaping in his eyes like a flame reaching out to touch her soul. Longing for what? Understanding? Forgiveness?

The flicker died in the space of a heartbeat, if it was ever there. His expression resumed its customary insouciance, a half-smile lifting the corners of his lovely lips.

Blast him. She'd been such a willing victim. A pathetic, lonely spinster who had fallen for his charm and his handsome good looks the moment he glanced her way. She'd succumbed to the faintest of promises and the demands of her body for something more than an empty bed. Not to mention the longings of her empty heart.

She lifted her chin and stared down her nose. 'Don't feel you have to leave England on my account.'

He opened his mouth to speak.

'Oh,' she said, her face flushing with embarrassment. 'It's not on my account, is it? This is your way of punishing Jaimie.'

His eyes blazed. 'How dare you suggest such a thing? I hold no grudge against Jaimie and he knows it.'

'I'm glad to hear it. He worships you, I think.'

He flinched as if she'd struck him. 'He's a fool.'

The self-loathing in his voice shocked her into silence. The emptiness mirrored in his gaze caused her heart to ache for his pain. 'Perhaps I was wrong to condemn you out of hand, Michael. You acted based on a misapprehension. You were angry. Under similar circumstances I might have done the same.'

A derisive sneer curled his lip. 'Always kind-hearted.' He cut off her protest with a savage swipe of his hand. 'No platitudes, if you please.' His gaze clashed with hers, wild, angry, like a storm at sea, and full of a hunger she didn't understand.

Then he bowed. 'I truly wish you the happiness you deserve. Please present my apologies to Lady Selina.'

It all seemed to happen so fast. One moment he was standing by the window, the next he was out of the front door before she had made it halfway down the passage with his name hovering on her lips. What had she intended to say? *I don't care what you did. I love you?*

Had she lost every shred of pride? Could he have spelled it out any more clearly? He didn't want her.

It was over. She had money and freedom. She could dance till dawn and bed whomsoever she wished.

But what good was that when there could never be anyone else but Michael?

She touched the gold circle at her neck. She should have given it back.

Selina met her on her way back to the drawing room.

'What happened?' she asked breathlessly, reaching out and touching Alice's arm. 'I heard him leave. I was hoping…'

'What?' Alice said. 'That it would all end happily ever after?'

She hurried to the window and looked down into the street. He'd gone and she'd never see him again. Never look into those turquoise depths and see the heat of his desire. The only thing they'd shared was a brief torrid affair. Yet she felt torn in two, as if she'd never be whole again.

Nonsense. There were things to do. Father to be brought home. Richard to ready for school. A new operating room to plan at St Thomas's. Practical things.

Commonsensical Alice things.

The old enthusiasm refused to surface.

Haunted by the memory of his gaze, she stared down into the empty street. A deep, dark well of sadness opened up at her feet. It would swallow her up if she let it. She could sink into its darkness and dwell in misery.

Only this time it wasn't her pride on the floor in shreds, it was her heart.

And what little was left was madly telling her not to give up.

He'd said he wanted her happiness. Then why was he leaving?

Only one person could shed any light on Michael's true state of mind. Father would be safe for a day or two. Michael, on the other hand, would soon be lost to her forever.

'Alice?' Selina touched her arm. 'Are you all right? Did he tell you where your father is?'

'Yes.' Alice swung around. 'I need to borrow your carriage.'

The Albright carriage pulled up outside Sandford House. Alice waited impatiently for the footman to let down the steps. Selina had insisted on an escort of three of her father's footmen. When she stepped down from the carriage, she could feel the disapproval of all three pairs of eyes.

Ladies did not travel across the countryside at breakneck speed.

Ladies didn't chase their husbands to find out why they were being abandoned.

She stared at the house and bit her lip. What if he was here? Then she would ask him to look in her eyes and tell her the truth, because what he had said in London did not make any sense. He'd given her permission to take any man to her bed. And he had looked so dashed bleak.

Had he found her wanton nature distasteful in a wife? He hadn't seemed to mind. Or did he think she could not remain faithful, given that she had already taken a lover before him? Could that be what was driving him away? He certainly hadn't looked happy. Or did he resent being trapped in a marriage he'd engineered on a false assumption?

Or was there something else? Something to do with that brief glimpse of hunger in his eyes?

The questions had been going around and around in her head on the journey until she thought she might go mad.

All the time she was haunted by the bleakness in his face and the feeling she had missed a vital piece of information.

She squared her shoulders. She would have the truth, no matter how much it hurt.

The footman proceeded ahead to knock on the door. A horseman trotted around the corner, coming from the stables. The black mare snorted and danced at the sight of the carriage, showing the whites of its eyes. The horseman reined the animal in with a firm hand.

He raised his hat. 'Lady Hawkhurst?'

'Lord Sandford?' It was the first time she'd seen him off his pile of cushions, his dark hair ruffled by the breeze, his face tinged with colour. He looked quite handsome.

He swung down from his horse. 'What a pleasure,' he said, sounding wary.

Lord, he was unexpectedly tall. Nearly as tall as Michael, but slender, less powerful in his shoulders.

'I need to talk to you about Michael.' She glanced at the servants. 'Is there somewhere we can speak privately?'

'Walk with me,' he murmured. 'Here, you,' he addressed the snooty footman. 'Hold my mare.' The man took the reins as if he expected the horse to bite.

Sandford held out his arm and led her off the drive and across the wide open sweep of lawn. When they were out of earshot of the servants, he looked down at her. 'How may I be of service?'

Where to begin? How to ask? Lord, he would think her such a besotted fool.

'Michael is leaving England.'

His mouth tightened; he looked desperately sad. 'I know.'

'Do you…is it…'? This was harder than she expected, but there really wasn't much time. 'Do you know why?'

'He came to tell me he was leaving a few days ago.' He looked off into the distance, his voice husky and strained. 'I begged him not to go.' His voice broke. 'It's all my fault.' His words trailed away and he looked down at her. 'Did he tell you I was the one who caused the fire?'

He sounded so miserable, her heart went out to him

and she placed her hand on his forearm. 'He said it was an accident.'

'But it wasn't an accident when I lied,' he said forcefully, as if the truth was too hard to keep inside. 'If I had not tried so hard to please him… If I had dared admit the truth…' He blinked rapidly. 'He hates me. He says he does not, but why else would he leave?'

'I think he resents being trapped into marriage.' It was all she could admit.

He stopped walking, his dark eyes still moist from his own sorrow, but his expression held shock. 'He loves you.'

'No,' she said, her heart aching for hopes she should never have entertained. 'Never once has he spoken of love.' Not even when she'd admitted her own feelings.

'I never saw him so happy as the day after your marriage,' he said earnestly. 'Never. Not even when he found me again, for then he had only just learned of his family's deaths. It was as if he'd lost them twice. First when he thought they'd abandoned him, and again when he came home and found them gone. He was so angry at what Fate had done to him. He believed it was punishment for disobeying his father's orders.'

He closed his eyes for a long moment. 'I encouraged him to hate your father, because he seemed to need someone to blame and I didn't want it to be me. I never gave a thought to the consequences.' He gave a sharp laugh. 'The smoke can lead one astray.'

Alice mulled over his words, laying them alongside what she knew of Michael and what he had said in London. 'Do you think he has gone back to blaming himself?' If that was it, and only that, perhaps there was still hope.

He looked down at the ground and pushed at the head of a daisy with the toe of his boot. 'I don't know. It hardly seems rational.'

Pain wasn't rational. He'd clearly much rather blame himself than blame Jaimie. Much as she had blamed herself for what had happened with Andrew. And still did.

There was really only one way to know for sure how he felt. If she dared take the risk.

'Where is Michael now?' she asked.

'Portsmouth, if he hasn't already sailed.' He looked at her, his fine mouth drawn down. 'He suggested I go with him. How could I give myself such a gift, knowing what I'd done? Knowing my actions drove him from England?'

Men. Who understood them and their pride? If Michael had offered her a berth on his ship, she would have jumped in the long boat without a second's thought. And if she wanted to get to the bottom of Michael's decision, that might be what she needed to do.

She turned to face him, took both his hands in hers and gazed up into his misery-filled dark eyes. He looked younger than his years and so very vulnerable. Her heart, bruised and broken though it was, welled with sympathy. 'I honestly don't believe Michael blames you for the past, and you must not blame yourself.'

He flashed her a brief smile of thanks, but she wasn't sure he accepted her advice. 'What will you do now?'

'Well,' she said, with sudden insight, 'I was planning to go to Portsmouth anyway. My father is there.'

He blinked. His eyebrows shot up. 'He did say you were a clever woman. May I wish you luck?'

She nodded. She was going to need more than luck, but she would take whatever she could get.

The *Gryphon*, renamed the *Alice*, was ready to put to sea. Why the hell had he done *that* to himself? Michael wondered as he inspected the repairs to his cabin. Every time someone said the name, his gut lurched. Sometimes he forgot and looked up, expecting to see her.

Well, he couldn't change it now. They were to sail on the tide.

'Someone to see you, Cap'n,' Simpson announced.

A tall young man strode into his cabin. Suntanned and broad, Richard looked more man than boy. He removed his hat and saluted smartly.

'Fulton.' Michael leaned back in his chair. 'Why aren't you on your way to Oxford?'

'I don't want to go to Oxford. I want to finish my training with Wishart.'

'Your sister wants you home,' he said roughly. 'Go away. Can't you see I'm busy?'

Richard shoved his fingers through brown curls. 'You are just like my father. He always does what Alice wants. When do I get to have a say in my life?'

'When you've finished school.'

'I hate it.'

'If you want to be a good officer, you'll need mathematics and astronomy.'

'You didn't go to university.'

'If you want the kind of training I had, join the navy.' He couldn't keep the sharp edge from his voice.

The boy glowered from beneath his eyebrows. Sulky bastard.

'Look, lad. Two years at school is nothing. You'll get to meet men your own age, kick up a few larks, learn about the world. If you want to go to sea after that, the navy will be glad to have you. By then the war should be well and truly over. Right now, your sister needs to know you are safe and well. Get on the next coach to London. She's waiting for you.'

'Two years,' Richard muttered. 'As soon as I'm eighteen, I'll be looking for a berth on a ship.'

'Ask Wishart for a reference.'

The rigid face eased into a rueful smile. He stuck out a hand. 'I wanted to thank you. For the opportunity to find out what I really want.'

An odd lump filled Michael's throat. God, he had so misjudged Fulton and his brood. 'You are welcome,' he said gruffly. 'Now be on your way before the press gangs do a sweep of the wharfs and you find yourself before a very different kind of mast.'

'Aye, aye, sir.' The boy executed a smart about-face and rolled out of the cabin with a sailor's swagger. In a year or so he would make a very good officer.

Michael unrolled the chart on his desk. He stared at it. Where to go? America? Africa? How far did he have to go to get Alice out of his head?

And, dammit, his heart.

She'd looked so damned wounded when he had told her what he'd done, he would have liked to have ripped his stupid heart out of his chest and hand it to her on a platter.

Not a good idea.

He was bad luck. Bad joss, a Chinese sailor had told him once. Jigger it. Bad luck always went in threes. It had been bad luck she'd been on the *Conchita*. Bad luck he'd won their chess game and bad luck she'd found out about the letters.

He wasn't going to risk sticking around for the next round in case Alice got hurt worse.

He rubbed his fingers across his collarbone. With a wry grin, he remembered he'd given his lucky piece to Alice. Hopefully, it would keep her safe.

As long as Michael stayed away from her, she'd be all right.

Two more hours and he'd cast off from England's shores. The only thing he regretted was not convincing Jaimie to come with him. The sea air might do the man some good. Get him away from that damned pipe of his and his less than savoury friends. After making provisions for Alice, he'd arrived at Jaimie's house to bid him farewell and found a bunch of hell-raisers in the throes of a highly suspect form of entertainment involving monks' robes and chanting. Not to mention the naked women.

He'd tossed them out.

Jaimie hadn't objected. Indeed, he'd welcomed Michael back with open arms, clearly relieved he'd been forgiven. Hell. Michael had nothing to forgive. He was the one who'd caused all the damage. Ruined everyone's lives.

He was lucky Alice wasn't carrying a child. His chest squeezed painfully. They would have made nice babies together.

Bugger. He swiped the trail of moisture from his cheek. Was he some sort of maudlin idiot in his cups? He forced his gaze back to the chart. He needed to decide. Never had he been so indecisive. Without a plan. Rudderless.

He picked up a pin, closed his eyes, waved it around in circles, and brought it down hard. India.

It was as good as anywhere else. He wouldn't mind a tangle or two with the East India Company. They'd had that corner of the world all their own way for far too long. And it was a good long voyage. About as far from England as he could get. And satisfyingly dangerous.

The only place worse was China. Perhaps he'd go there next.

He picked up his compass and ruler and began the delicate task of plotting.

Another knock on the door.

'What now?' he muttered.

The door opened. 'New cabin boy, Cap'n,' Simpson said. 'Seeing as how Wishart took Jacko on to replace the Fulton lad.'

'I don't need a cabin boy.' Michael had only taken Jacko on because he'd found the lad starving on the waterfront.

'Chuck him over the side for the fishes, shall I?'

A squeak of terror brought his gaze off the paper.

The barefoot, ragged boy, with dirt on his face and a disreputable cap pulled low over his forehead, kept his gaze fixed on the deck and his shoulders hunched.

There was something dreadfully familiar about the lad. He rose to his feet, supporting himself with his hands on the desk as he leaned forwards to get a better look. 'Alice?'

The boy raised his head. A pair of wide hazel eyes met his. 'How did you know?'

He felt very strange. Light-headed. Off kilter. Happy. He got a grip on himself. 'What the devil are you doing here? And looking like that? Damnation.

Come inside and close the door. Simpson, I don't want to be disturbed.'

'Aye, aye, Cap'n.'

Something in the steward's voice made Michael look at him again. The man had the broadest grin he'd ever seen, and Simpson was a master at grins.

'Out,' Michael said.

The door swung shut.

Alice took off her cap and fiddled with it. Her hair stuck straight up like a crest.

'What did you do to your hair?'

'Oh.' She smoothed it flat. It looked better. Actually it looked nice. Sexy. His blood stirred.

He stalked around his desk, stood in front of her, looking down at the wisps of hair sticking up on her head, the elegant shoulders in rough linen, her beautiful, slender bare feet.

Big mistake. Getting close. From here he could smell her. Amid the dirt and the odour of horses, he smelled lavender. 'If you are going to dress as a boy, it is a bad idea to use female perfume,' he growled. 'You might give sailors the wrong idea.'

'I'll remember that next time,' she said agreeably.

He grabbed her arm, tilted her chin with one finger until they were almost nose to nose, lip to lip. 'There isn't going to be a next time.'

She shook her head.

He stared into her eyes, saw the lost promises and cursed. He spun away, rubbing at the new growth of beard on his chin. He'd forgotten the itch of a new beard, but it wasn't the real reason his skin was tingling. Was she…? The air burst from his lungs. Wild hope rushed in. He turned. 'You are not with child?'

She shook her head.

Disappointment sent his stomach to the deck. Because he'd welcome the excuse to stay? He glowered. 'Then why are you here?'

Rather than being intimidated, she looked…defiant, even a little mischievous. He ought to put her over his knee and spank her bottom. His body pulsed with a burst of longing.

Lord, did he have no control when it came to this woman? He wanted her so badly he couldn't look at her. Seeing her in London had been bad enough. This was torture.

Somehow he had to make her leave.

'I went to visit Jaimie,' she said. 'He told me where to find you.'

'He did you no favours,' he said coldly, crossing his arms over his chest to keep from reaching for her, clenching his fists to stem the urge to sweep her up in his arms, to kiss her senseless and carry her to the replica of the bed he'd lost over the side. For some reason, right at that moment, the bed seemed to take up more than its fair share of the cabin.

'You should not be here.'

'I know.'

He did not like the way she was watching him, like a robin with its eye on a particularly juicy worm.

'But since I was in Portsmouth to collect Father, I thought to drop in.' She glanced around, her gaze coming to rest on the bed.

Drop in. Dressed like that?

Afraid she might see the desire in his eyes, he turned away, looked out over the moorings, at the forest of masts and spars held together by man-made webs. He grabbed at the back of the chair for support, squeezed until he could feel the carved wood biting into his flesh. 'You've seen me. Now go.' A deep breath steadied his legs. He strode around her, careful not to come in contact with her slim body, heading for the door. 'Your brother was here. If you hurry, you can catch him up. I'll have Simpson arrange for a carriage.'

As if he hadn't spoken, she prowled to the desk looking down at the scattered charts, poking at his compass.

He could bodily throw her out, but if he touched her, she'd be more likely to end up in his bed. And that would be a mistake of unimaginable proportions.

'India?' she asked, looking up.

'Yes. As soon as you are off my ship.'

'I went to India as a child. I wouldn't mind seeing it again.'

'I don't need a cabin boy.'

'Or a wife, apparently.'

He clenched his jaw so hard he thought his teeth might crumble.

He watched from the edge of his vision, pretending not to care, as she padded around his cabin, her bare feet a soft whisper on the rug, her bottom and thighs clearly outlined in her disgraceful breeches. Never had she looked more disreputable, or more desirable. He tried not to see the sway of her hips. Tried not to look at her at all, but no matter where he looked, her image burned the backs of his eyes. He had the feeling she was all he would ever see for the rest of his life.

Alice glanced at him sideways, over her shoulder, and caught him stealing a peak at her bottom. He frowned.

She stopped at the bed, staring at the carved gryphon. 'You replaced it.' She reached up and ran a hand over an outstretched wing.

He felt the brush of her fingers on his skin and shuddered inside. Blood rushed to his groin. He was burning up. He couldn't think. He held himself rigid, unmoving.

'Do you remember the shanty called "The Valiant Lady"?' She tilted her head on one side, staring at the gryphon's face.

It took a moment for his brain to sift through the words and recall the old song about a woman who follows her man to sea as a surgeon's assistant and saves his life. A flash of comprehension widened his eyes. 'You aren't signing on as ship's surgeon.'

Her brow furrowed. 'With Bones remaining behind to open a hospital for mariners, you could do worse.'

He swallowed a laugh at her bold assertion. 'It isn't a suitable occupation for…for a lady.' He had almost said for his wife, but he had given up all rights in that quarter.

She deserved so much more than a rough wreck of a man who left a swathe of death in his wake. God help him, but much more of this and he would go stark staring mad with wanting and lock the door with her on the inside.

He must not. He'd made his decision. He returned to his charts as if she was no longer there, watching her from beneath his lashes. Waiting for her to get fed up and leave.

She plonked down on the bed and hooked one ankle over her other knee, like a boy. The fabric of her breeches clung to her open thighs. His breath caught in his throat. He couldn't keep his gaze from the temptingly delicious invitation.

She was doing it on purpose. Bedevilling him. Letting him know what he'd be missing.

He forced himself to look away. Simpson had brought her, he would damned well row her back to the quay. Wrapped in something large. Like a sail. 'You must go. We weigh anchor with the tide.'

She cocked her head on one side. 'Why are you running away? I never took you for a coward.'

A blow to the solar plexus could not have knocked the wind from his lungs so effectively. It took a moment to recover, even as he acknowledged it as the truth. 'Think what you wish.'

'I think you are leaving because you regret our marriage.'

Behind the bravado of her outrageous costume, behind the careless wave of her hand, deep in her eyes he saw hurt. If he'd been a Roman he would have fallen on his sword, because there was nothing he could do to ease her pain. 'I regret everything I did this past year, but my leaving has nothing to do with you.' And everything.

'Then why?'

'Damnation.' He spun away, stared out of the window. 'You don't understand.'

'How can I, when you won't tell me?'

He heard the catch in her voice. It pierced the armour he'd built up to guard the soft, uncertain places in his heart. 'I'm bad luck.'

'What?' She laughed. Then faltered as he stared at her.

'A Jonah,' he said.

'What sailors' superstition is that?'

Put like that it sounded crazy, but he knew better. 'I don't want you on my conscience.'

Her eyes widened. 'How very selfish.'

Stung by her injustice, he thrust his face into hers. 'How is wanting to keep you safe selfish?' he shouted.

She put her hands flat on his chest. Holding him at bay, her womanly scent enticing him closer. 'It isn't about keeping me safe, it's about you feeling guilty.'

He laughed. Hard and bitter. 'What do you know about guilt?'

'Everyone makes mistakes,' she murmured. 'Some small, some large. You can't correct them by running away.' She spoke gently, as if she feared he might break.

He'd been broken and mended so many times there wasn't anything of him left straight or whole. There was nothing left to repair and the pity in her gaze was worse than if she'd been angry.

He walked to the door. 'My decision is made.'

She bit her lip, stared at him for a long moment, sadness filling her eyes. She shook her head. 'Very well. I wish you godspeed.' Her voice shook, but she took a deep breath and continued in husky tones. 'For my sake, Michael, don't come back. It would hurt too much.' She brushed past him on her way through the door.

His heart stopped beating as if she'd ripped it from his body. The pain almost brought him to his knees.

How he remained standing, watching her coolly, without a word, he didn't know. But he did it for her sake.

He did it to keep her safe from the ill fortune that hung about him like a cloud. The old Chinese sailor had warned him years ago not to tempt the gods. He had. By leaving, he could always remember her safe in the arms of her family. He'd told Jaimie to watch over her. Made him swear.

He snatched up the quilt from the bed and followed her out on deck. A salt breeze caressed his cheek. The sails snapped their impatience to be gone. This was his life. His penance.

No matter how much he wished it different.

'Simpson,' he roared. 'Lower the boat.'

While Simpson plied the oars towards the quay, Alice huddled in the quilt. The ache in her chest had grown more painful with each stroke of the oars. She could scarcely draw more than a sip of air without crying out. As if to torture her further, the scent of sandalwood on the quilt invaded each breath she took. Tears chilled by the wind ran down her face. She scraped them away.

So much for Jaimie's assertion that he was sure Michael cared for her deeply. The disguise had been her idea. A very unsubtle reminder of their last night of lovemaking.

Sadly, Michael had not been the least bit pleased to see her. Most of the time he looked as if he barely remembered who she was. All his talk of luck was an excuse. She'd done exactly what she said she would. Learned the truth. He would never have married her, if not for his revenge. He didn't love her. Not even a little.

No wonder he couldn't wait to get her off his ship and out of his life. She'd gone to him and he'd thrown her out. Like rubbish.

She touched his ring at her throat. She should have returned it. She should toss it over the side. She closed her fingers around it.

She'd keep it. As a reminder.

Simpson missed his stroke. The boat wobbled. He was staring behind her, his jaw slack.

She glanced back. A launch rowed by four men was gaining on them, making for the quay. In the stern, an officer hunched beneath an oilskin and his tricorn hat pulled low. A big man. While she couldn't make out his features, his form looked remarkably familiar. When she looked back at Simpson, he gave a grin and a wink and continued pulling for shore.

'Avast there!' one of the oarsmen hailed them.

Simpson squinted through the spray. An odd expression came over his face.

'What is it?' Alice gripped the gunnels of the rocking boat and looked over her shoulder.

'Er…Navy bastards,' Simpson said, shipping his oars and looking puzzled. 'Or the coast guard?'

Not Michael, then. Lord, would her foolish heart never give up hope. Not even after he'd bundled her off his ship like yesterday's laundry.

Staring back at the boat, Simpson had the look of utter bemusment. He raised a hand as if acknowledging a signal.

'What do they want?' She started to rise.

Simpson grabbed her and thrust her into the bottom of the boat and covered her with the quilt. 'Stay down, my lady.'

'Don't be ridiculous.' She tried to fight him off. 'I've nothing to hide.' Nothing except her rather odd costume. Not the sort of thing to be caught in by a bunch of rough sailors. She stopped struggling.

The other boat bumped theirs. Simpson said nothing and nor did they. A pair of strong arms wrapped around her waist, holding her tight inside the quilt.

Familiar arms. And a very familiar large strong body held her close and leaped with her into the other boat.

'Michael?' she squeaked. 'What are you doing?'

'Quiet,' Simpson hissed. 'Blasted pirates. Just do what they wants.'

Inside her warm dark cave, she narrowed her eyes.

It was Michael who was holding her. She knew it. Otherwise she'd be terrified.

And they'd played this game before.

She pressed her mouth against the fabric to stifle her urge to giggle and went limp.

'Looks like we got ourselves a powder monkey and a sail hand,' a rough voice said. Not Michael. One of the other men. 'Back to the ship wi'em.'

A strong firm hand pushed down on her back, pressing her against the boats planks. The splash of the oars told her they were under way.

Where was he taking her? Back to the ship? Had he changed his mind? Or? Or what?

Or what if it wasn't Michael?

Simpson had given up far too easily for it to be anyone else. Hadn't he?

What if she was wrong and this really was some press gang looking for new crew? Wouldn't they be in for a surprise? Dash it. They might be only too pleased to discover they'd captured a female disreputable enough to visit a ship in breeches.

This had better be Michael or she was in trouble.

'Up we goes.' Ah, now that was Michael's voice, even if he was trying to disguise it with a low accent.

He flung her over his shoulder. There had been a lot of shoulder tossing in her life just lately. Finally it was by the right man.

She could hear men's voices all around her, muffled laughter and the thump of boots on the wooden deck.

Finally her captor set her down on her feet and whipped her covering away.

She opened her eyes to a familiar scene, his stateroom and a fierce-looking Michael with his hand on his hips, glaring at her.

'Oh, my word. It is you.' She reached out.

Hands behind his back, his face stern, he stared at her. 'Stand to attention, sailor. I'll have no sloppiness on board my ship.' The twinkle in his eyes belied his fierce expression. The corner of his mouth flickered.

He was trying not to laugh, the rogue.

She snapped upright, gazed straight ahead. 'Aye, aye, sir.'

He gazed at her for a long moment. Then his eyes ran down her length, skimmed her body. She felt hot all over.

She swallowed. This was the privateer and the maiden game. Wasn't it?

His gaze lifted back to her face. 'I am a fool,' he softly.

Her stomach fell.

He smiled then. Sweetly. Boyishly. Apologetically. Her heart seemed to melt inside her chest. 'A purely selfish fool.'

'Oh, Michael.'

'Let me finish. When I left you at Hawkhurst Place, I thought you'd be safe.' He heaved a sigh. 'But would you stay? No. And when I locked you in a room, you climbed out of a window.' He glared at her from under his brows. 'You could have been killed climbing down. Then you travelled alone on horseback to London of all places. Do you have no sense of danger?'

'I rented a post-chaise in the nearest town, for goodness' sake, with the money you had left me.'

'Hardly safe late at night.'

She winced. 'I—'

He held up a hand. 'I finally found the perfect solution. I paid for an army of men and left you in their care.'

She blinked. 'An army?'

'A small army of footmen at the town house. Old soldiers most of them. They have their instructions.'

'Why would I need a small army?'

'I've lost so many people in my life.' His voice grew rough. 'I thought if I left you at Hawkhurst, kept you in ignorance of my revenge, that I wouldn't have to lose you too. But you wouldn't stay where I put you.' He let go a heavy sigh. 'And of course when you discovered the truth…' his voice cracked '…you were magnificent in your loyalty to your father. I was so damned jealous when you stood up for him, but you were right. I'd done a terrible thing.'

'Father doesn't seem to have suffered too much. I have never seen him looking so well.'

'Don't make excuses for me, Alice. I ruined an innocent man and planned worse. I deserved to lose you.'

He gazed at the window, his throat working as if it was hard for him to speak. Yet she knew she had to let him finish.

His voice was a mere murmur when he started speaking again. 'I decided it was better for you to hate me and for me to lose you now than at some time in the future. Better to get it over with than always be wondering.'

She frowned. 'Wondering about what?'

He shrugged as if the question was foolish. 'I don't know. A carriage accident. A fall. Death in childbirth. Anything can happen. And so I arranged for your father and brother's return, money for the hospital. I thought that no matter where I went, I could always imagine you happy and safe, with all your heart's desires.'

She shook her head. 'Not quite,' she whispered. 'Without you, they are but a shadow of my heart's desires.'

His eyes glimmered with moisture in the lamplight. He swallowed. 'You married the wrong man. I grew up rough. I am not one for balls and routs.'

She bit her lip. Tears burned in her throat. 'Are you sure you want me, with my less than spotless past? I thought that was perhaps what drove you away.'

In a second she was folded in his arms. 'God, Alice. I value you beyond price. What happened occurred long before we met. I won't say I didn't think about killing the selfish bastard. But he never stood between us.'

'Oh, Michael.' She raised her face and his lips descended on her mouth, gentle at first, wooing, velvet soft against her lips, his tongue plying for entry. She happily obliged. He groaned. The sound vibrated against her breasts. She dissolved against him. Grabbed his shoulders and feverishly kissed him back.

Slowly, Michael broke the kiss. He felt so dammed happy and so utterly selfish. What if something went wrong? 'You are taking a terrible risk, Alice. My luck has run out. This ship could sink tomorrow.'

'I have this.' She pulled on the chain around her neck, revealing the child's signet ring. 'It is waiting for the next Hawkhurst heir. And besides—' she cast him a teasing glance '—we haven't tried out the bed. To see if it is as good as the old one.'

He kissed her furrowed brow, the tip of her nose, the full bottom lip, her chin, and dropped down to one knee, took her hand and kissed the palm. 'Can you indeed tolerate a buffle-headed, rough-mannered sailor in your life?'

'There is one thing I need to know before I decide.'

His gut lurched.

'Why did you change your mind?'

A wry chuckle forced its way up from his chest. 'If you must know, these last weeks have been hellish. I couldn't stop wondering what you were doing. How you were feeling. Hoping you missed me. When I watched that damned boat pulling away, I realised it doesn't matter how far away I go, I'm going to be worried mindless.'

'Not a good enough reason, I'm afraid.' Her smile teased, but a seriousness filled her eyes.

If he didn't take the final risk he would lose her for ever this time. He could see it in the determined set of her chin.

He pressed her hand against his cheek, breathing deeply while he formed the words in his head and forced them into his throat. 'I love you,' he whispered.

No bolt of lightning struck them down.

'I didn't hear you,' she whispered back.

A dam broke somewhere in his chest, but surprisingly it didn't hurt. It felt good. Warm. Joyful.

'I love you,' he said, his voice firm and sure. He leaped to his feet. 'I bloody well love you.'

Her arms went around his neck. 'I love you too, Michael.'

He kissed her, held her close, felt her slight, lean body in her ridiculous clothes, and for the first time he could remember, he felt as if he belonged.

It didn't matter where they went. As long as they were together, he would be home.

Humbled, he lifted his head and she stared at him with worried eyes.

'I love you with all my heart, Lady Hawkhurst,' he whispered. 'I hope you don't live to regret this wild start of yours.'

'Never,' she whispered against his lips. 'I'd go to the ends of the earth with you.'

'Ah, yes. The small matter of our course.' He set her on her feet. 'Wait here a moment.'

'Where are you going?' The panicky note in her voice made his heart ache. He had yet to earn her trust. But he would, if it took the rest of his life. 'I have some orders to give.' His voice roughened. 'I'll be no more than a minute or two.'

The moment he left, Alice felt all her old fears return. She paced the cabin. Would she be able to keep such a handsome, virile man happy? Common sense told her it wasn't possible. Her heart refused to listen.

The door swung back. Outside the men were shouting and running back and forth, while he stood just inside the doorway looking at her. Quiet joy glowed in his sea-tinted eyes as his gaze rested on her face. It warmed her through and provided the strength she needed to believe.

'I hope your crew aren't too disappointed,' she said.

He cocked his head on one side. 'Why should they be?'

'They expected to go to sea.'

'Yes.'

She blinked. 'We are going to India?'

He shook his head. 'Bermuda. On our honeymoon. Our real honeymoon.'

'Michael, we can't. Father is expecting me to take him to London.'

'I sent word when I went to fetch you back.'

'I don't have any clothes.'

He put an arm around her waist and nuzzled her neck. 'You aren't going to need any. Not for days and days. Perhaps never.'

She glanced over at the bed and shrugged. 'It would be a shame to waste a brand new bed.'

He swung her up in his arms and in a few long strides he reached the bed. 'I don't deserve you, wife, but I love you with all my heart.'

She raised her face for his blissful kiss. 'As I love you.'

* * * * *

MILLS & BOON

Historical

On sale 2nd July 2010

Regency

THE EARL'S RUNAWAY BRIDE
by Sarah Mallory

Five years on from fleeing her marriage, Felicity has just taken the hand of a dangerously handsome dance partner. She's about to come face to face with Major Nathan Carraway – her commanding husband back to claim his runaway bride!

Regency

THE WAYWARD DEBUTANTE
by Sarah Elliott

Eleanor Sinclair craved escape from the stuffy ballrooms of society, so she donned a wig and disappeared into the night. Catching the eye of handsome devil James Bentley, a game of seduction begins that tempts Eleanor to forsake all honour...

Regency

MARRIED: THE VIRGIN WIDOW
by Deborah Hale

The woman who betrayed Ford Barrett, Lord Kingsfold, has a debt to pay – Laura Penrose owes him a wedding...and a wedding night! Can she tell dark and dangerous Ford the truth, before he discovers her innocent secret?

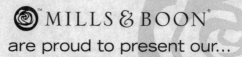

Three gorgeous and sexy Mediterranean men

RAYE MORGAN

CAROL GRACE

DONNA ALWARD

MEDITERRANEAN
Men & Marriage

– but are they marriage material?

The Italian's Forgotten Baby
by Raye Morgan

The Sicilian's Bride by Carol Grace

Hired: The Italian's Bride by Donna Alward

Available 2nd July 2010

www.millsandboon.co.uk

M&B

2 FREE BOOKS
AND A SURPRISE GIFT

We would like to take this opportunity to thank you for reading this Mills & Boon® book by offering you the chance to take TWO more specially selected books from the Historical series absolutely FREE! We're also making this offer to introduce you to the benefits of the Mills & Boon® Book Club™—

- **FREE home delivery**
- **FREE gifts and competitions**
- **FREE monthly Newsletter**
- **Exclusive Mills & Boon Book Club offers**
- **Books available before they're in the shops**

Accepting these FREE books and gift places you under no obligation to buy, you may cancel at any time, even after receiving your free books. Simply complete your details below and return the entire page to the address below. You don't even need a stamp!

YES Please send me 2 free Historical books and a surprise gift. I understand that unless you hear from me, I will receive 4 superb new books every month for just £3.79 each, postage and packing free. I am under no obligation to purchase any books and may cancel my subscription at any time. The free books and gift will be mine to keep in any case.

Ms/Mrs/Miss/Mr ——————— Initials ———————

Surname ————————————————————

Address ————————————————————

————————————————————

——————————— Postcode ———————

E-mail ————————————————————

Send this whole page to: Mills & Boon Book Club, Free Book Offer, FREEPOST NAT 10298, Richmond, TW9 1BR